Louis Zangwill

I0585143

Cleo The Magnificent

Outlook

Louis Zangwill

Cleo The Magnificent

1. Auflage | ISBN: 978-3-73261-734-0

Erscheinungsort: Paderborn, Deutschland

Erscheinungsjahr: 2018

Outlook Verlag GmbH, Paderborn.

Reproduction of the original.

Louis Zangwill

Cleo The Magnificent

Outlook

CLEO THE MAGNIFICENT

or

THE MUSE OF THE REAL

A Novel

by

Louis Zangwill

AUTHOR OF "THE BEAUTIFUL MISS BROOKE," "THE WORLD AND A MAN," ETC., ETC.

NEW YORK:
G. W. Dillingham Co., Publishers.
LONDON: WM. HEINEMANN.

MDCCCXCVIII.

Entered according to Act of Congress, in the year 1897, by
G. W. DILLINGHAM CO.,
In the office of the Librarian of Congress at Washington, D. C.

Cleo the Magnificent.

1

BOOK I.

CHAPTER I.

It was past midnight, and both men were smoking leisurely by the study fireside. Morgan Druce sat just on the edge of a low chair, his long, slim body bent forward, his clean-shaven boyish face well within the glow of the fire. Though he appeared to be looking at it, he was only conscious of its warmth.

Robert Ingram, middle-aged and bearded, lolled back in sensuous comfort. "The long and the short of it is," he resumed, "you've a soul-crisis on just at present. Crises are bad for the digestion, and I took care to grow out of them long ago."

"Our temperaments are very different," said Morgan.

"That's what makes your case so difficult to meet," returned Ingram. "It's your infernal temperament. One never knows how to take it. In fact, you're the sort of person in whose existence I never really believed; for though, as you know, I once had ideals and a literary conscience, I was always aware they would go as soon as I had a market for everything I could manufacture. You are the genuine incorruptible artist, to whom art is sacred. I really don't know whether to be doubtful of my cynicism or your sanity."

"That my case *is* a pretty bad one I've already admitted," put in Morgan.

"Now, if you were only some poor devil who was alone in the world," went on Ingram without heeding his remark, "I could take you in hand and make something of you, for you've quite brains enough. Poor devils are generally more reasonable in their views than you, even when they're geniuses. You simply keep on wearing out your heart day after day. Why? For fame? What is it worth? Well, I won't answer the question—I deal quite enough in platitudes."

"You don't understand, Ingram. What do you really know of me?"

"Well, if I don't know you by this time, you must be an uncommonly deep person—or perhaps I am an uncommonly shallow one."

Morgan Druce did not answer. His last remark had been more of a reflection than an interrogation. What did Ingram really know of him, he asked himself again, despite the five years of the indefinable relation between them? Admitting that the man beneath the cynic was kindly and sympathetic, yet he could not but be aware that Ingram's treason to the aspirations of his youth had destroyed the finer edge of feeling. His vision did not respond to subtler vibrations; his judgment was broad and coarse.

Such was Morgan's intuition about Robert Ingram. He believed the man to be sincere with him and he trusted him. And yet, as he looked up now and saw Ingram, relapsed into his luxurious arm chair, blowing rings of smoke, he seemed to detect something in his expression that filled him with a vague distrust about the genuineness of his professed interest in him. There was a sort of swagger in his whole posture, a slickness about his well-dressed, well- fed body, and a self-satisfaction in his somewhat burly face, nay, even in the manner his fat fingers held his fat cigar, that set Morgan wondering for the first time whether Ingram's attitude to literature did not in truth sum up the whole man; whether that popular novelist and dramatist could really have a place in his heart for anything that was of unimportance to his own personal existence—for a poor devil of a poetaster, for instance.

It was one of those sudden doubts that are created by a chance glimpse from an accidental new point of view; and Morgan thrust it from him as absurd and unjust. It could have no foundation, else why had Ingram responded to his appeal at the beginning? Why had he tolerated his calls all these years? Why were they talking together in that room now?

He had often been puzzled about this relation between them, though, as with his friendship with Lady Thiselton, its very strangeness and originality pleased him. His relation to that charming woman was, he felt, both indefinable and incredible; and his relation to the man beside him, though less odd, could be included neither in the category of acquaintanceship nor in that of friendship. Morgan was ignorant of Ingram's personal life, even as Ingram was ignorant of such a large fact in his own as Lady Thiselton. Their coming together had been always on the ground of their one common interest; otherwise there was the most absolute mutual exclusiveness between their existences. True that Morgan's periodical appearance at this Albert Gate flat, of which Ingram had made for himself a luxurious bachelor's home, had eventually resulted in a certain frankness of speech and familiarity of manner between them. But here their intercourse began and ended.

Perhaps Morgan had all along seen the position a little bit out of perspective; the very freedom with which Ingram had come to unmask himself before him and the intimacy with which they addressed each other had perhaps misled him. The cheery breeziness of Ingram had attracted him a good deal from the first, and he had liked the man for the ready good nature he had displayed towards him. And altogether it had been easy for him to think that he had done more than just rub up against the surface of Ingram's life, the depth and fullness of which he had scarcely realised.

At the beginning he had looked upon his being allowed to come and see the older man now and again as a privilege. It had never struck him to look at these visits of his from the other's point of view. It was precisely this point of view that now forced itself upon him as he struggled with the suspicion that had come to him. Had Ingram looked upon him merely as somebody who deserved to be good-humouredly tolerated? And was his openness only due to the consciousness of his (Morgan's) being an outsider, into whose ears he had got into the habit of speaking thoughts he would have told to no other living person, pretty much as he might have written them in a diary? Such a habit was easy to acquire with regard to an outsider whom one came into contact with periodically, and with whom one had a long talk each time.

He was not pleased, however, that such a train of thought should have come to him, and, urged by something akin to remorse, his mind went travelling back over the past five years in search of arguments in favour of Ingram.

There was a long interval during which both smoked in silence.

"Do you remember," asked Morgan, at length, "the circumstances under which we first became acquainted?"

"Perfectly," responded Ingram. "You wrote me a long letter, a rather pathetic one. That was the first intimation I had of your existence."

"Did you destroy that letter?"

"I never destroy letters—compromising ones, of course, always excepted."

"Then I may assume it still exists. Would it give you very much trouble to find it now?"

"I pride myself upon my system," answered Ingram.

"Please put it to the test, then."

"Your system is excellent," admitted Morgan, as at the end of about five minutes Ingram held up the sheets in triumph. "Now I wonder if you'd read it to me. I want to hear how it sounds."

"Certainly, you amusing beggar," said Ingram. "You wrote it during your last crisis and you want to compare your feelings then with now."

"I forget what I wrote," said Morgan, with an attempt at gaiety. "It must be very dramatic, so please put the proper expression into it, just as if it were a passage in one of your plays."

"Dear Mr. Ingram," read out that gentleman. "For nearly six years I have been trying to live by writing verse—ever since I was seventeen. Six years of passionate hope and longing, failure and failure, all years of wandering in the desert, of groping in the dark. I know no one—no one to criticise me—no one to encourage, to blame, or to praise; only the voice of purpose in my breast.

7

Amid loneliness this passion for fruitless labour has grown strong, frenzied, blind. Perhaps one day I shall penetrate—if I live. But for life one must have food; for work one must have shelter. At twenty-three one does not want to die; not when one has lived always in the future, when one has striven and toiled for recognition that may yet come. Not mere recognition of genius or talent, of knack or gift, but recognition of Truth as opposed to Imposture, of my right to life, of my right to give free and full expression of the individuality that is mine.

"As matters are now—I am utterly friendless so far as my inner life is concerned—I can see no other end than fall. God knows what shape that fall is destined to take; into what mire my soul must plunge in the fight for life. I could bear anything if I were not so utterly alone and helpless. I would do hack-work if I but knew Grub Street. I would sell my soul to a publisher for fifty pounds a year. Anything to get my foot on the lowest rung of the ladder! Anything to help me on the way to freedom!

"If you could see me, speak to me, help me in any way! Believe me, I do not wish to force my personality on you. I do not want you to give me any material thing. I only beg of you to aid me in asserting my claim on life by telling how I may win bread.

"I should be deeply grateful for a word from you. In any case, pardon this intrusion. Yours, etc., Morgan Druce."

———————

Ingram drew a long breath and threw the sheets on to the table.

"Have I read it nicely?" he asked.

"And I wrote that—to you, Robert Ingram!" exclaimed Morgan, brokenly.

"You did," said Ingram, quietly. "And you know what the sequel was."

"You were moved by my appeal. You came to seek me out."

"Well, your letter interested me. It was not the letter of a duffer or a swindler —the sort of thing you can tell by its ornate pompousness; and it just caught me when I was somewhat bored by things, so that I rather welcomed it as an excitement. I expected to find you lodging in some miserable cottage—a Chatterton in a garret. I came to bring food to the hungry. Instead——"

"You found me living in a palace standing in a fine park, with no lack of loaves and fishes, of milk and honey."

"It was the greatest surprise of my life. When I could no longer doubt that the only people called Druce in the neighbourhood lived in the magnificent Elizabethan mansion, whose name was that of the supposed cottage from which you addressed your letter, I began to think the family kept a skeleton in one of the cupboards. In plain language——"

"You thought one of the members of the family must be a lunatic."

"Anyway, the champagne was first-class, the cigars were worth half-a-crown apiece," said Ingram, laughing.

"And when you had gone into the matter you thought that if I wasn't quite a lunatic, I was not far short of one for disagreeing with my father."

"Frankly, I did."

"You never really sympathised."

"I did—all the time I conceived of you as a Chatterton."

"A palace is worse than a garret," asserted Morgan, "under the conditions in which I lived."

"Bah! You know nothing about garrets. And, as I pointed out to you, even if, in spite of the competition, you did sell your soul to a publisher for fifty pounds a year, he'd take care to stick to it. You were hopelessly wrong in your ideas about getting your foot on the first rung of the ladder."

"I am ashamed of ever having had those ideas—of ever having been willing to suppress my individuality, if only temporarily, for the sake of living. It all ought to have ended then. Why did you advise me to go on?"

"I only advised you to go on writing—I took the other thing for granted. In the light of my experience of myself at the same age, I judged it was the only advice you would take. And then having entered on the adventure, I wanted to finish it; so naturally I set about making peace between father and son. Excellent man, your father! So open to reason! You must have been deuced clumsy to irritate him. To refuse to enter such a business! You'd have been a rich man in a few years. But I'm sorry to see your last remark implied a sort of reproach."

"It was a stupid remark," admitted Morgan. "Of course I wanted to go on. At twenty-three one does not want to die."

"If there is still a prospect of being allowed to write poetry," added Ingram. "You wanted to be put in the way of earning fifty pounds a year, and naturally you invoked the assistance of the man who was reputed to have a weakness for embryo genius. However, at the age of twenty-eight, it appears, one does want to die. I helped you over the last crisis; perhaps I may help you over this one. Let us look at the facts. You've had a good chance and you've been defeated. Your poetry is not wanted. As I've told you before, I am not competent to say whether it's great or whether it's downright drivel—it's years since I discovered my limitations. You've been imprudent enough to pay the expenses of publishing two small volumes, and certain it is that nobody found any greatness in them. I admit I couldn't make head or tail of the bulk of the stuff—I'm satisfied myself to write what plain folk can understand. To put the matter bluntly, you send work to market that most people would look on as the ravings of a lunatic. Now, my advice is—cut poetry. There is plenty in the world for you to live for. Go and travel awhile. See men and cities, sculpture and paintings. Study humanity instead of merely thinking about it. Sail over the wide seas; breathe in the good air; be true to your youth and fall in love right bravely. You are rich—all this is in your power. I am sure your father will be pleased."

Morgan was touched by the other's enthusiasm.

"I have always misunderstood you," he cried, remorsefully; "you are not the mere gross tradesman you boast of being."

"Really, you embarrass me. Anyway, I hope that, now your opinion of me has gone up, my advice will bear fruit. After which I shall not mind confessing that that last nice bit is a quotation from my first novel. I could have invented nothing more apropos."

"You give me advice I am powerless to act on," said Morgan, after some hesitation. "I spent my last shilling to-day."

"No money!" ejaculated Ingram. "The deuce! Don't you draw a regular income from your father?"

"That was not the arrangement," said Morgan. "I was the first-born, and he was mortally offended by my refusal to enter the bank and carry on the name and the tradition of the house. During all those six years there had been friction and bitterness between us. At last came an appalling outbreak, and I was suffering from the full pain of my wounds when I wrote to you. You were good enough to tell him that genius sometimes earned quite considerable amounts, and the ultimate result of your intercession, of which you only knew the happy issue, not the details, was that he agreed to give me six thousand pounds, with the understanding I was never to expect another penny from him. My brother was to take my commercial birthright and I the responsibility for my whole future. I've earned nothing save an odd few shillings now and again, and all I had from my father I've somehow managed to mess away."

"Good God!" shrieked Ingram. "Six thousand pounds in five years! An exemplary young man of simple habits like you! What could you have done with it all? You're not a spendthrift. You don't gamble, do you?"

"I don't know how it has gone," said Morgan, helplessly. "I made bad investments, I lent some of it away, and I suppose I spent the rest."

"And you wanted to sell your soul to a publisher for fifty pounds a year! The fact is, I suppose, you don't know the value of money at all—it just melts away."

"For me money has no value. I don't care a pin about it," said Morgan, doggedly.

"That's scarcely the point," said Ingram. "Whether you care about it or not, you'll have to raise some of it. Let me interview your father. The fault is his. He knew you were a poet, and yet he was imprudent enough to give you capital instead of an income."

"It was my doing. I wanted to be perfectly free and independent of him—not to be worried by sordid complaints and lectures and warnings with each quarter's cheque. I told him so frankly, and I so annoyed him even at the end that he gave me the money, saying he did not care what I did with it. I certainly intend to stand by the arrangement I made with him. That money was to be the last, and the last it shall be."

"You are difficult," said Ingram.

"You must be indulgent."

Ingram lighted a new cigar and appeared lost in reflection a little while.

"There is only one thing, then, I can suggest," he said at last.

"And that is?" asked Morgan, in a tone that clearly indicated his belief that he was beyond all suggestions.

"You can be my ghost. Don't be alarmed—you must do some work, you know, and that is the only work I can think of for you. I have to refuse very many commissions. Try your hand at some of them and I'll run over the work and sign. As I've said before, you've got brains enough if you'll only use them in the right direction."

"You mean it for the best; but I could not be party to a fraud."

"How so? My business in life is to manufacture stories and plays for the people. My signature merely guarantees the quality just as the name of a maker on a pianoforte guarantees the instrument. But every such maker employs others whose names do not appear in connection with the finished product."

"The whole thing is impossible. Forgive me for ignoring your arguments. I ought never to have troubled you with my miserable concerns. It would, perhaps, have been better if I had never written you this."

And Morgan took up his own letter from the table, morbidly fascinated by it, and impelled to read again the words that had been wrung from him five years before by his torturing sense of his position in life.

But, as he began to read, an odour he had been vaguely conscious of inhaling all along was wafted very perceptibly to his nostrils. Then he became aware that the letter was subtly scented.

An unreasoning anger came upon him.

"Some woman has had this in her possession," he exclaimed.

Ingram looked at him strangely, hesitated, then seemed finally to comprehend.

"You are a veritable Lecoq," he said coolly.

Then that conception of Ingram that had before begun to hover in Morgan's mind now forced itself upon him wholly. He had always understood that the man had been inclined to take him somewhat as a good joke, but this he had not minded so much, so long as he believed that his personality and his aspirations really interested him. Now his sense of not having been looked upon seriously predominated, and with it came an exaggerated consciousness of everything in Ingram that was obnoxious to his spirit. If the re-reading of the letter had been a torture for him, the knowledge that it had been ruthlessly exposed to other eyes aggravated the pain tenfold, especially at this particular moment.

"And so this person, whose vile scent impregnates this, has had my soul laid bare before her for her amusement!"

"Whose vile scent?" repeated Ingram, angrily. "I must ask you not to use such language about any friend of mine."

"You went to her, no doubt, to be praised and fawned upon for your generosity to me, and afterwards——"

"Don't be a fool!" exclaimed Ingram, cutting him short.

"Thank you. I shall take the advice. I have been a fool long enough."

Morgan moved out of the room, leaving Ingram flushed and motionless.

CHAPTER II.

As Morgan had told Ingram, he had that day spent his last shilling. He had thus no option but to walk home to his rooms in Chester Terrace, Regent's Park. It was a long walk, and one had already struck, but he did not hurry. The night was a fine one of early spring, and it suited his mood to linger in the free air.

He had not really gone to Ingram for advice, though he had been unable to prevent his despair from showing itself. He was sorry that the exhaustion of his funds should have come just at the moment when he had resigned himself to the final abandonment of the ambition that had determined his whole life. He was sure now that a mind like Ingram's would inevitably set down his despair to his money difficulties. But the next moment he told himself it was grotesque on his part to care just then what inference Ingram might draw about him. Ingram and he would be concerned with each other but little in the future!

But what was the future to be? Were there not others who would be fully as astonished as Ingram at learning the truth? And even if it were possible for him to hide besides there was Margaret Medhurst. What meaning could the future have for him without her?

His old inner life had at length come to an end and he was now to pass from it into he knew not what—perhaps a raw, cold air. And yet his feeling now was not so entirely one of despair as when he had that evening rung Ingram's bell. He seemed to have been stung out of his terrible apathy. The smart had stirred up his deadened nerves. He was trying to set in order the jumble that possessed his mind and to think clear and straight.

The vague figure of a scented woman reading his letter haunted him, and at moments Ingram was added to the picture, and he saw them uniting in mockery of him—prosaic, prosperous author, and strange, romantic serpent- woman!

Though that letter of five years before had been wrung from him, he had written it with but the vaguest idea of sending it. A romantic impulse had dictated its form as an appeal to a prominent novelist, and it was only when he had finished it that the same romantic impulse urged him to post it. His feeling about it was purely poetic, and he scarcely realised he was addressing a real, living person. The commercial world of literature was to him a mysterious, far-off chaos, and at very bottom he had no belief the letter would be the means of his getting nearer to it.

So far as he was concerned at the moment, he had sent his bolt flying into the clouds, and the contingency of its being shown about had never occurred to him; moreover, if Ingram had left his appeal unanswered, the fact he now resented so much would never have come within the sphere of his consciousness. But to become cognisant of it years later at a moment of despair humiliated him unbearably. The mere re-reading of the letter had already humiliated him, for the lapse of time, the change of circumstance, the literary degeneration of Ingram, and his very acquaintance with the man, had made him feel the words very differently than when they had come spontaneously out of his blood. His sense of their futility added to his resentment.

But as he now walked along he was beginning to be conscious that, side by side with this resentment, had come something fantastic, something luring, immanent in the far faintness of the scent that had perfumed his letter.

He found himself repeating Browning's lines with a sense of the thrill and romance of life.

> "Heap cassia, sandal-buds and stripes
> Of labdanum, and aloe balls,
> Smeared with dull nard an Indian wipes
> From out her hair: such balsam falls
> Down seaside mountain pedestals,
> From treetops, where tired winds are fain,
> Spent with the vast and howling main,
> To treasure half their island-gain.
>
> "And strew faint sweetness from some old
> Egyptian's fine worm-eaten shroud,
> Which breaks to dust when once unrolled;
> Or shredded perfume, like a cloud
> From closet long to quiet vowed,
> With mothed and dropping arras hung,
> Mouldering her lute and books among,
> As when a queen, long dead, was young."

If his sense of overwhelming defeat made for despair, he was conscious of his nature being effectively appealed to from another direction. If he had that evening determined to throttle his ambition and write poetry no more, he seemed to have become aware of the stirring of a new motive for existence. But what it was he could not definitely tell himself.

And always before him rose the figure of the scented serpent-woman holding his letter in her long fingers, her white teeth gleaming in mockery!

"I shall live—live!" he exclaimed, as he entered his own door at last.

He lighted the gas in his large, comfortable sitting-room, and noticed there were letters for him on the mantel resting against the clock, whose hands pointed to half-past two.

But he would not look at them just yet. His was a strange mood just then and he did not wish his thoughts disturbed. There was something he had to do at once. Let the letters wait till he had finished.

Again he heard Ingram's voice reading. Every word had branded itself on him.

Soon he had the large table littered with bundles of manuscript. They represented his poetic output. Many of them had travelled far and wide; never again should they be sent forth into the world to bring him that which his heart had most desired. He took up one here and there and ran his eye through it. Considering the years he had worked, the output—for a young man's muse —was perhaps not large. But then he had only taken up his pen when inspiration had come. Certainly during the earlier years most of his time had been spent in reading and study. Otherwise he had had a habit of losing himself in the play of his imagination, awaking after having lived in worlds innumerable. Thus the actual amount of verse he had produced in the first years was really quite small.

He could not help dawdling a little before proceeding with the work of destruction. They were strange products, most of these poems of his; mirroring vague metaphysical moods, unseizable mystic fancies; incomprehensible save to one whose own inwardness they suggested, or to one of infinite emotional sympathy. A blurred, shapeless spirit brooded behind these melodious masses of words, these outpourings of disconnected ideas—a spirit invisible for reason and responsive only to divination, as love responds to love. Sometimes it was hidden amid a flow of sensuous images; sometimes in an impression of a landscape, of an atmospheric effect, of a play of light and shade. Such impression was never pure and complete, such visual effect never pictured for its own sake; for here and there amid it would lurk a phrase that was not of it, that struck a note—an elusive key-note—which set vibrating something haunting in its familiarity, terrifying in its strangeness; something mocking and meaningless, that went echoing away into the infinite.

He had not been able to find contentment in the mere presentation of beauty. Even where he dealt with the concrete there was always something to destroy the semblance of reality. The world that was revealed to his vision was a surface-world, for he had not pierced it by experience, but only dimly through the medium of books, and the elements it gave him he used freely. But his combinations of them were seldom along the lines of the possible. Here a colour would flash out at one; there a jewel would sparkle; now a perfume would be wafted; now a bird would sing. But all this individual definiteness was merged into a general blur, or formed itself into a sort of kaleidoscopic pattern that subtly suggested a meaning to be seized.

And all that Morgan now looked over again gave back to him the spirit he had put into them. The gaps in his expression of that spirit he was blind to. Shaped in the mould of his peculiar fantasy, these poems lived for the mind that had created them, that had been compelled by its own inner necessity to give them what was to him their particular form, to others their very formlessness.

His belief that this poetry was of immortal quality was unshaken, but he had been born into a wrong world, he now told himself. He was aware that he did not know the world of every-day affairs; that he was not fitted to know it. The very thought of its swirling incomprehensible activities turned him giddy; and if he walked amid it daily it was for him pure visual perception. Beyond that perception he did not seek to look and so he escaped discomfort.

Well, let him not linger. His old life—the singer's life—was over, and nothing of it must remain.

The grate was a big one, but even then the work of destruction would take some time. A fire had been laid that morning, but had not been lighted. He put back the coals into the vase and filled the grate with his manuscripts. Then, striking a match, he watched the blaze blackening and curling up the edges of the sheets.

When eventually the table was bare, he reflected it was strange he should now feel so little emotion. His predominating sense was one of physical fatigue, but the figure of the scented woman was still with him. Would it not be splendid, he asked himself, now that his past life lay there in a charred heap, to enter with his new life into the life of this woman—nay, to win her away from Ingram?

He took his letters. There were three of them, and they read as follows:

"My Dear Morgan:—This is to let you know I shall be in town to-morrow. I want you to come and meet me at Victoria at one o'clock and we shall lunch together before I go on to my hotel. My chief business is to see friend Medhurst about my eyes. I fear my present reading-glasses no longer suit me. By the way, I've some splendid ideas for you to work out. It's quite clear to me now from whom you inherited your genius. Mind you are in time. Your dad, Archibald D.

"P. S.—The 'Pleiad' to-day publishes that little poem of yours about Diana. I feel very proud of being your father. Present my regards to Mr. Ingram."

Morgan merely smiled. He had not had a poem published for many months, and this was his first indication that the one in point had been accepted. Curious, he reflected, it should just appear that day.

"Dear Prince Charming," ran the second. "This is to reproach you for not coming yesterday afternoon. For two hours I waited without giving up hope. Softest-hearted of mortals, for me alone is your heart a stone! I had all the sensations of Mariana in the moated grange, but whilst you are in the world, I certainly shall not wish myself dead.

"When are you going to take me to Whitechapel? My mind wanders longingly from this prosaic Belgrave Square to yon fantastic region. It's quite a month since we last got lost together. I have next Monday and Thursday free. I wonder whether it will occur to you to connect the two last sentences. Either day—or both—will suit me. This doesn't count as a letter. I shall write you a real one this evening. Helen."

"Dear Morgan," read the last. "As you have probably heard, your father is coming to town to see Mr. Medhurst professionally, and of course he is to dine here to-morrow evening. Come in and join us; we shall be strictly en famille. By the way, Margaret has not only finished 'Chiron' and the 'Spanish Marauder,' but she has actually sold both! They look very well, indeed, in bronze. Yours ever, Kate Medhurst.

"P. S.—Diana sends her love and hopes that if you have any more stamps you will bring them with you."

This postscript was in the writing of the young lady herself.

The reading of these letters did not give him any pleasure just then. These other lives in whose round he was an important figure were going on without any intuition of his inner tragedy, without any suspicion that they would henceforwards have to go on without him; that he could no more carry them forward into his vague, new life than those equally vital elements of his old self—his poems! How strangely did their moods contrast with his—his father's playful good-humour, Lady Thiselton's sprightly *camaraderie* and Mrs. Medhurst's cheerful domesticity!

But the last letter made him wince. It was only a simple invitation, but it hurt him as though a finger had been put on a raw wound. For he, who had made a failure of his existence, whose one remaining link with life was a mere grotesque possibility of an adventure with an unknown serpent-woman, loved Margaret Medhurst with a poet's despairing love.

The figure of the scented woman floated up again. She had let the letter fall into her lap now and her wonderful face seemed to smile at him.

CHAPTER III.

He awoke in the morning, acceptant of what he had done in the night. A calmness had set in and with it had come a clarification of his thought. His grasp of the position was more definite, and his feeling was that, to meet it adequately, he must disattach himself completely from the past.

But the future was mystic and seductive.

However, his tendency to dwell on it had to be put aside in favour of commonplace things that must be done immediately. As Ingram had pointed out to him, he might be as indifferent to money as he pleased, yet he must give it his first attention. Though ready cash was exhausted, he remembered almost with surprise he had several possessions that might be converted into it.

His breakfast was served to him as usual, but he did not open the promised letter which duly arrived from Lady Thiselton. His general sense of things filled his mind sufficiently.

His first business was to wait upon the family jeweller in Oxford Street, from whom he had made occasional purchases for birthday presents. The experience was a strange one for him, and he felt somewhat timid about it. However, when he had explained what he wanted, he was agreeably astonished at the man's insisting, with a great show of goodwill towards him, he must accommodate him with fifty pounds, and before Morgan had recovered from his flurry, he had given an I. O. U. for the amount and had bank notes in his pocket.

"Why, I shouldn't think of charging *you* any interest," the jeweller had declared, and Morgan was much puzzled to understand why. Nor did he quite know what this piece of paper he had signed represented.

He had now accomplished all the action his brain had planned, and it was time to go and meet his father. And then it struck him as curious that life seemed to be ignoring his ideas and to be taking him forward despite himself. With all his intense feeling that he must complete his disattachment from the past, its impetus was stronger than he. Somehow he *must* go and meet his father; he *must* dine with the Medhursts that evening.

As was clear from Archibald Druce's note, the relation between father and son was scarcely so theatrical as Ingram might have gathered from Morgan's talk the evening before, a fact of which Morgan was well aware. He had not really intended to give Ingram a theatrical impression, but the somewhat subtle truth could never have been conveyed in the few words they had had together, apart from the fact that it must inevitably have got coloured by the mood of the moment.

There had been many vicissitudes between father and son. The latter well remembered the moment when, unable to keep his big idea to himself any longer, he had divulged it to his father as they were strolling together in the grounds one sunny afternoon. The two had always been on the best of terms. Now Archibald Druce's ideas about his Morgan's career had been definitely shaped for years. He intended that the boy should, after passing through the University, enter the banking business with which his whole life had been associated, and ultimately become a partner therein. But Morgan's own idea of his mission in life seemed to the banker so extraordinary that it made him laugh outright. Unfortunately, too, in addition to pooh-poohing his son's unexpected ambition, he went on, by way of implanting in him sensible and serious views of life, to point out that the right to spend money had to be acquired by effort expended.

Morgan had made up his mind at a very boyish age that he was destined to become an immortal bard; the conceptions he had then formed had remained with him in all their boyish freshness. They were pure conceptions, detached from the realities, of which he then knew nothing. Poetry was a great and glorious thing, and when he first decided that his whole life could be devoted to nothing nobler, he had selected it away from the actual material circumstances from which existence cannot be extricated.

But in this first talk with his father he had already been brought into collision with these sordid complications. Archibald's well-intentioned scorn had inflicted a wound that pained still after the lapse of years. Moreover, by raising financial questions, he had unwittingly poured poison into that wound. Morgan, however, refused to have his eyes opened and clung desperately to his detached conception of poetry and the poet's life.

The thought of his being destined for business terrified the lad. He felt he could never live in the atmosphere of an office. He was born to sing, to charm, to enchant. What had he to do with money? He must argue with his father and convince him. And he effectually did succeed in making him understand he was serious. The banker was upset, and Morgan, carried along by the freshness and purity of his enthusiasm, made an altogether wrong judgment of the position. For the first opposition and the first clash of wills represented a bigger fact to Morgan than it did to the father, who, not entirely understanding the force of the ferment in his son's mind, as yet took it for granted that time was only needed to eradicate this strange, startling madness. He therefore pressed Morgan to proceed at once to the University, in the belief he would take a more sensible view of things when he was a few years older. But Morgan refused. He held to his ambition with frenzied persistence, and he had felt the bitterness of dependence. He determined, therefore, to try his wings at once, remembering that money *was* attached to success, and, in the optimism of enthusiasm, forming impossible hopes of supporting himself before long.

Archibald Druce did not mind his being apparently idle for awhile, and, by a sort of common understanding, the subject was not touched upon between them for some time. Morgan perforce had to live at home, and, as time went by, this very fact caused him a great deal of misery. Perhaps the very magnificence of his surroundings made matters worse for him.

His mother, too, was against him, and, after awhile she seemed to expend all the time she could spare from playing the rôle of *grande dame* in the county, in egging on his father against him. The sense of her injustice embittered him, for he knew he could not fairly be accused of spending his time unprofitably. He was studying perhaps harder than he would have done at college, for he was a student almost as much as he was poet. Of recreation, though, he had no stint. He rode, fished, swam and boated; but always alone, for his instinct made for solitude. With his brother he was not unfriendly, but there was no intimate sympathy between the two.

During the years that followed there were many fallings-out and reconciliations between father and son. If the banker had been entirely able to rid his mind of the plans he had so long cherished for his son, he would have been quite content that the latter should go through life as a gentleman of wealth and leisure. But he was wedded to the business to which he had given the best energies of his life, and the idea that Morgan must eventually take his place in it amounted almost to an obsession. A reconciliation always made Morgan happy, for its own sake quite as much as for the belief that his ambition was being recognised. Estrangement and friction were always terrible things to him and caused him unspeakable suffering.

His letter to Ingram was the culmination. It was sincere and expressed exactly what he felt. The immediate cause of the mood which prompted it had been Archibald's putting before him again all the old propositions and his letting it be clearly seen he had never really abandoned them.

Then followed a few months of happiness in London. At last he felt master of his own destiny—free of all that had vexed him, free to succeed. But the routine of his days was much the same as before. He studied and wrote and dreamed. Now and again he was allowed to come and chat with Ingram. Friends of the family made him welcome at their houses whenever he chose to emerge from the isolation that was natural to him. At the Medhurst's, in lay claim to merit for the talents he possesses, and is it immodest of him to let others perceive by his conversation that he is quite aware he possesses them? Or, on the contrary, is not the fact that he is talented purely a piece of good fortune, and would it not be the merest humbug on his part to pretend to be blind to it? Again, if a man performs what is called a good deed, ought he to claim merit for that? Does not the performance of such a deed give one pleasure, and is not that pleasure the real end in view? It has struck me of late that on such points there's a great confusion of thinking, and between ourselves, Morgan, I've been lately arriving at conclusions that most people would call revolutionary and dangerous. But I set truth above all things, and I can't do better than devote my remaining years to its service. Now, I think I have really sufficient material for an original and interesting volume. I have been a man of affairs all my days, and I think the views of such a man who has lived in contact with the world should at least be as valuable as those of a college professor who has been secluded from it. It is really about this volume I propose to write that I want to consult you. I have made a memorandum of a few points I should like to thresh out thoroughly with you."

Morgan was rather startled at this sudden and serious awakening of literary ambition in his father, though he had before now had many a hint that he was wrestling with formidable ethical and moral difficulties. He could see Archibald had set his heart on writing the book, so he could not do otherwise than encourage him. It would simply keep him enjoyably occupied, and, as the task would no doubt cause him to dip into accredited works on ethical science, he would ultimately discover that the problems he had chanced upon were not quite so original as he supposed.

But even while Morgan discussed the idea with his father, he had a curious dream-like consciousness of his own affairs, which somehow seemed to be retarded by this appearance of the banker in London. And, all the time he was endeavoring to concentrate himself on the conversation, he was aware of that floating vision which had never ceased to haunt him.

Minute details respecting the work were gone into, even to the colour of the paper on which it was to be written. Morgan did not know whether blue or buff was the more restful for the eyes, and the question was left open for John Medhurst to decide. Archibald looked tremendously pleased at his son's reception of his project, and it certainly raised his opinion of Morgan's judgment.

"I'm glad to see you've not been spoiled by success, Morgan," he could not help saying.

It was a strange irony, Morgan thought, that his father's acceptance of him should be so complete just when he himself had finally abandoned all hope.

The reflection would have been a bitter one had he not found Archibald's pride in him amusing, in view of the latter's new theories about "merit."

Later on, at the hotel, Archibald produced the copy of the "Pleiad," which contained the verses inspired by Margaret Medhurst's younger sister, and insisted on reading them aloud. His paternal pride was more than satisfied by the small sum total of Morgan's published work, and each little addition to it furnished an occasion of great excitement for him.

Of course, Ingram was mentioned before long, and Morgan had to say that that gentleman and he were no longer friends. Archibald said he was sorry, and looked it. He considered Ingram a great author, and the breach rather a misfortune.

"Is there no hope of smoothing things over?" he asked. "Why not take me into your confidence? I flatter myself I have had some experience in patching up even serious differences between people, and you know I'm at your disposal."

Time had, indeed, brought about a strange reversal of rôle between the banker and Ingram.

Morgan explained that Ingram had behaved in such a way as to make him revise his estimate of him, but that it would scarcely serve any purpose to go into details.

The banker again said he was sorry, and looked it still more than before. Anyhow, as the subject was so obviously disagreeable to Morgan, he would not allude to it again.

In the afternoon they took a little stroll together, and, after partaking of a cup of tea, they parted, promising to see each other at Wimpole Street.

"By the way," said his father, at the last moment, "I hear from Katie that they haven't seen very much of you of late, and that you had struck them as preoccupied. She even seemed rather doubtful about your coming this evening. I hope you don't stick too long at your desk. I've long since found out that sort of thing is a mistake."

calculating effects, whose business has always been poetry? Let your business still be poetry, but weave it out of life instead of words. Abandon yourself without underthought. Live in that wonderful region which is here, even as it is everywhere, but in which only the souls of poets may wander and rejoice." And his temperament prevailed over his will. He allowed the full flow of love to flood his spirit. Great poems were summed up in one quick flash; in a second he lived through a century of fine words.

And, as if divining his thought, she turned to him and spoke. Her words seemed softly to ring through the din, and he gave himself up to the full delight of the moment.

"Do you know, Morgan"—for he was always "Morgan" to everybody there —"a great change has occurred in my dignity the last few days?"

"You are to marry a peer," he hazarded.

"I have risen much higher than that."

"You were at the utmost height."

"I only moved in yesterday, with my benches and mess and clay and wax and tools. Pa had a hole made in the roof and a top light put in. I feel so pleased with my studio, and, of course, I mean to entertain there. We shall have such gay times, and I've a fine excuse for keeping the company young and select."

"Too high up for old legs?"

"How shrewd!" she exclaimed. "I see that for real worldly insight one must go to a poet."

"Thank you. This is the first time I've been accused of common sense."

"That is hardly to be wondered at. Your poems have every other quality. You'll come up and see my studio anyhow?"

"By moonlight?"

"No, by candle light. And you the bearer, like the Latin motto on one of my old school books."

Meanwhile the combat opposite still raged, and in the end Archibald and Diana had to be parted almost by force. Diana sent a final shot from the door, and then scampered away.

"The little rogue!" murmured Archibald, and then broke into one of those unrestrained laughs which he usually reserved for his own witticisms.

The three men drew near the fire. Medhurst said something about taking Diana in hand. She had been somewhat spoiled at school, being looked upon as a sort of demi-goddess by her classmates. Archibald declared he wouldn't have her any different for the world. What was the good of a girl if she was just the same as any other girl? Thence, proceeding to attack convention, Archibald eventually steered the conversation round to the contribution he himself purposed making to ethical philosophy, for he had been waiting for an opportunity to let Medhurst into the secret.

"It's curious that the more one thinks, John, the more one gets one's notions upset. I know quite well that most people would think it a highly dangerous doctrine to put forward, but I really cannot see that the man who is a saint deserves any more to be praised than the man who is a murderer. The murderer is simply unfortunate and ought to be pitied. Nature gave him the impulse to murder—in fact, on a closer analysis, all personal responsibility seems to disappear."

"And what does your wife say to all this? Isn't she rather alarmed?" asked Medhurst.

"My wife!" exclaimed the banker, contemptuously. "She's hopelessly behind the times. Why, she's a perfect child. She takes no interest in anything beyond the tittle-tattle of the county. We had quite a scene the other day because I gave expression to my opinion that young people should be properly instructed in life by means of explanatory handbooks, instead of being left to gather their knowledge haphazard. I have never known her to make a single original remark—her observations are invariably the most obvious. Morgan should be thankful for the happy hazard of nature which fashioned his brain rather in the mould of mine than in that of his mother."

"And so you really intend publishing?" said Medhurst.

"I am not afraid. People must be taught to look the problems of life straight in the face. Truth must be driven home, my dear John, and it is my intention to say some pretty straight things to the world."

"Have you yet fixed on a title?" asked Medhurst, secretly amused at this sudden, strange development on the part of his old friend.

"Ah! there's just the difficulty. It was one of the first questions I put to myself —what about the title? The thing is to get a good striking one, and that's by no means an easy task. The title of a book is almost as important as its contents, and, confound it all, my dear John, I'm blessed if it doesn't take nearly as long to manufacture. I've been cudgelling my brains for the last three months, and I must confess my mind is an absolute blank so far."

"Why not call it 'Plain Thoughts of a Practical Thinker?'" suggested Morgan. "And perhaps you might add a sub-title—'An attempt to investigate some questions of primary importance that are usually shelved.' How does that strike you?"

"Splendid!" exclaimed Archibald, enthusiastically. "'Plain Thoughts of a Practical Thinker'—the very thing. 'An attempt to investigate some questions of primary importance that are usually shelved.' Admirable! 'Practical Thinker!' That is just the idea I want to convey to the world. I am not one of your mere dreamers, your theorists, your college professors. I speak as one who has had a large experience of men and affairs, as one who has for years administered the fortunes of a great house. And yet I have sufficient of the thinker and the idealist in me to have begotten a son whose name will live in English letters. It will, Morgan, I tell you. You are a little bit misunderstood now, but what great man has ever escaped misunderstanding? I expect to be misunderstood, but if they think I am to be howled down—'Plain Thoughts of a Practical Thinker!' A perfect inspiration! Suppose we join the ladies. I want to tell Kate about it."

CHAPTER VI.

While Archibald unfolded his literary scheme to Mrs. Medhurst, Diana mimicking his enthusiastic gestures at a safe distance, Morgan and Margaret sat apart in that region of the drawing-room which lay nearest the door. She had been telling him about some parties she had gone to, and he, terribly jealous of the men who had danced with her, made pretence to rally her about them. She, however, remained quite calm, admitting cheerfully she *had* a good many admirers, who filled her programme, and whom it was always pleasant to meet. Then they were both silent and looked at each other.

"Once upon a time," said Margaret, deciding at length to speak her mind; "*you* used to be one of those who wrote on my programme. Now you never appear anywhere. I suppose you are afraid you might have to talk to me a little."

"You are unjust," he said somewhat bitterly. "It is not kind of you to say such things."

"If a friend suddenly develops a distaste for one's company and manifests it as markedly as you have, how can one be blind to it? You are a changed man, Morgan. In two months you have come here once to tea, and you had not even the decency to put on a cheerful face. Such a lackadaisical expression you had! And not even an enquiry about my great works. You seemed to be saying the whole time, 'How you commonplace people depress me—me, the genius, the genius; you are killing my inspiration.'"

Something in his look checked her.

"Genius suffers from fits of melancholy as well as from fits of inspiration," he reminded her.

"Poor Morgan!" said Margaret, softening. "And so you've had a fit of melancholy! What a long one, too! All the same, I ought to reproach you for not believing in our sympathy. Well, I suppose now I may tell mamma not to be afraid to send you a card for our dance next month."

"I had no idea your mamma was so timid a person," he said, with successful evasion. "And how goes Chiron, how the Spanish marauder? And how much did you get for them?" he went on gaily, in one breath. "You see I am well posted in your affairs."

"Well, since you *are* a little bit interested, come."

Instinctively they looked towards the other group. Archibald still harangued

35

Mrs. Medhurst, endeavouring to prove to her that John's abilities were no merit of his, any more than her beauty was a merit of hers. A happy accident was the cause of either, and he had been intellectually wrong in lavishing so many compliments on her during all these years.

Morgan and Margaret left the room quietly, and stole up the stairs on tip-toe, like two children at play. Right on the top landing Margaret threw open a door, and Morgan peered into a shadowy abyss, for the one gaslight was round a corner by which its rays were cut off from this part of the landing.

"The candle is on a ledge in the hall," explained Margaret, disappearing within the darkness; and in a second he heard her strike a light.

"This is the hall," she went on. "I insisted on pa having it partitioned off from the rest of the room—though, as you see, only by a sort of green baize screen that doesn't reach to the ceiling. But it makes the place ever so much more romantic."

Morgan stepped into the tiny vestibule, which was fitted with a little oak table, and passed through a door in the green baize into the attic itself.

"Was I not to be the candle-bearer?" he asked, taking the light from her. "What a tremendous place!"

"It's perfectly ripping," said Margaret, "though I reckon it won't hold more than four of us when we're in a gay mood. That's an old piano. It takes up a lot of room, but there's still a good deal of thumping to be got out of it. As yet the place is quite bare, but all next week I'm going to hunt up odd things in back streets, and when you come again you'll be astonished at the transformation. All that mess there covered up in the corner—well, you can guess what it consists of."

"And where are Chiron and the Spanish gentleman?"

"The first casts are on the mantel yonder—lost in the gloom. Pa wants them for the drawing-room, but I am so childishly pleased, I can't part with them yet. The moulds were to be destroyed after sixty examples of each had been taken. I have received twenty-five pounds each. You see, Morgan, I, too, am a genius."

On closer examination Morgan found he could conscientiously extol Margaret's handiwork. From a technical point of view both figures were excellent, and there was a virility and vigour in the handling which one would scarcely have associated with the work of a young lady modeller, and which certainly showed she had towered above her material. The Spanish Marauder swaggered along in helmet, breast-plate, doublet and hose, a hare and pheasant slung jauntily over his shoulder, and his jolly, devil-may-care face, that had evidently smelt powder, full of an arrogant self-satisfaction. The Chiron was a strong piece of anatomical modelling. The ancient centaur, indeed, looked very wise and very noble, and the horse into which he merged was arranged with quiet skill in its lying posture, so that not a line, limb, hoof or muscle struck a note of awkwardness.

"Then you think I really am worth talking to—a little?" asked Margaret.

He set down the light on the mantelshelf and somehow found himself holding her hand. Neither appeared to be aware of the fact.

"My dear Margaret, I was hoping you had accepted my fit of melancholy ——"

"You stupid Morgan! I only wanted you to tell me how clever I am. I am so greedy for praise—because I haven't any of those melancholy fits, and my vanity must be gratified *somehow*. At least, when I do have the mopes I always know the reason, and it has never been anything connected with my genius."

"What! you don't mean to say that you ever——"

"Sometimes," she interrupted. "A good deal of late, only, unlike you, I never let anybody guess."

"I thought you were a perfectly happy girl in the first flood of enthusiasm for your work and with all those nice men to admire you."

Her fingers tightened perceptibly on his.

"If you continue to plague me about those nice men, Morgan, you shall not have a single dance next time, but you'll just see those nice men get them all."

"I am sure you don't look a bit as if you could devise such cruel torture."

"Would it be a very terrible punishment?"

"I would do any penance to avoid it."

"You'd look too comic in sackcloth and ashes. Come to my studio-warming instead."

"A charming penance, Margaret."

"Perhaps we ought to go down now," she suggested, irrelevantly.

He took up the light again.

"Have you fixed the date for the warming?"

"Impossible yet. But I'll send you——"

"Not cards—now you've moved up into Bohemia!"

"Oh, no. A little pink note. I hope that is the correct thing in Bohemia, or, at least, that it isn't incorrect."

"In Bohemia there are no correct things."

"What an awful place it must be. Whatever one does is wrong."

"On the contrary, whatever one does is right."

"Then all things are correct in Bohemia!"

"How can that be, Margaret? There are things—no, there aren't, and—and— I'm afraid I've got myself into an awful tangle. You've quite turned my head with your logic."

He began to move across the room towards the door.

"If it's only my logic that turns your head, then I take everything back. I won't speak to you ever again."

"My goodness!" began Morgan, losing his wits, forgetting he held the candle and letting it fall. The light vanished like a spectre. "I beg your pardon," he ejaculated, in some astonishment, whilst Margaret's laugh rang out.

Just as he stooped down to recover the candle, they became aware of footsteps, and in a moment the handle of the outer door was being turned.

"All dark," said Diana's voice. "Then I suppose they're not here—or, at least, I shouldn't like to think they were. I fancy Marjy put a candle and matches on the table."

They heard the sound of her fumbling, and, as if by common understanding, they remained still as mice. Then Diana declared the things weren't there, and Archibald suggested they might inspect the place in the dark.

"I certainly shall do nothing so improper," returned Diana severely. "There must be match-light at least. I draw the line at that. Produce your pretty, golden box."

Diana opened the green baize door, and Archibald struck a light.

"Ho, ho!" he said, playfully.

"We are evidently *de trop*" said Diana. "Let us retire."

"Be careful," called Margaret. "You'll burn your fingers."

But the mischief was already done. Archibald uttered a "d—n," threw down the end of the match and stamped on it wrathfully.

Morgan picked up the fallen candle, lighted it and replaced it on the mantelshelf. The wax was broken in the middle, and the top part leaned disconsolately to one side.

"We are sorry to have unwittingly interfered with your little arrangement," said Margaret, curtseying in mock apology. "But you are quite welcome to make free of my humble abode, so we shall leave you in possession. Come, Morgan." And the two swept out of the room.

"Come and lunch with me to-morrow at the hotel," said Archibald to Morgan, as he got into a hansom an hour later. "We'll spend the afternoon together. There are some points about my book I want to settle. 'Plain Thoughts of a Practical Thinker!' Splendid title! Morgan, you're indeed a genius. 'An attempt to investigate some questions of primary importance that are usually shelved.' That just hits it off—the very book I intended to write!"

CHAPTER VII.

When his father had driven off, Morgan, seized with a restlessness, began to stroll slowly homeward. He had at least wrung some happiness from the evening. His love for Margaret had been strong enough to absorb him, save when at moments his sense of his general position had obtruded. But now he surrendered himself once more to the mood which the events of the day had interrupted.

He was again conscious of the tragedy of his past life with its culminating episode of the evening before, and of the infinite possibility that life held of mystery and fantasy—a mystery and fantasy into which he was going to plunge. The hours he had just enjoyed, he told himself, must not be allowed to influence him. They must be sternly isolated from the future; the disattachment of the new life before him from the wreckage of the old must be complete.

Wreckage! He used the word deliberately, though he was aware there were elements in the position that would have made his estimate of it seem grotesque to many ears.

He was the son of a father of unlimited wealth, who idolised him now. In addition to very many acquaintanceships, both in London and the country, that were pleasant even if they did not occupy the centre of his consciousness, he had the friendship of Lady Thiselton and the more intimate though less fantastic relation with the Medhursts. And, moreover, he was in love with a beautiful and talented girl, who, he modestly felt, had a great esteem for him —though any other eyes than those of the diffident lover would have seen at a glance that she loved him in return.

How could all these things fail to make a man happy, especially when the man was only twenty-eight years old?

But Morgan's happiness was dependent on his attitude towards things, not on the things themselves. And just now he but perceived all these elements that might have made another life enviable as so many ironies. His ambition—his self-realisation and its recognition by his fellows—had been all in all to him; its abandonment had been the culmination of anguish infinite. The best years of his youth had been lost in vain effort, and some of the bitterness of early opposition that success might have purged still lingered in his spirit. His nature was proud and sensitive and his very failure made it impossible for him to ask for more money, even though he knew it would be forthcoming without stint. What wonder now if he perceived his life as a tragedy!

Common Sense would have advised him to put on one side all emotions and moods that arose out of and summed up the past, all the subtle feelings that possessed and mastered him; would have urged him to begin a new epoch, seek the paternal aid, retain his friendships, and persevere in his love; would have given him assurance of a perfectly satisfactory outlook if he would but readjust his mental focus.

But Common Sense is obtuse and safe. Morgan was a mass of fine sensibility; his temperament was full of subtle light and shade—therefore dangerous. Plain-souled, clumsy-handed Common Sense, with perception limited to the thick outlines of character, could not have comprehended him, and would unwittingly have confessed it by classifying him contemptuously.

Morgan had lived his own life—felt it. His present estimation of it was, therefore, spontaneous; not a cold estimation by mere intellect, but a living one by his whole complex being. And, as the result, he was meditating, at this period of pause and summing-up, to carry forward all that Common Sense would have suppressed, and to suppress all that Common Sense would have carried forward, to sacrifice all the inter-relations with others that constituted his outer life—even as he had already sacrificed the expression of his corresponding inner life; retaining only his emotional unrest.

And the seductive picture of the scented serpent-woman, ever smiling at him now with gleaming teeth, symbolised the future for him, and alone preserved the continuity of interest that stimulated him to go forward at all. His attitude, in some respects, was analogous to that of a romantic boy playing with the idea of running away from home, drawn by visions of marvellous adventures in strange lands. The sequel might be vague and in the clouds, but that very fact only made it the more fascinating.

His temperament had said to him that evening: "Let your business still be poetry, but weave it out of life instead of out of words." The thought resurged in his brain and then it struck him as crystallising his whole feeling about the future course of his existence, as furnishing the key to his position.

To make of life a fantasy, a poem, a dream! The idea was an illumination.

But beyond a half-considered intention of changing to humbler rooms and hiding therein from his world, he did not meditate any definite activity. The feeling at the bottom of his mind was rather that events would shape themselves. To this attitude of passivity his whole life had tended. His will-strength had gone into his passionate desire of poetic achievement, and were it not that he had, so to speak, grown into relation with others, his life would have been utterly static. The movement of their lives alone had taken his along. He had not the least idea now how he was going to become acquainted with the strange woman who filled his thoughts, but, without actually translating his feelings on the point into definite terms, he counted it as a certainty that a path would somehow be opened. It pleased him, too, to think that he owed his cognisance of her existence to that first impulse which had caused him to write to Ingram. That fantastic initiation had set in motion fantastic life-waves that were now flowing back to him.

For others the regularities of existence, the steady round of work, the care and hoarding of money; for him the mystery and the colour of life!

And in a flash of insight he seemed to understand that the poet in him had already asserted itself in his life as well as in his work. Was it not the very curiousness of his relationship with Ingram had made it so palatable? Was it not the strangeness of his friendship with Lady Thiselton and the originality of her personality that appealed to him so much, and was it not his imaginative side that had always been so pleased with both? Was it not his peculiar temperament that had always made him keep his relation with each person a thing apart, so that each was unaware of the others; that had made him like to feel that his life, in a manner, was cut up into strips, along each of which he could look back with a certain sense of completeness, though it was only by the nice fusion of all these isolated completenesses that his existence could be seen as a whole?

But underneath the imaginative spirit of the poet lay the human spirit of the man. And if the former predominated the latter was not entirely dormant. If the poet in him coloured his life and thought, it was the man in him that felt the results, so that the instincts of the poet often clashed with the sympathies and affections of the man. Of this discord within himself he could not help being aware, but he knew it purely by its effect, for he had never searched deeply into the complexity of his nature.

Thus it was that the man in him was grieved at his having had to make promises of further visits to the Medhursts; was paying for every grain of happiness wrung from the evening by a reaction of pain unspeakable. But the poet in him governed, was trying to suppress the man.

He was roused from his meditations by a familiar voice when he was but a few feet from his own door.

"I have been hovering about for a quarter of an hour."

He was startled, then laughed. The veiled woman stood on tip-toe and kissed him on the forehead, he stooping mechanically to meet her movement.

"You don't mind the veil?" she said.

"How did you know I was not indoors and abed by this time?" he asked.

"I didn't know. I only came to meditate in the moonlight. I have been enjoying such exquisite emotions. Are you too tired for a promenade round the circle?"

He fell in with her humour.

"Morgan, reproaches have been accumulating. To save time—you know I never waste any—you shall have them all in one ferocious phrase. You have been brutal to me of late. I don't mean to say that you've ever ceased to be charming, but—why, at least, didn't you answer my note?"

"It only came this morning," he stammered, "and I haven't had time to read it yet."

"In other words, you wrinkled your brow as soon as you saw it, made up your mind I was beginning to be somewhat of a nuisance, and threw it aside unopened. Of course, you forgot all about it afterwards. You have a perfect genius for putting crude facts in a delicate way."

"Another new discovery about me."

"That is but the natural result of the profound thought I bestow upon you."

"Your profound thought contradicts itself. It declares me brutal and charming with the same breath."

"Profound thought always contradicts itself. I know it for a fact, because I've been looking up Hegel. The nice things and nasty things I say about you arise equally from my love for you, which is thus the unifying principle. The apparent contradictoriness, therefore, disappears in a higher synthesis."

"Quarter! A man can't stand having philosophers hurled at his head."

"But I kiss your head sometimes. I'm sure I'd much prefer that always, only you goad me into the other thing."

"I goad?"

"Yes. By your masterly inactivity when I am concerned. I have to force myself into your life, and after we've been chums for three years, you, left to yourself, ignore my existence. You have such a terrible power of negative resistance against poor, strong-willed me. But, after all, you admire me tremendously, don't you, dear Morgan?"

"I have told you scores of times you are the cleverest woman in the kingdom."

"I am the only woman who understands your poetry. I don't mean that as a bit of sarcasm at the expense of your compliment—I merely want to show you I deserve it."

He made no reply. For a few moments there was a silence.

"How reticent you are to-night!" she said at length. "You usually have quite a deal to tell me. Are the sentimental chapters preying on your mind? I do so much want to know about those sentimental chapters, but you always evade the subject. Tell me, *are* there any in your life?"

"Ours was to be an intellectual companionship only."

"Comprising intellectual sympathy and kissing on the forehead—both of them chaste, stony, saint-like, tantalising things. But I'd be content for the time being if I were only sure your heart were perfectly free. I couldn't bear the thought of your making love to another woman."

"You are amusing."

"I am jealous."

"Then you have been imagining sentimental chapters for me."

"Well, being a woman of the world, thirty-three years of age—no deception, Morgan—and, knowing you have lived twenty-eight, I naturally suspect the existence of those chapters, you darling sphinx. And when I suddenly come across a poem from your pen about a sweet little girl, my suspicion becomes almost a certainty."

He could not help laughing.

"That sweet little girl is too concrete, too much away from your metaphysical manner, to be a mere creation of your brain. What vexed me particularly was that the most stupid woman I know—I mean my dear friend Laura—admired the thing and called it a gem. Now I don't like my monopoly threatened in that way. I have always prayed against your own prayer. I don't want the world at large to admire you—yet. I want you, disgusted with the world's non-acceptance of you, to find consolation in my love. There is a fair proposal for you, Morgan. Love me, marry me—and after that you may become as great as you like. Your poetry as yet is my friend, but I begin to feel afraid of it when you start pictures of sweet little girls."

He did not take her the least bit seriously—he never did. Her occasional courtship of him had been always so light and airy, so dispassionately epigrammatic, that he looked on it as mere whimsical banter and rather good amusement. She had plagued him into consenting to that kiss on the forehead which she gave him each time they met, referring to it constantly as an advantage won by hard effort. The circumstance of their first meeting had been commonplace enough—a chance introduction at an afternoon tea. They were friends whilst yet utter strangers to each other, for a mutual personal magnetism had acted immediately. He understood that her playfulness did but conceal fine qualities of character that would have pleased even the aphoristic moralist, whose conception of the ideal woman she mercilessly outraged. That she had really understood and appreciated his work naturally counted a good deal in her favour. He knew her worth, but of course he did not want to marry her. If to-day there was a more earnest ring than usual in her love- making, he had got too indurated to it to believe in it.

"Who *is* the sweet little girl?" she insisted. "I repeat, I am jealous. This is my first experience of that queer emotion, for you are the first man I have ever loved."

He found this most amusing of all.

"Really, Morgan, it is perfectly harassing to have one's tragedy taken for light comedy. You know my wedded life was unhappy. The late baronet was absolutely ignorant of Schopenhauer, and even cursed him to my face for a madman, just because he happened to be my favourite philosopher. Since I've dipped into Hegel, I've come largely to agree with my husband's denunciation, though not on the same grounds. Not that I profess to know anything either about Hegel or Schopenhauer. Edward always thought me a blue-stocking— me, who have only a woman's tea-table smattering of philosophy! Why, it takes all the fun out of life to be a blue-stocking! Edward hadn't any brains. I married him without love, and in face of his attitude towards Schopenhauer, you may guess what chance it had of springing up. During the brilliant years of my widow-hood—eight in number—my heart has remained positively untouched by anybody but you. It's your childlike helplessness that fascinates me."

"You flatter me."

"There are other things, of course. You've splendid large eyes and nice, soft, silky hair, and such a pretty curl to your lip. And you've such a charming, innocent look. If only you'd promise not to write any more poems about sweet little girls, you'd be perfect."

Whether it was that her proximity at this moment of inner perturbation and suffering roused in him an overmastering desire for her sympathy, or whether her last remark exercised an insidious drawing power, he did not quite know, but he found himself saying immediately:

"I can make that promise very easily. I made a bonfire last night."

She understood at once.

"Which explains much for which I've been reproaching you!" she exclaimed sympathetically. "You have been suffering, dear Morgan."

Her voice had grown soft and coaxing. His determination to shun everybody could not stand against this real concern for him. In a few words he told her of his despair and of the dubiousness of his position. But he could not bring himself to speak of his hopeless love, or to raise the veil that concealed his other friendships from her. His comradeship with her had always stood for him as a thing apart; and this attitude of his towards it had made it the more charming. It had been quite natural for him to take it entirely by itself and as unrelated to the rest of his external life.

"But, my dear Morgan," she protested, "this can't go on. How do you intend to live?"

He was glad she did not have recourse to that crude, obvious suggestion of his begging a replenishment from the paternal coffers. But he did not know how to reply to her question, which rather made him regret the turn the conversation had taken. The one future for him was that in which floated mystically the figure of the scented serpent-woman, and he felt that that drift of things he was relying on had begun by a wrong move.

"Perhaps I shall write stories," he hazarded.

"You alarm me," she cried. "Your idea is hopelessly impracticable. How could you possibly hope to rival the Robert Ingrams?"

"The Ingrams!" he echoed, glancing at her sharply.

"I only mention him because he happens to be as popular as all the rest put together, and because I happened to make his acquaintance some time back."

Morgan made no remark. He was relieved at her explanation, about which there was nothing surprising, for he well knew that Ingram moved in high social latitudes.

"Besides," she went on, "you would naturally be tempted to draw women like me, which would simply be courting extinction. Of course, in Ingram's novels no fashionable lady ever does the things I do, and the critics would insist I was an utter impossibility. Now, as to the fifty pounds you've got—before long the sin of that borrowing will rise up against you and you'll be signing again, signing away whole pounds of your flesh. And I daresay you overlook you've various little debts. No doubt you owe your tailor, say a year's account, and then your rooms are pretty expensive, and quarter-day has a spiteful habit of swooping down on one four times a year, and—and you mustn't have to bother your pretty head about all these sordid things."

This was somewhat of an appalling speech for Morgan, who certainly did not want to cheat his creditors. And, indeed, it now occurred to him that he must be indebted to his tailor for quite a large amount. Although his horror of debts was far above the average, he never realised the conception "money" as ordinary people realise it. So far as it figured in his thoughts at all, money was a gorgeous, poetic unit—the treasure of romance, the gold and silver of fairyland. In practice, the very abundance of it at his command had till lately kept his attention from dwelling on it; just as it did not dwell on, say, the second toe of his left foot—an equally constant factor in his existence—till some pain might make him aware it was there. His present forced awareness of the prosaic side of the notion "money" gave him somewhat of a sense of being caught amid a swirl of storm-blown icicles.

"The remedy is simple," he said, at last.

"It is. I have forty thousand a year. Marry me for my money."

"Declined, with thanks."

"So blunt, yet so pointed. A pity it's not original. But I know what you meant by your remedy. You don't see it would be a double crime, and you are too good a man even to commit a single one."

"You mean——"

"I mean I should follow you. It would be just lovely to be rowed across the Styx together. Of course, I should have to pay your obolus."

"It is getting late. I really think we ought to turn back."

Lady Thiselton sighed.

"I must confess I am dejected," she said. "I should like to have a quiet cry. What are you going to do, Morgan?"

"Nothing."

But he knew that would mean bankruptcy, and he had also an unpleasant conviction that she meant what she said about following him.

"And even if we did go to throw sugar to Cerberus, your father would step in and inherit your debts, and you will have sacrificed us both in vain. The result is the same, whether we go to Whitechapel or to the other place. You can't make it otherwise. Now, if you won't let me be your wife, at least let me be a sort of mother to you."

Her thought met his just at the right junction. He did not answer because her argument was unanswerable. How else avoid coming on the paternal purse again?

"I am only asking you, Morgan, to let me help you live just as you want to live."

48

She spoke with pleading and humility.

"We shall be towards each other just as we are now," she continued, "and although I intended to torment you till you agreed I was worth an occasional kiss on the forehead in return for mine—which would not at all take us out of the platonic, or rather plutonic, regions in which you so sternly insist we must abide—I shall give you my word to cease from active hostilities for six whole months. Just think—I undertake to be content for the next six months with kissing you on the forehead once each time. Is that not sufficiently an earnest of my good faith?"

Again he gave her no answer, and, in the silence that followed, their footsteps seemed to be echoed back to them. Since to die were futile, let it be she rather than another that helped him to live. She was a good friend and a loyal one. Of course, it was repugnant to take money from a woman, but to take it from anybody else would be still more repugnant.

"As is usually the case in life," she again chimed in his thought, "the choice is not between the good and the less good, but between the bad and the worse. Believe me, I understand and sympathise with your hesitations. But between such friends as we are and such original people to boot, scruples of a conventional kind ought not to enter. With us money should count for nothing. So please don't choose 'the worse,' and perhaps 'the bad' won't turn out so very bad after all."

Still he could not prevail upon himself to accept her generosity, though conscious he was undeserving of her long-sufferance.

"If I could but see the least prospect of repaying you, I should not hesitate so much," he said at last.

"My dear Morgan, in life one mustn't look too far ahead, else existence becomes impossible. Let us not bother too much about the future, but let us seize the flying moments; which means we ought to go to Whitechapel on Thursday and spend a happy day."

He was still lost in thought.

"And your silence—may I put the usual interpretation on it?"

"I suppose so," he said, shame-facedly. "Please don't think me ungracious," he added.

"You very dear person!" she cried; and after that they walked for fully five minutes without exchanging a word.

The matter had been decided and, according to their wont, there was no further manifestation, no further reference to it on either side. Each understood the other's emotions, and that sufficed.

CHAPTER VIII.

"Shall I put you into a hansom?" said Morgan, looking at his watch as they passed out of the park. "It is getting on towards two."

"Mayn't I come in and smoke a cigarette?" pleaded Lady Thiselton. "My nerves have been tried a little, and a few minutes' rest will soothe me."

"I fear the lady of the house would not approve."

"Oh! we shall creep in quietly without disturbing her pious dreams. Do be nice, Morgan. You know I never smoke any other cigarettes than yours—I am never wicked except in your company."

They entered almost noiselessly.

"How silent the night is," she remarked, "and what a feeling of sleeping multitudes there is in the air! Suppose the morrow should dawn and they should never awaken. I am shivering. Your room is cold, though the moonlight is quite pretty."

He lighted his reading lamp under its big, green shade. She would not have the gas—she liked the room full of dusk and shadow. The fire was ready laid, and Morgan put a match to it, after which he proceeded to look for the cigarettes. When eventually he turned towards her, he uttered a suppressed exclamation.

She had taken off her heavy cloak and her hat and thrown them carelessly on a chair. She now stood a little to the left of the fire, her face half turned towards it, and was busy removing her long gloves. Her features, amid which nestled mystic trembling shadows, showed bloodless, as though carved of ivory, and her great, dark brown eyes were wonderfully soft and caressing. Her hair ran in a flowing curve off the warm white pallor of her brow till it was lost beyond the ear. Almost on top of her head it lay in a coil, bound with a wide, green velvet band that was fastened in front with a great emerald. Her throat, neck and shoulders rose with the same dull, smooth whiteness, and with an exquisite firmness, from the strange, green velvet costume it had pleased her to wear, and were set in its gold border that glowed and sparkled with smaller emeralds. The robe curved in at the waist, defining the adorable grace of her figure and falling to the ground in gleaming folds and strange contrasts of light and shade. And on each side hung a long, open sleeve with bright yellow lining spread out to the view—a wide, descending sweep of gold in glistening contrast with the deep green of the costume.

She had now placed her gloves on the same chair, and her long, bare arms showed in all the firm beauty of warm ivory tones, without a touch of rose in their whole length, even to the very finger tips. A thick, gold bracelet encircled the wrist of her right hand. On the other hand the gleam of ornament was given by the wedding ring and a similar ring on the same finger set with a limpid diamond.

"Well," she said, smiling.

"You have taken me unawares. One moment you are a soberly clad person, and the next a queenly blaze."

"The moonlight is really wonderful. Turn out the lamp and let me play the 'Moonlight Sonata.'"

"No, smoke your cigarette instead," he suggested.

"You are afraid I might cause the good lady pleasant dreams instead of pious ones. Thank you, dear."

He held her a light, and, after she had taken a puff or two, she passed her cigarette to him.

"Your tribute, Morgan," she demanded.

He took a puff and passed it back to her. Then, when she had smoked a little:

"It is delicious," she said. "Your lips have given it their sweetness of honey, their fragrance of myrrh."

She leaned leisurely against the mantel, whilst he drew a chair for himself to the opposite corner of the fire. The great emerald gleamed through a dainty cloud of smoke.

"It is lovely here," she said at last. "Such moments as these are the happiest of my life. One's nature must rebel sometimes against being driven along the prescribed lines. There are sides to one's soul, absolutely unallowed for in the ordinary scheme of civilized existence. But instead of letting me moralise, you might be saying some nice things."

"About what?"

"About me, of course."

"Oh! I am enjoying the spectacle you present."

"I built a palace in the air, and, lo and behold! it has proved to be a real palace. I went up to my room to-night and was feeling fanciful and sentimental, which means, of course, I was thinking about you. And then I imagined this whole scene—only a little different; I in this dress, and you at my feet, worshipping me and calling me all sorts of sweet names. And I was coy and held back!"

She paused a moment and laughed merrily.

"Of course," she went on, "I could not resist putting on the costume in order to get nearer the real feeling of such a scene, and it was so delicious that I at once wrapped myself up and come here in a cab. The maid told me you were not expected till late. It's very amusing, by the way—that girl really believes I'm your sister! So I made a descent on dear, stupid Laura—the admirer of your sweet-little-girl poem—and whiled away an hour or so. All muffled up, of course. Her heart's weak, you know. Then I strolled back here. And now my imaginary scene is being enacted. Not exactly as I imagined it, but I know the realities of existence and the usual tragic fate of expectations, and so I have reason to feel ecstatic over the result. Besides, I think I really do look very nice. The contractor for the clay must accidentally have supplied a little of the first quality at the time I was made. He must have torn his hair on finding out the mistake. Come, Morgan, kiss me on the forehead."

She put the cigarette on the mantel, prettily blew away the smoke, and held her two splendid arms towards him. But he did not move.

"I'll even put on the veil and keep my hands behind me, like a good child."

"Helen! Please," he protested.

"Forgive me," she said, and there was a strain of pathos in her voice. "For the moment I forgot my promise—I was fancying this was a mere continuation of my vision. But I shall not do it again—I shall bite out my tongue first."

He was moved, and awoke to the understanding that he had not yet estimated, according to the ordinary reckoning of the world, the pecuniary favour he had accepted from her. The fact that he felt shame at the resource of which circumstances forced him to avail himself could not affect his sense of her nobility, and it was a true instinct of gratitude that made him rise in order to bestow what she had ceased to demand. But, somewhat to his astonishment, she waved him back.

"No, Morgan; I really meant what I said, and you must not think I am only tricky."

After which he felt forced to pin her to her request, protesting her honesty was not in dispute.

"You know I am to be trusted," she whispered demurely. "I am so glad you did not insist on the veil. I must really smoke another cigarette to get calm; I am as agitated as a girl getting her first kiss."

"And I'll smoke another to keep you company," he said.

"Let us meet clandestinely somewhere on Thursday about ten o'clock," she said a little later. "It makes it ever so much more piquant to proceed mysteriously. We shall lunch in those parts. I must be home again by five, as I have a small dinner-party. I have an idea, Morgan. One of my men writes he won't be able to turn up. You've never dined at my house in state. Come and fill the vacant place."

He shook his head. His instinct was to refuse without considering. She insisted a little, but, seeing his heart was against it, left the subject, turning gaily to something else.

Soon he went out with her and saw her into a hansom. It was past two when he bade her good-night, having agreed to a rendezvous for Thursday in the heart of the city.

CHAPTER IX.

It was a little past mid-day, and Archibald Druce, who had returned an hour before from an early morning professional appointment with Medhurst, was feeling restless and lonely. Morgan was not due till half-past one, and so the old man wandered disconsolately about the hotel, seeking some congenial spirit with whom to hold converse. At length, peering into the smoking-room, he discovered a white-haired, stately gentleman, with a somewhat military air, whose grave appearance was encouraging. With him Archibald began an exchange of civilities, and very soon launched out into an account of his interview of that morning.

"I assure you, my dear sir," said the banker, though the other had not questioned the fact in any way, "I can see absolutely nothing. The room is a perfect blur, and I fear I dare not venture out into these crowded London thoroughfares for the rest of the day. The worst of it is that the introduction of the cocaine into my eyes has been of no avail. Of course my eminent friend could not know I was possessed of such remarkable eyes, and as it was necessary for him to see into them, no blame attaches to him for having adopted the usual means of causing my extremely small pupils to expand. Now the curious point is that my pupils were totally unaffected by the cocaine, and I fear my eminent friend had to work on me under difficulties. The couple of hours I spent with him in his wonderful workroom have, however, proved exceedingly profitable to me. I assure you, my dear sir, they have been most instructive."

"No doubt," said the military person, his fingers fidgetting uneasily with his newspaper.

"Between ourselves," continued Archibald confidentially, "I rather imagine that my friend enjoyed the time I spent with him. It is not often he gets a really intelligent patient to work on—in fact, he found me so appreciative that he exhibited especially some profoundly interesting experiments. Amongst other things, he threw a gigantic representation of my retinal system of blood vessels on to a white screen merely by turning a strong light sideways into my eye. And the explanation of it was quite simple. The retinal vessels stand out slightly in relief, and thus a perfect shadow of the system is cast on the retina. It was this shadow I saw, and the white screen was merely a convenient background for it. I don't know if I make myself clear."

"Perfectly clear, perfectly," said the military person.

"Indeed, John Medhurst seemed quite loth to part with me. I quite believe he enjoyed the experiments as much as I did. He brought out his books and very kindly allowed me to inspect the plates—and extraordinarily fine plates they are!—and thus acquire some idea of the inner mechanism of the human eye. What a truly wonderful place the universe is—wonderful!"

"That no intelligent man can deny," said the military person.

"My friend holds a most distinguished position in his profession, and I esteem it a great honour and privilege to be on such intimate terms with him," said Archibald, offering a cigar to the other and lighting one himself. "Now you know," he went on, in a somewhat softened and more intimate tone; "there's quite a little bit of a romance in the story of our friendship."

"Indeed," said the military person more genially, his palate savouring the exquisite aroma of the cigar.

Archibald smiled tenderly.

"His wife's an old flame of mine," he explained, veiling his emotion with jocular phraseology. "An old flame, did I say? I'm still over head and heels in love with her. But I was too late—she and John had already made their little arrangements. And very soon after John and I became friends, and friends we've remained to this day. Kate has two of the loveliest girls, and I'm hanged if I'm not head over heels in love with them as well. The younger one is a regular little she-devil!"

"Ha! ha! ha!" guffawed the military person.

"Upon my honour she is," insisted Archibald. "Why, she flirts outrageously with me. I'm sure I don't know how many heads the little witch is going to turn when she grows up. And her sister, Margaret—I couldn't tell you which of the two I like the better—has quite an extraordinary talent for plastic art. I mean to give her a commission before I return to my place. I'd like for one thing to have a bust of her mother in my study—that would be so inspiring. And long ago I took a fancy to have a nice sphinx. A thing of that kind, you know, is good to remind one of man's intellectual limitations."

"I suppose so," said the military person, vaguely.

"Her figures are extremely lifelike. Just imagine, a thing cast in dead bronze to have all the reality of life so that you would almost expect it to move."

"She must be a highly-gifted young lady."

"You will scarcely credit it, my dear sir, but she is only nineteen—on my word of honour," said Archibald with growing enthusiasm. "Only the other day she sold two of her things for twenty-five pounds apiece. Twenty-five pounds apiece!" he repeated slowly, as if that represented to him a gigantic amount. "The examples are to be strictly limited to sixty of each, after which the moulds are to be destroyed. They are both magnificent pieces of work. Why, you fancy you almost hear Chiron's voice and the twanging of his harp."

"Indeed," said the military person.

"She is perfectly sweet and beautiful as well as clever," went on Archibald. "Now my dog of a boy, between ourselves—ha! ha! ha!——"

"He's a bit smitten?" suggested the military person.

Archibald laughed gleefully. "And I fancy that a certain clever young lady of nineteen who knows how to model is also a bit smitten. Only my boy doesn't seem to come to the point. But then he's a poet."

"A what?" inquired the military person, startled.

"A poet," stoutly repeated Archibald. "And a very great poet, I venture to assert, he will be one of these fine days. Naturally he is not a man of action—he is a dreamer. But when I wanted Kate I wasn't satisfied just to go on dreaming about her—ha! ha! Now if my boy would only stop dreaming and just get married instead, I'd settle as much on them as ever they'd want. You see, a genius like my son," he went on, lowering his voice almost to a whisper, "must be exempt from the sordid cares of money-earning, and my eminent friend, though his position in life is an extremely honourable one, is not a man of means. He may have put by a bit out of his hard-earned income, but, as I always say to him, he wants that against a rainy day. But it's no use my talking to him—he will keep on worrying about his girls having no fortunes. 'And suppose they don't marry,' says he; and I have positively to laugh him into a more cheerful mood. 'Don't be a fool, John,' I say to him, 'those two girls are worth all the fortunes in the world, and the man who didn't think as much wouldn't be worth marrying.'"

"Your views are extremely generous," said the military person. "They do you credit."

"Not at all, my dear sir," said Archibald, looking pleased; "my views are simply rational. I consider the blind worship of mere money an utter mistake. There are higher things in life. I may say I am in entire sympathy with my son's aspirations. By the way, it occurs to me that the extraordinary refusal of my pupils to expand under cocaine may be but another manifestation of the remarkable nervous system that characterises my family. It may be connected in some mysterious way with my son's genius. But possibly, sir, you may know my son?"

"I fear I have not that honour. I know only one literary gentleman—he is the editor of the 'Christian Bugle.' Might I suggest that we exchange cards?"

"Willingly," said Archibald. "Very happy to make your acquaintance, Major Hemming," he resumed, after the mutual self-introduction had been effected. "My son is to be here shortly, when you will have the opportunity of meeting him. Perhaps you will do us the honour of lunching with us?"

"I should be delighted, but unfortunately I am lunching with a friend."

"I am sorry we are not to have the pleasure," said Archibald. "But perhaps you would like a copy of my son's book. It is but a small volume, as you see." And Archibald pulled the parchment-bound, deckle-edged booklet from his outer breast pocket. "Don't hesitate, my dear sir, it will give me pleasure if you will accept it."

"You are most kind," said the Major. "I shall look forward to reading it with the utmost pleasure."

"I am sure you will agree that only a genius could have written those poems," said Archibald.

"I have no doubt but what I shall form a high opinion of your son's gifts," said the Major.

"Being of a literary temperament myself," went on Archibald, "I happily have been able to appreciate his. I do not want him to work for money, and I have, therefore, put him on a sound financial basis. So far, he appeals only to a very select section of the public. But he has not written a line which he has not been inspired to write. As regards the general public—I myself, in my humble way, have become aware of the indifference and stupidity of the general public. When, after thorough re-examination of every point of my mental position, I try and speak plainly to such of my fellow-men as I have the opportunity of addressing, I am met with an absolute want of intelligent comprehension. However, I intend to say what I have to say, and I am now at work on a volume, the nature of which you will sufficiently gather from its title: 'Plain Thoughts of a Practical Thinker—an attempt to investigate some questions of primary importance that are usually shelved.'"

"An excellent idea, sir."

"To give you an example of the narrowness even of people who occupy a high position in the social sphere, whenever I have ventured to assert my sincere belief that children should be instructed in life by means of competent handbooks instead of being allowed to pick up their knowledge in a haphazard, more or less dangerous fashion, I have been met with a frigid politeness, behind which the shocked disapproval was but too manifest."

"Humph!" said the Major. "I must confess your proposition is certainly a startling one."

"It is a common-sense one," said Archibald, curtly.

"Pardon me," said the Major, somewhat stiffly, "but I do think that in the interests of morality and religion it would be exceedingly unfortunate if your ideas were generally adopted."

"I am perfectly prepared to argue the point," said Archibald, drawing himself up, whilst his eye flashed with the light of battle.

"I fear I have no time just now," said the Major, glancing at his watch. "I must be off. I wish you a very good morning, sir."

"Morgan, my boy," cried the banker, when that gentleman at last appeared, "I've spent the last hour tackling one of the most terrible Philistines I have ever met."

END OF BOOK I.

BOOK II.

CHAPTER I

"Which way do we go?" asked Lady Thisleton, as they stood hesitating at a crossing-stage in Broad Street, City. "Wouldn't it be nice to stay here and philosophise?"

She was dressed as plainly as possible in a dark brown coat and skirt, and wore a small hat and veil, so that she was not in the least conspicuous. Both she and Morgan, having entered on the day's adventure, were determined to enjoy it, though his mood was far from being whole-hearted. And, as they surveyed the slow medley of omnibuses that moved between them and the pavement they were struck by the scene in the same impersonal way. They did not feel that they formed any part of it; they saw it as with the eyes of a floating, invisible spirit. To them it was collective movement and colour— movement in the hurrying streams pouring from every exit of the giant stations, in the massed chaos of vehicles, in the sense of bustle and business and purpose; colour in the crudities of blue, green, yellow, red, that flared from omnibuses and shop windows, and that yet were fused into the dun monochrome of town, to the overwhelming sense of which asphalt and paving and street lamp and stone buildings and sober costumes all contributed, and with which the very hubbub seemed to blend.

A vague feeling of tragedy seemed to invade them as their eyes rested on all this life; but it was the result of an intellectual perception, not of a sympathetic realisation and comprehension of this throbbing reality. As for Morgan, the scene made him remember he had once tried to wrestle with political economy and had disliked it tremendously, and the thought made him smile.

"Why do you smile?" said Lady Thiselton. "Certainly it is not gay here. I feel quite overwhelmed. All these faces—pre-occupied, cheerful, sad, worn, despairing, hopeful, starved, well-fed—suggest such a whirl. I invent a whole biography for each one that catches my eye. I wonder how far I am right—I who am only a woman of the world; which means I know nothing of life outside of my own four walls and a few other four walls that more or less resemble them. But it's all really lovely, isn't it, Morgan? What suffering must be here! You can't imagine how I'm enjoying everything. Of course I sympathise as well. But mine is a sort of artistic sympathy. I'm not noble enough to feel the real thing. Isn't it all interesting?"

"There's a policeman staring at us suspiciously."

"Then we'd better move on. The good policeman's dream of paradise must be a place in which he is the one static soul and in which the blest keep passing on to all eternity."

They crossed the road and moved along with the crowd. The bells of St. Botolph's struck ten as they turned into Bishopsgate.

"I feel the mediæval spirit coming on and begin to see visions of highly-coloured Lord Mayors and aldermen and burghers and beef-eaters. And somehow Dick Whittington and his cat are mixed up with it all, and exhibitions with glass roofs and careful craftsmen and apprentices, and Christopher Wren. Alas and alack! Where is old London?"

"I don't know," said Morgan. "But I do know where Whitechapel is. We have to pass through Houndsditch. I looked it up on the map to refresh my memory. I have always found Houndsditch a disappointment."

"So have I," said Lady Thiselton. "It is every bit as uninspiring as a West End street. Some of the side alleys look interesting though, but then such strange people seem to be in absolute possession, and you feel you have no right to set foot within their territory. I am really a fearful coward."

They walked on silently.

"Why don't you contradict me, Morgan, and tell me I'm brave? You never voluntarily pay me a compliment. If I want compliments I have to put them before you as so many propositions, to which, being a truthful person, you are forced to give your assent."

"You are brave," said Morgan.

"Thank you. Every stone in this part of the city has its associations, its traditions, its history. And then there are venerable churches isolated amid the serried buildings of commerce, with charming bits of hidden green and trees. I'm chattering away like a country cousin come up to see the sights of London town and to carry back its fifteenth century flavour. Let us forget history and tradition, and let us get an unadulterated vision of the modern. Here is a nice place to stand."

They had turned into Aldgate and had gone some distance in the direction of Whitechapel, and the new scene had a character of its own. Both felt the spirit of toil here, where the grime of industry struck a coarser and somberer note.

"I feel a million miles from home, which is just what I want to feel," declared Lady Thiselton. "And there is quite a market place opposite, and bookstalls. This is just what Browning could have described. Why did he not come here for inspiration? Here, too, he might have found a square, old yellow book and paid eightpence for it, and tossed it in the air and caught it again and twirled it about by the crumpled vellum covers, and could have wandered on reading it through a perilous path of fire-irons, tribes of tongs, shovels in sheaves, skeleton bedsteads, wardrobe drawers agape, and cast clothes a-sweetening in the sun. But the crowd is really too thick to walk amongst. As we are on pleasure bent, let us be recklessly extravagant and take a twopenny ride on top of a tram-car."

Morgan admitted he was beginning to find it unpleasant to be at such close quarters with the crowd. Some of the people he was brushing up against, he complained, were not too scrupulously clean.

"No doubt," he added, "I shall find them with their mysterious bundles more picturesque from a distance."

"Why some of them are quite spick and span with their polished silk hats, and there are any number of pretty girls. The shops, too, seem quite attractive. I can even imagine myself living here for a time, cannot you?"

"Let us get on our tram car. That may give my imagination the necessary stimulus."

At first they had the top all to themselves, and were borne smoothly onwards, cutting through the very centre of the turmoil. The red brick church was the furthest point she had ever reached in the East of London, Lady Thiselton informed Morgan. She had been in the neighbourhood two or three times in company with her husband, who had been interested in a sort of mission and dispensary combined, his idea being not only to make wicked people religious, but to irritate the devil by keeping their souls out of his clutch as long as possible.

"Now it is only like the High Street of a big provincial town," she commented, after they had passed the London Hospital. "I think it's getting monotonous."

Three begrimed, strapping youths came clambering up noisily and, sitting immediately in front of them, continued a conversation about a certain "she." Their vocabulary became so offensive that Lady Thiselton whispered she thought it perfectly improper for a lady to keep on looking at the backs of men's necks on the top of a car, in full view of the whole world.

They descended and strolled on further. There was no crowd now to hinder them, and they were curious to see what this far-stretching thoroughfare led to.

"So far it seems a broad stretch of mean quaintness. I had no idea London was so big. And what grimy side streets! I shudder to think of the grimy network that lies on either hand. Morgan, I feel a very immoral person."

"Your emotions are strangely unpredictable."

"What right have I to forty thousand a year when there are people starving in these back streets?" asked Lady Thiselton indignantly. "I am going to turn Socialist."

"You are not."

"I am."

"You'll never abandon individualism."

"Of course not. I'd never think of parting with that. But I really don't see why I shouldn't be a Socialist as well. I pity those poor, benighted beings that have room in their narrow souls for only one set of opinions. I like to be everything, to hold every 'ism,' and to be labelled all over with every 'ist,' like the window of that 'eating-house' yonder. Which reminds me of my dinner party to-night. Isn't it terrible to eat in Belgrave Square when some people have to eat in a place like that. It's positively wicked. I have an idea. I think I can't do better than inaugurate my new 'ism' by lunching there to-day. Suppose we do so on our way back."

"But *I* never confessed to be converted to socialism," he protested.

"Why it's a dear little eating-house, a perfect love of a place."

"I take it for granted you wish to meet your guests to-night with a smiling face," he warned her.

"The consciousness of having had the courage of my 'ism' will fill me with such a glow of goodness that I cannot fail to appear a veritable Madonna. Of course, you know I am counting on you."

"No."

"Yes."

"No."

"But I haven't filled up the place. I've been relying on nagging you into coming."

"You know I don't want to," he grumbled yieldingly.

"But I want you to. Don't be angry, dear," she went on, coaxingly. "Haven't I amused you the whole time?"

He ended by promising to come, if not incapacitated by the lunch, and felt fairly secure of passing the evening at home.

After they had wandered about for some time longer and had paid pennies to see a curious compound animal, a sort of ox, sheep, horse, donkey and goat rolled into one, and an abnormally fat woman, more decently clad than the life-size coloured picture of her in the window had led them to imagine, they invaded the love of an eating-house. They stepped within the threshold firmly enough, but then stood hesitant. The place gave them a general sense of brownness. It was the old-fashioned style of coffee-house, with a sanded pathway down the middle and a row of stalls on either side, each separated from its neighbours by tall partitions. Everything was of a dirty brown, panelling, partitions, benches and the bare tables. A brown light came through the dingy windows, and the very odours that hung in the dingy atmosphere suggested the same tint.

A coatless, aproned waiter emerged from the back to greet the first mid-day customers, and, in reply to their enquiry for lunch, invited them to be seated within one of the stalls. After he had wiped their table he disappeared, and he returned in a moment with a table cloth, followed by a shorter and stouter man, also in shirt sleeves. They began to see they had made an impression, and were to be served in accordance with the host's sense of the fitness of things.

The proprietor—for such the stout man was—by way of special civility, remarked that it was fine weather, and asked what he might get them.

"The correct thing," said Lady Thiselton; and, on the man staring, "what everybody usually has here," she added, in explanation.

"Boiled beef and suet to-day, or roast beef and Yorkshire, or chops and steaks," enumerated the man.

So "boiled beef and suet" was ordered on the assumption it was the correct thing, and, while the waiter was busy getting it, the proprietor felt it his duty to entertain them till it came.

"His intentions were no doubt strictly honourable, but, Morgan, do you think we shall have to talk to people like that when socialism is established? My goodness!" she exclaimed, examining the slices of meat closely. "What are those green streaks?"

"Perhaps that's perfectly right. The green streaks—like the boiled carrot—may be just a little surprise by way of extra. Neither is included in the description of the dish."

"Morgan, I really don't think I can eat this," she said faintly.

"Backsliding already?"

"Not at all. You forget I'm a bundle of 'isms,' and in practice one can only be true to one at a time. When that one begins to make me feel uncomfortable, I become true to another. Thus I am always true to myself. All the mutually contradictory 'isms' unite in a higher synthesis. Am I not the most lovely higher synthesis you ever saw?"

"All of which Hegelian dialectics mean that I'd better tell them to take this stuff away."

"If you think they won't maltreat us. They look terribly fierce; and they may have any number of myrmidons within call. That sort of people, you know, doesn't like to have its cooking criticised."

"So long as we pay, we'll not find them too sensitive."

The matter was soon arranged, they adopting the man's suggestion of a "nice, juicy steak." And when it arrived they felt compelled to pronounce it excellent.

"I shouldn't be surprised if those green streaks were the proper thing after all," said Lady Thiselton.

"Doubtless we have missed some extraordinary delicacy," said Morgan. "But please tell me which particular 'ism' is in possession at the moment. I am not quite clear on the point."

"That is just my state of mind. But I fancy that, at the present moment, I am given over to emotion rather than to thought. This interior is affecting me artistically. I was just thinking what a lovely Dutch picture it would make. But I really am sincere about my 'isms.' The arguments in favour of any one 'ism' are unanswerable, and I have to admit the truth of each, whenever I consider it. All human thought ends in the blind alley of Paradox. Hegel was a word-juggler. Nice phrases are pleasing, but let us not take them seriously."

And Lady Thiselton proceeded to utter a good many "nice phrases," which Morgan found pleasing, and did not take seriously. Customers dropped in by ones and twos till at length all the other stalls were filled, everybody instinctively avoiding the stall where a tablecloth gleamed its white warning. When some men, having eaten, began smoking their clays, Lady Thiselton's sharp ear detected some speculative remarks about herself and Morgan, tinged with facetiousness and gore. She thereupon suggested she was pining for something mystic and spiritualistic, being quite tired of this realistic interior.

"I am trying to banish it by contemplating the Blessed Damozel," she said, and quoted whisperingly:

> "'The Blessed Damozel leaned out
> From the gold bar of Heaven;

Her eyes were deeper than the depth
Of waters stilled at even;
She had three lilies in her hand,
And the stars in her hair were seven.'"

A moment later they stepped out into the afternoon light that nearly blinded them with its mournful glare. But a heavy sadness had descended on Morgan. The lines Lady Thiselton had whispered to him had set him thinking of Margaret.

CHAPTER II.

The same evening, Morgan, not feeling any alarming symptoms, had to carry out his promise to join Lady Thiselton's little dinner party. She received him with a formality that made him laugh inwardly—and almost outwardly. But the impulse died away as with a start he perceived that Robert Ingram was in the drawing-room. He reflected, however, that, though the encounter was an unexpected one, there was nothing very astonishing about it. Helen had herself told him she had made the novelist's acquaintance, and to find him dining at her house was no matter for surprise. The position, nevertheless, was a most curious one, especially when their hostess unsuspectingly introduced the two men. Ingram's manner was a little bit bewildered, as if—from his knowledge of Morgan—he feared the latter might make a scene by dramatically cutting him.

However, nothing of the kind happened, Morgan behaving with perfect gravity. He had to give his arm to Mrs. Blackstone—Helen's dear friend, Laura, of whom she had spoken to him as the most stupid woman she knew. He would have welcomed the opportunity of talking to her—for he was sure her conception of Helen would be astonishingly amusing, but he had a feeling that something important was going to arise from his coming here to-night, and that there were possibilities of explosion in the position. This gave him a general sense of expectant excitement, so that at first he was a little bit impatient of Mrs. Blackstone's remarks. He learnt that she admired intensely that sweet little poem of his, and that she had been longing to meet the writer; also that reading was a great blessing when one felt miserable. Did he not admire Mr. Ingram? She herself adored his work. He was constrained to reply that Ingram was one of his literary heresies, whereupon she, with ready resource, supposed that tastes differed, and then, as the result of a luminous thought, she added that a poet would naturally not be so much interested in mere prose. Of course poetry ranked the higher, but she was ashamed to confess—she made the confession without any sign of shame—she scarcely ever read any at all. She had several favourite novelists who each published so many books a year that it took all the time she could spare to keep pace with them.

"And indeed I'm glad they manage to write so much. They help to fight against the flood of nasty realistic works we get nowadays. I should like to see those all burnt."

Mrs. Blackstone went on to observe that she couldn't make out why people went on writing such filth. She preferred books of a sound, moral tone.

Morgan, feeling himself called upon to make common cause against the Philistine, put in a tentative word of defence.

"That's true," admitted Mrs. Blackstone.

He soon drew further admissions from her, she never suspecting the extent of the ground she was yielding till, just at the moment of rising, she apparently gave up her whole position with the naïve statement:

"I always thought they had a reason for introducing that sort of thing. Thank you so much, Mr. Druce, for explaining it to me."

He was not quite sure whether he had been bored or amused. All the same he now felt glad he had come; he seemed to be so much more actively interested in what was to follow. Instinctively he looked at Ingram, and the novelist came to talk to him whilst the other men discussed the hygienic aspects of smoking.

"Well, have you got over your temper yet?"

The phrasing was unfortunate, though its conciliatory intention was obvious. Morgan felt he was being addressed as if he were a sulky child, and his resentment leapt up afresh.

"I beg you will not interest yourself further in me," he said.

"Suppose we omit some of the conversation," suggested Ingram, "and assume all that sort of thing to have been said. You are hurt because I showed your letter to a friend. Aren't you taking a distorted view of the matter? Recollect that at the time you were an utter stranger, and your letter was a bolt from the blue. I cannot see that I committed so very great a crime."

"It is as great or as little as you feel it to be."

"And how may it be purged?" asked Ingram ironically.

"Ponder over it till you perceive its enormity, then apologize to me in the presence of the woman."

Morgan scarcely realised what he was saying till the words were out. Apparently he had spoken without hesitating and without thinking, but he knew that his utterance was the result of all that had occupied his mind for many days past. He felt now he was on the road towards the realisation of that fantastic future, that poem in life that was to take the place of the poetry in words he had abandoned.

Ingram gave him a strange, piercing look. Morgan had never before seen in his face such an expression as he saw in it now. There was a pregnant pause before the reply came.

"Very well, then. We will go to her to-night. No doubt the others will now be glad to hear our views on tobacco smoke."

Morgan was conscious of a strange glow of pleasure, of a strange satisfaction. All his sense of romance and mystery was astir. How charming was the promise of the phantasy to come! The smiling, scented serpent-woman was holding her arms to him! And again those lines of Browning echoed through him, and his whole being seemed invaded as by a "faint sweetness from some old Egyptian's fine, worm-eaten shroud."

He defended moderate smoking with vivacity.

Afterwards, the guests being disposed for conversation in the drawing-room, Helen managed to sit with Morgan a little apart.

"What do you think of Mr. Ingram?" she asked. "Did you talk to him at all?"

"He seems fairly intelligent," replied Morgan; "more intelligent, in fact, than his work would lead one to suppose. You told me the other day, did you not, that you have known him some little time?"

"It is only during the last few months that I have cultivated him or rather he me."

"I see Mrs. Blackstone has possession of him now. She must be very happy."

"She is his greatest confidante. That I am *her* greatest confidante, you know already, *ergo*—well, I'll leave you to make the deduction. She is really a good soul, and a marked success as an ear trumpet."

"But is Mr. Ingram aware of that?"

"Quite. That is why he speaks into her such a deal. He finds me perfectly deaf otherwise."

All this was a revelation to Morgan.

"You seem to be hinting at something," he could not help exclaiming.

"Of course. Mr. Ingram is anxious to marry a title, and, since he does not object to having a good-looking person attached to it, he has done me the honour to pretend to be in love with me. He has been proposing for the last six weeks, and has offered to purify his books still further to suit my virginal soul."

"And you professed to be telling me everything interesting," he reproached her.

"Why, I left off telling you about my wooers and proposals at your own request. You insisted they would never make you jealous, and they rather bored you. So I did not say a word about this one. Of course Laura is anxious to further his cause. She thinks me a good woman and somewhat of a prude. Poor soul! She doesn't suspect the wedding ring with the diamond in it you've seen me sometimes wear! You know it's the sort of thing wicked women affect when they want to be cynical about the marriage tie. Well, Laura is doing her best to persuade me to be the instrument of Mr. Ingram's reform. She thinks it such a pity his life has not been so wholesome in tone as his novels. Her admiration of him is so great that she wants him to live up to her conception of the author of his novels, and I am to be sacrificed for the purpose. She is ten years my senior, and you will observe her interest in me is quite maternal. But I must tell you more about it another time. The doctor's looking bored. I must go and amuse him."

CHAPTER III.

Shortly after midnight Morgan and Ingram were driving towards Hampstead, in which vicinity, the latter explained, resided the lady upon whom they were going to call. For a long time the two sat silent—they seemed to have nothing to say to each other.

And even while Morgan was thrilled through and through with expectancy of romance, he could not help his brain playing a little with the general position, which, in face of what he had learnt to-night, was far more complicated than he had imagined. He smiled as it occurred to him how easily he could annoy Ingram by marrying Helen. Curious, he thought, that Ingram had not the least suspicion of it!

"May I not ask who is the lady?" he said at last.

"She is nobody in particular," said Ingram. "I call her 'Cleo,' which is sufficient for all practical purposes. There is really no reason why I should not tell you now that Cleo, in fact, has been the companion of my leisure for the past six years. I will leave you to form your own impression of her."

Ingram spoke with an exaggerated air of bluntness, as if to indicate his indifference to whatever effect his statement might produce on Morgan. The latter, however, was not very much surprised. His active feeling was rather one of bewilderment as to the part Ingram was playing in this tangle of relations. The fact that Ingram had turned up as a suitor for Helen's hand, when he himself had been all these years in active relation with either unknown to the other, had exhausted all the possibilities of astonishment in him. But he found it strange that Ingram, in spite of his matrimonial intention, should still continue on such terms with this 'Cleo' as to be able to bring a friend to see her in the way he was doing now. Ingram's very readiness to fall in with the suggestion struck him as bearing some significance he could not yet fathom.

Yet, though his mind was thus occupied, Morgan cared little about Ingram's private designs. It satisfied him to feel that Ingram was his unconscious tool, and that he was at length drifting in the right direction. On rattled the vehicle through empty, dark streets, where the very street lamps looked lonely and subtly fostered his mood.

They drew up at length in a narrow street of stucco houses, and Morgan followed Ingram through a wooden gate up a glass-covered stairway that led to an ordinary front door. Ingram opened it with a latch-key, and they stood in a square, little hall, prettily furnished and dimly lighted by an antique hanging lamp.

"Cleo expects me," said Ingram, "but I must ascertain if she will receive both of us."

He disappeared through a door at the back of the hall, and, returning soon, led Morgan through a sort of anteroom into a large inner apartment, on the threshold of which they were met by a waft of strange perfume which Morgan recognised immediately, though for a moment it somewhat overpowered him. The scene, too, was so bizarre that his perception of it lacked sharpness, and his first impression was a dreamy one of fusing colour.

The room itself was large and square, and more than half of the marble inlaid floor was raised several inches above the other part—that on which Morgan stood as he entered. In the centre of this lower part was a small marble fountain, with two tiers of basins, beautifully carved. The water played prettily, overflowing from the lower and larger basin into a daintily-bordered square tank set in the floor. Against the wall beyond the fountain was built a marble slab, supported by a double arch, under which stood ewers and vases. And higher up in this same wall were set two pairs of tiny windows, divided into little coloured panes, with designs of flowers and peacocks.

The ceiling seemed a quaint, flat, immense tangle of gold, green, red and blue thread work, each line of which could be followed till the eye lost it in the maze; and three lamps, suspended by brass chains, filled the room with a ruby light that came through the interstices of fine brass and silver work. The walls were marked out in panelling and covered with a strange, decorative pattern. The raised part of the floor was spread with richly woven rugs of warm tints, and a few stools of curious workmanship stood about. Books lay scattered here and there, as if thrown carelessly on the ground after perusal. In the centre was a gilded couch, upholstered in silk, and, as Ingram mentioned his name, Morgan found himself bowing to the wonderful woman who reclined on it.

She rose at his greeting, tall and of a gipsy-like brown, and clad in a straight terra-cotta robe tied in front with a broad, gold girdle, whose long ends fell floating to the ground. Her feet were sandalled. Her hair was of a rich, golden red, and somehow showed up in contrast to the blue grey of her eyes. Her lips were full and of a startling scarlet, as though they bled. She smiled to Morgan, displaying two rows of tiny white teeth, and held out to him a long, brown hand.

He took it in his, and the contact set vibrating every chord of his nature that had been strung up during the past days. At last he was face to face with the dream-woman who had haunted him, and she was even as he had seen her! And with all his emotion at this sacred moment there mingled a sense of pride that his poet's instinct had divined true.

"I am happy to know you, Mr. Druce. Mr. Ingram has just explained to me why he has brought you. I am so sorry to be the cause of your anger."

Her voice was curiously soft, without the least ring or even suggestion of firmness; warm and yielding as a summer wavelet.

Morgan was somewhat startled at her words; he had almost expected some strange, rich, musical language to fall from her lips.

Ingram drew over a stool, and Cleo bade him be seated. There was somewhat of an embarrassed silence. Morgan scarcely knew how to meet the occasion. It struck him that perhaps he ought to be grateful to Ingram, for he had now a conviction that the letter of his which Cleo had had in her possession had really interested her in him—had touched some sympathetic chord in her— and that the task of cultivating her would not, for that very reason, prove a difficult one. He was certain that her nature had much in common with his own, and that the future which was now to be unrolled was to be a series of tableaux as charming as this first one.

He felt it incumbent upon him to dispose of the matter for which nominally he had come, and murmured that Ingram had now sufficiently shown his good faith, and that he personally was quite satisfied. As he spoke he looked at Cleo again, and her eyes and lips gleamed at him strangely. He was aware she wished to say a good deal to him, but that the presence of Ingram hindered. And as the same constrained silence once more fell upon them, the elusive odour of her perfume seemed to obtrude again, as though taking the opportunity to assert itself.

Ingram at length remarked that the hour was late, and that if Cleo would excuse them he would escort Mr. Druce back. He was glad that harmony had been re-established, and he expressed his thanks to Cleo for so willingly receiving his friend and helping to heal the breach.

Morgan did not mind having this first interview with Cleo thus cut short, especially as he could not talk with Ingram there to listen. He was, moreover, uncomfortably aware that Ingram was watching him closely the whole time, and he did not fail to detect the tinge of irony in the novelist's last little speech. But he felt he had closed his account with the man, and he would not trouble his brains any more about his motives or meaning. He therefore rose to say good-night to Cleo. She offered them wine, but both men refused, so she smilingly gave her hand again without striving to detain them.

Outside, each seemed given up to his own thoughts. Morgan would make no comment on what had been revealed to him, nor apparently did Ingram want to hear any.

They separated at a cab rank, each taking a separate vehicle. And only as they were about to part did Ingram break the silence:

"I need hardly tell you you have seen a hidden side of my life. I look to you to forget."

CHAPTER IV.

The very rapidity of the glimpse that Morgan had had into that Hampstead interior made it the more fascinating to dwell upon in imagination, and, though the definite figure of Cleo now took the place of the vague, smiling woman who had always been with him, it seemed to him that he had discerned Cleo's every feature from the beginning.

The general flow of his thoughts and moods were coloured by this fantastic adventure on which, he now felt, he was fairly embarked. Nevertheless his life was not proceeding precisely on the lines he had conceived when he had resolved to transport his imaginative combinations from the field of paper to the field of life, to weave dreams from reality instead of from thought. That disattachment he had decided on in order that he might abandon himself wholly to the urging of his temperament was proving a much more gradual process than he had supposed.

For as yet the old relations were being continued; the man in him—which the poet was unable to suppress entirely—could not break these off abruptly. Thus, when Margaret's pink note announcing the studio-warming arrived, he could not possibly accept the notion of ignoring it, for was he not her true and healthy lover? His friendship, too, with Lady Thiselton, had even become strengthened in spite of himself. He could not help telling himself again and again that she was as firm and true as a rock. And the very man in him that appreciated her sterling qualities had still a sense of shame at his having taken money from her, forced though his hand had been. The vagueness and nebulousness of the future that suited the poet made the man with his healthy repugnance to debt extremely uncomfortable.

The flow of his existence had thus split up into two currents, but the stronger by far was the poetic force in him that made for a desperate playing with life.

Yet several days passed without his being impelled to go to Cleo again. Even as he had been wont to wait for inspiration, so he waited now for the spirit to move him to the next step in this life-fantasy. His time got frittered away, he scarcely knew how. He replied to several letters from his father, who wrote to him at great length on particular points of ethics, for the banker had by now seriously set to work on his *magnum opus*. Two or three times Helen ran in to see him at tea-time, and did her best to amuse him. The mere reflection that Ingram must suppose he was but the most casual acquaintance of Helen's was sufficient for that; so that she had not a very difficult task, and expressed herself highly pleased at the agreeable mood in which she was now finding him. She chatted quite freely about Ingram and the latest developments of his courtship of her. She had refused him for the fifth time, but he didn't seem the least bit discouraged yet.

"By the way," she went on, "I've just been reading his biography in a magazine. Evidently he has not been as frank with his interviewer as he has been with me. The way I made him confess was just lovely, though now he makes that a grievance, much to my indignation. All I said was I couldn't possibly begin to consider his case till I knew all about him. I made no promise at all. At first, indeed, he was foolish enough to insist his record was spotless. A man who writes novels of such sound moral tone! If only he had written naturalistic novels, I might have believed him."

Morgan wondered if Ingram had included Cleo in his "confession." He was rather inclined to doubt it, because he felt sure that the very strangeness of that *liaison* would have made Helen want to tell him about it.

"And what do you intend to do with him ultimately?" he asked.

"Well, if I thought it would make you the least bit jealous, I should announce that I intended to accept him. But as there is no possible advantage to be gained by such a falsehood, it would be very extravagant of me to waste it. I've scattered so many of them in my time that I must be economical for the rest of my life."

Though he had never for a moment believed there was any possibility of her marrying Ingram, he was yet relieved to hear her state her intentions so definitely. Such was his sense of Ingram's unworthiness of her!

A couple of days later he went to Margaret's studio-warming. Both the experience and the anticipation of it were emotionally exciting. But as a good many of Margaret's particular friends were there, her attention had to be spread out a great deal, and he did not have to talk to her much at first. Certainly there was nothing between them that could be called conversation.

He found it soothing to talk a little with Mrs. Medhurst, who was always equable, nice, and apparently in a pleased mood. She also had been receiving long confidential letters from his father, and she expressed the fear that at the rate the latter was now going in the direction of iconoclasm he was courting public suppression.

"He is very much in earnest," she added. "I have written him at length about the bringing up of daughters—he insisted on having my views. He is very modest, though—just ventures to hope for success. 'If I only had Morgan's pen,' he once wrote, yearningly."

To be reminded now how completely his father had been won over to belief in him was but to have all the bitterness of his failure again concentrated in one moment.

During the rest of the time he found himself carrying on a half-hearted conversation here and there, yet with all his attention on Margaret. He followed her with his eyes, watching her every movement and gesture, noting her every smile, catching her laughter and the sound of her voice. Something that was light, that was sunshine, seemed to detach itself from her and to fill the whole room; something that brought a sense of happiness to mingle with his strange mood.

He felt that happiness as a sick man feels a cool, soft caress on his brow.

CHAPTER V.

One afternoon Morgan took a hansom and drove to Hampstead. He entered the glass-covered way that led up to Cleo's door and knocked unhesitatingly. The servant who responded to his summons stared at him in undisguised astonishment.

"Is your mistress at home?" he asked, for he did not know by what name to enquire for Cleo. He sent in his own, however, and was immediately ushered into her presence. This gave him no elation, because he had taken it for granted she would receive him.

"I had a sort of presentiment you would come to-day," said Cleo, throwing on one side the novel she had been reading, and the cover of which, illumined with seven mystic stars and a veiled floating figure, just caught his eye.

"And I just felt that I *must* come," he said as, at her invitation, he took a seat on one of the quaint stools with somewhat of an air of long habituation to this strange Egyptian chamber.

Cleo was lounging on her gilded settee, obviously arrayed to receive him in the hope of his calling. A vague, mystic light that compelled an almost religious emotion came through the tiny window panes. The fountain played with a soft splash.

"Do you know I am what the vulgar call 'superstitious?'" she continued. "I always knew you would come into my life."

As she spoke her eyes seemed to shine with a greater fire. The scarlet of her lips to-day was somewhat concealed by the half shadows; her hair, too, seemed silkier and more restrained in tone than his first impression of it. Her gown was of a vague colour—a sort of blue-grey, in which the element of blue was suggested as a light continuous tinge. A crimson silk scarf, fastened with an opal buckle, formed a pleasing sash, and fell to the knee. As before, her feet were sandalled.

"That letter of yours Robert showed me—years ago now—made me love you at once," she explained. "Only a man of genius could have written it. How my heart bled for you when you said, 'I see no other end to the comedy than fall. God knows what shape that fall will take, into what mud my soul plunge in the fight for life. I could bear anything if I were not so utterly alone and helpless…. If you could see me, speak to me—help me in any way!' Yes, I wanted to see you—speak to you—help you. It was I who made Robert respond to your appeal. I remember how disgusted I was with him when he insisted on taking the whole thing as a splendid joke, just because he found you had a rich father."

Her strange, soft voice seemed almost informed with dramatic passion as she quoted his letter. It was clear she knew the whole of it by heart. So Ingram's violation of his confidence, he reflected, had been responsible for this interweaving of his life with Cleo's, and his presence here to-day was but the natural continuation of the beginning then made. He confessed to having been angered with Ingram.

"My blundering vision could not see how the strands were being woven," he added.

"I was certain all along they *were* being woven," she returned. "The incident at the time made a great impression on me, and I knew that one day we should come together."

It gave him a thrill of joy to learn that he had been occupying her thoughts for years past; that, having once come within her consciousness, he had remained in her vision as a never-fading image.

"I am encouraged to ask you about yourself," he said. "You know I love you, too."

This last statement was not an insincere one, for he did not conceive it as a real statement made to a real human being. Cleo was his wonderful dream- woman, and he had no notion at all of getting any insight into her as a real woman playing an actual rôle in actual life. He did not think of her as an element of real life at all; she was simply the heroine of the fantasy he was busy weaving. His declaration represented exactly his sentiment towards her in that rôle; it expressed his sense of the fitness of things at the moment, was the requisite correct touch the position demanded—this position which he had mentally isolated from the rest of reality, and in which for the time being he had lost himself.

"I know, dear," she answered. "I will tell you gladly, for I want you to understand and appreciate me. Like you I have always been conscious of genius, but I have had to wait long, bitter years. 'Tis always so with genius. I have ever felt myself a chosen spirit, and I am sure I am destined to become the greatest actress that has yet charmed and captivated the world. Am I not tall, surpassingly beautiful, lithe and supple as a reed—graceful as a lily? But that is not all. In me is reincarnated the spirit of the ancient East, and it is my mission to interpret that spirit to the modern world. I will help you, dear, to realize that same spirit, and then one day, in a grand burst of inspiration you shall write the play of my life. Then shall I break upon the civilized world as a revelation.

"I can remember no time at which I have not been conscious of my mission. But six years ago, when I set out on my journey into the world, I was scarcely more than a child. I had no influence—I knew nobody; and so I had no chance of making a real appearance at once. I had to begin by joining a touring company, and that only to play the rôle of a servant girl. At the time I was glad of any beginning, for I was confident I should make my way. But I soon found myself stranded. Then what do you think I did?"

"You wrote a letter to Ingram—just as I did?" he exclaimed excitedly.

She laughed.

"That is very clever of you. It is exactly what I did. He had a successful play running at one theatre and I read that he was at work on a new play for another manager. I thought that, if I could only induce him to see me, I might get a real chance. My letter produced the desired effect, for in it I had told him exactly what my future was to be. We had an interview and he perfectly agreed with everything I had said about myself. But he swore he could do nothing for me. His plays, he asserted, contained no fit part for me—it would be a thousand pities if I let my strength and energies be dissipated in playing minor parts that any intelligent school girl with a pair of bright eyes could do ample justice to. Then he confided to me that he, too, had plans and ambitions, but that he was not making nearly so much money as he was said to be doing in the personal paragraphs of the newspapers. He was putting aside, however, all he could spare, so that he might have a vast theatre of his own; and if that came to pass I was the one being on earth to be associated with him in such a mighty undertaking. Would I stay with him and wait?

"So I stayed with him, and I have waited—six years! We have built our vast theatre again and again—it was to be the vastest in the world, so that my audience should be worthy of my great gifts. Time after time have we gone together into every detail of the scheme, I always believing that at last we were getting ready in earnest. You will wonder, perhaps, how it is I have allowed myself to be deceived for so long. It was because I believed in him during the first three years, and during the second three I had already lost so much time that I *dared* not disbelieve in him. It was always: 'Just six months more, Cleo, dear, and then we shall astonish the world.' And then the vision of that vast theatre was too fascinating for me to abandon. His excuses were always plausible. Now he had made some terribly bad investment, now a publisher had gone bankrupt, now the sales of his books had fallen tremendously. Besides, he kept complaining bitterly that he was being forced to suppress his genius and individuality and to work for money. Just as he was waiting patiently, so must I wait patiently. He was to write me my great piece, and I was to interpret it. He bought this house for me and had this room rebuilt to suit my ideas, so that the spirit in me should be nourished by a congenial environment. By sitting here each day and meditating, I have ministered to my sacred moods and I have kept pure the essence of the ages which I am to revive for the modern world. Thus the years have not been wasted. I have matured. I am confident my powers have increased, and I have never felt more eager to exercise them than now. Let me but appear in a suitable rôle and both fame and fortune are assured to me, for I shall easily eclipse every living actress.

"Of course, I have recognised now that Robert has been playing me false, at least of late. I should not like to think that he did not really have those ideas in the first years, but I realise now he has abandoned them and hasn't the courage to confess the truth. Of course, he says that his year's finances have all gone wrong again, and that he had seriously underestimated the capital necessary for the undertaking.

"I am not a prisoner, of course. I have always had perfect liberty, and I engaged the maids myself. They are too well paid not to be attached to me. Robert is supposed to be my husband. Of course, they know he isn't. Altogether, I have not been so very unhappy here. This room has been a great comfort to me, and Robert and I have always got on well together. But now we must part. He will miss me after all this time, but there is no reason why we should not part in peace."

She related all this with the greatest naïveté, so that her absolute faith in herself, her genius, and her mission, did not astonish him. The words seemed to flow naturally from the personality.

He was aware she had scarcely given him a biography, but he liked to take her as a mystical figure floating out of a sort of nebula. Such personal details as might have been relatable of any other woman he did not want to know; they would have interfered with this purely artistic vision of her.

"I wish that I had a fortune to place at your disposal," he murmured. "You should have your theatre at once."

"My vast theatre!" she sighed. "I fear I must dismiss that as a hopeless dream. But I could take a theatre and make a less ambitious beginning with very little money, indeed," she added, yearningly.

Then Morgan told her the condition of his finances; how he had exhausted his own resources, and how "a friend"—he referred to Helen in this highly general manner—had lent him five hundred pounds, of which he had scarcely spent anything yet, but which he had not the slightest idea how he was going to repay. Of course, he could not and would not apply to his father again; on which point Cleo readily expressed her sympathy with him.

Asked by him how much she thought would be sufficient to launch her on her career, she could not say at once, but promised to think about it and discuss the matter with him when he came again. She explained that whatever the amount was, it would only be necessary to have it to draw upon in case of need. Success being certain from the first, money would come flowing in immediately, and, if they did decide to embark on the adventure, he would certainly be able to repay his friend very soon.

Her words to him were so many oracular statements, and he no more thought of questioning them than a child thinks of questioning its teacher about the names of the strange marks that constitute the alphabet.

"You will be coming again, then, on Thursday," said Cleo, as he stooped to kiss her hand in token of farewell.

CHAPTER VI.

"My dear," said Cleo, when Morgan came again, "I want to bind you to me for always. Let us marry at once, or, at least, as soon as possible. Then, since we shall have thrown in our lots for good and always, we shall achieve together what we have been unable to do separately. My spirit shall act on yours, and one day your genius shall fashion the great masterpiece of my life. As soon as we are married we shall take a theatre and I shall put on the most suitable play I can find. As I have already told you, I have given up those idle dreams of a vast theatre of my own, in which to make my début. But never before have I felt my powers to be so ripe. Let me but appear for one evening in a part that will enable me to do justice to my gifts and I shall bring the world to my feet. I look to you to help me now, and, by making myself yours for always I shall at least be showing my gratitude and my confidence in you. It is but right that two geniuses should be mated. The fact that we both thought of the same resource under similar conditions—for were you not as forlorn and alone as I?—was prophetic, and clearly indicated it was fated your life and mine were to be cast together."

Her masterful definiteness hypnotised him. Her will was strong enough to do what his own had failed to complete, to draw him away from the rest of the world and absorb his life in hers.

Cleo had entered into his spirit and had at length not only silenced but won over the man in him. She had seized on his whole being, appropriated his every thought, and had attuned to hers every chord of his complex nature. Her perfume and colour, her exotic beauty, had entwined themselves in his every fibre, had enslaved his senses, and intoxicated the thinking part of him. Her genius, too, cast an added glamour of enchantment over the new life that lay before him—a dream-life into which this marriage would take him entirely, and by contrast with which, apart from its anguish, the real life behind him lay dull and leaden.

To link his life with hers! To launch Cleo as a great actress! To win renown side by side! He yielded himself to the prospect with eager enthusiasm!

The notion of taking a theatre that Cleo had put before him at their last meeting had already led him to make a rough calculation of his present resources, and he had estimated that a financial clearing-up would leave him with but little more than three hundred pounds. He mentioned this now somewhat hesitatingly, for he feared that sum might be quite inadequate. He was relieved to hear Cleo say that she could make it suffice; and with her clever management he would very soon be able to discharge his debt to his friend. She knew exactly how to go to work and would make all arrangements, but of course she would let him help her as much as he could.

"We shall set to work the very day we marry, for we must not lose any time. All I shall take away from here are my costumes. I have some money that Robert has given me from time to time, but that I am going to return to him. It would be a desecration for us to use a penny of his in our new life. Of course we must make our home temporarily in furnished rooms."

The next day Morgan paid all his odd, floating debts, and got his particular possessions together; all of which did not occupy him very long. When he saw Cleo again it was arranged that she should take the requisite formal steps for their marriage before the registrar, and that she should also begin negotiations for the renting of a Strand theatre. She had had her final reckoning with Ingram, who had assumed an air of indifference, and had not wanted to know anything about her plans or future movements.

"'Since you have made up your mind,' he said, 'I have no option but to bow to your wishes.' But I could see that his lips were drawn as if his heart ached at having to lose me. I must have meant so much to him all this time. Poor Robert!"

"Of course, I gave him back his money," she went on, when her emotion had subsided. "He took that with the same indifference. He said he could quite appreciate my feeling about it and he would not oppose my wishes on the point."

As regards his family and friends, Morgan made up his mind to write to his father, to Lady Thiselton, and to Mrs. Medhurst, simply announcing the mere fact that he had married. He would not give any particulars nor say a word as to the personality of Cleo. The rest of his acquaintances he would simply ignore.

CHAPTER VII.

However, on the day before his marriage, Morgan happened to come across Mrs. Medhurst's dance card amid a heap of papers he was about to destroy, and somewhat to his surprise found it was for that very evening. He had accepted the invitation verbally, when talking to Mrs. Medhurst at the studio-warming. And now a strange notion seemed to come whizzing at him and he arrested it with a clutch.

Why should he not go and dance with Margaret for the last time?

In a moment his mind was made up. And shortly after ten o'clock he found himself being received by Mrs. Medhurst. A half-dizziness came over him as he shook hands with her—the festal atmosphere that pervaded the rooms seemed to blur his senses. He would have stumbled had it not been that Margaret's voice fell upon his ear just then, and he became aware that her hand was in his. He saw her, as she stood at her mother's side, a clear and gracious figure against the mist of things.

She was in white to-night with just a lily in her hair, and it showed graciously in a dainty setting of green. An adorable tiny edge of arm peeped between sleeve and glove. Morgan thought of the lines Helen had whispered to him at the Whitechapel Coffee House:

"The Blessed Damozel leaned out
From the gold bar of Heaven;
Her eyes were deeper than the depth
Of waters stilled at even."

He wrote his name on her programme. He was feeling timid and self-distrustful, and having taken a dance near the beginning he hesitated perceptibly before taking another lower down. She thanked him gravely as he returned her the card and he thought he detected a half-sorrowful expression in her face. No doubt she had been quick to observe the constraint of his manner, and he felt she must be suspecting something.

He was glad that the arriving guests were claiming her attention, and he moved away and mingled with the crowd. But he was indifferent to the scene, to the music and dancing, to all but Margaret. He could not turn his eyes away from her. He took note of every man that asked a dance of her. One of them kept writing on her programme for what seemed to Morgan an unbearable time, Margaret looking on with a tolerant half-smile. He knew the fellow well and hated him. Fledgling at one or other of the learned professions, always aggressively smooth and well-bred, a veritable paragon of polish without a single redeeming mannerism, to Morgan he represented one large swagger. There was something in the pose of the eye-glasses and in the clean-shaven upper lip that told of boundless conceit and infinite self-assurance. What right had he, was Morgan's indignant thought—and he made the criticism as of a mere external fact from which he stood aloof—to be so friendly with Margaret? How was it that she should show such little insight as to be imposed upon by so specious a personality? No doubt she thought him perfectly charming!

He was very angry and bitter, and already half-repented the impulse that had driven him here. If the experience, in all its emotional bearings, was a unique one, it was likewise a disagreeable one. When the time came round for him to dance with Margaret he tried hard to appear perfectly at his ease, and to make a show of good spirits. Exercising the privilege of an old friend, he began to tease her about the rapidity with which her programme had got filled.

"A girl must flirt a little," she asserted calmly, after a short passage-at-arms. "You're not jealous, Morgan, are you?"

"I am only observant," he answered evasively.

"Your gift of observation must be truly wonderful—you manage to exercise it at so great a distance, or perhaps you send out your astral body to do the observing, which must be the reason why it's invisible to me."

"I dare not speak at all. You turn my every word into a scourge against me."

"Don't you feel you deserve the scourging?"

"I have had another melancholy fit," he urged, forced to defend himself.

"Poor Morgan!" she said, pityingly. "I do believe you have some trouble that you are keeping to yourself. Do you know, I've been thinking so for some time now. You don't trust your friends sufficiently. Come now, isn't my surmise near the truth?"

The tears almost welled up to his eyes. He did not answer her, for he could not speak at all; but his silence was tantamount to an admission.

"Poor Morgan!" she repeated softly, as if to herself, and the sympathy in her voice troubled him still more. "And the trouble? Of course, you are going to tell me first."

"Well, not to-night," he answered, closing his heart against her with a superhuman effort. "I must not spoil your evening."

"Do you think I shall enjoy it, now that I know?"

"Why should you not?" he asked, and there was a shade of rebuff in his tone. A half-savage impulse was urging him to pick a sort of quarrel with her.

"You are unkind," she exclaimed in distress. "Is my friendship nothing to you? Perhaps I am wrong to show you that I care about yours. I ought not to have let you see I was so concerned about your trouble, but I could not know that was going to vex you."

He did not answer, because her words disarmed him.

"Forgive me, Morgan," she went on gently. "Of course, you are irritable and all unstrung, and I ought to be very much more patient instead of flying at you. It would be wicked for us two to quarrel, but I really do want you to be nice to me."

She was led away just then, and he felt glad to be relieved of the responsibility of carrying on the conversation.

Dance after dance went by. It hurt him to see that eye-glassed plausible young man dancing with Margaret. His mood grew hateful. The hours at length became unendurable. He slipped away quietly and went home.

But all through the evening he had been conscious in the back part of his mind of the new life he had embarked upon. And even whilst he held the sweet lily in his arms, his very love for her bringing him anguish and bitterness, he was yet aware of scenes that sought to obtrude—scenes in which figured the wonderful woman with whom he had thrown in his lot, in which she stood in the glare of the footlights with a dense packed theatre applauding to madness; scenes not outlined clear and projected in space, but which were to him shapeless silhouettes and dazzling formless patches of light flitting across the extreme background of his consciousness.

About mid-day Morgan Druce and Selina Mary Kettering were united in holy matrimony. She had given her true name for the occasion, but Morgan, intent on signing his own, scarcely noticed hers. She was Cleo to him, and Cleo she would remain. It was not till about an hour later, when they were lunching at a West End restaurant, that his mind began to play about the fact that he really was married now. Yet it seemed incredible. For him marriage had always connoted something large and elaborate, a substantial experience with which were involved complicated preliminaries, a process so transforming that one almost expected one's very chemical composition to be changed by it.

But all had been so astonishingly simple. The whole morning had been singularly like other mornings. The visit to the registrar's office had been short and unimpressive. His bone and tissue were perfectly unaffected by it. Cleo and he had lunched here before. How then was his relation to her so different from what it had been?

He argued with himself. He told himself he *was* married, but he refused to believe it. With all his knowledge and certainty of the fact, he failed to convince himself. And yet that certainty set him speculating as to what his father and mother would say when they read the curt announcement he intended dispatching that afternoon. He wondered what Helen would think, what Margaret. The fragrance and beauty of the lily seemed suddenly to invade his spirit. He had a sense of sweetness and light, followed by a reaction of pain. Perhaps Margaret would be crushed by the news; perhaps— and he could not help the thought, grotesque though it was—she would marry that smooth, eye-glassed young man.

There was a strange ringing in his ears; he was conscious of his whole being soaring far away, a floating, palpitating spirit amid great spaces of mystery and dream. A universal music was swelling around him, a mighty concerto bursting full upon him from the stillness of infinite distances—the sobbing of violins, the blare of brazen instruments, an orchestral clash and clang.

"You may smoke," said Cleo.

With a start he found himself amid the garish mirrors of the gilded restaurant.

END OF BOOK II.

BOOK III.

CHAPTER I.

Had the transition from bachelorhood to the married state been less easy and less quickly achieved, Morgan might perhaps have realised that the pattern of life he was weaving had not the same undetachedness from the real as a pattern woven in dream, but that it was a part and parcel of the real. As it was, he was not the man to stop and think, once he had made his plunge into the strange, vague future that had appealed to him. And now this theatrical enterprise, with Cleo as the star, loomed ahead of him not only as the redemption of his empty life, but wrapped in that seductive romance which his mood and temperament demanded.

For the present, they had taken furnished rooms in Bloomsbury, where they lived under an assumed name. Morgan did not leave his new address at his old quarters, for he did not want any letters to follow him, no matter from whom they came. He felt he had done all he could in writing the three letters he had decided to write. And with the sending of those letters, he seemed to be detaching himself from his old life with one clean cut; his imagination left free to construct the tableaux of what he believed—such was the impression Cleo's personality had made on him—was going to be a gorgeous panoramic future, a triumphant historic march through the civilised world. The fact that Cleo now went about clothed like any other mortal did not detract from his estimate of her genius, for the mere dispensation with such extraneous splendour left untouched the splendour of the woman herself.

And, from this mere moving from one London street to another, he had all the feeling of having placed a thousand miles between himself and everybody who knew him. In the theatrical enterprise he was to figure under his present assumed name, though that was only likely to come within the public cognizance as the name borne by Cleo's husband, a personage none of his friends would think of associating with himself. He thought he might thus fairly count on remaining undiscovered, though, of course, he could not provide against chance encounters. But he felt he would be very angry if any attempt were made to follow him up and interfere in any way with the destiny he had chosen.

Meanwhile, with an exaggerated sense of his own helplessness, he looked up to Cleo with an unshakable confidence, placing an oracular value on her every word. She symbolised for him an all-conquering power before which destiny itself could make no front. Had he been an artist he would have painted her as the triumphant figure of allegory, standing amid the stars with one foot planted on the terrestrial globe. His attitude towards her was one of wondering admiration and blind assent; with so much deliberateness did she turn her vision on that seething world which she was preparing to conquer, and which had always been to him such a whirling, giddy, incomprehensible chaos that he had never been able to look steadily at it. Now, timidly peeping from behind her skirts, he ventured to open his eyes on it. Alone, he would never have known where to touch the heterogeneous, noisy mass, but she, displaying a definite and intimate knowledge of its constituents, at once began to establish relations with it here and there. These efforts of hers seemed to him at first random and isolated, and he watched with interested expectancy for the light-giving result as a child might watch the preparations for an elaborate conjuring trick. Eventually he began to see, with a pleased sort of surprise, that the floating set of relations entered into by Cleo was assuming recognisable shape as a theatrical enterprise.

The marvel she inspired in him deepened daily, so wonderful seemed her purposefulness, her energy, her faith in herself. And though, beside these qualities of hers, his diffidence compelled him to self-effacement, he yet seemed to draw something from her very superabundance.

From the beginning he had given up all the money to her, only too pleased to be rid of the control of it. But when the arrangements were fairly advanced, she insisted on his mastering the details of the expenditure she was making and on going into the figures with him each time she drew up what she considered a likely profit and loss account, which she did at least once each evening. The result was always on the right side and always large, and he was not quite clear that it did not necessarily represent a sure fact, if a future one. Figures had always irritated him, but, as she performed all the arithmetical processes and he simply had to exert his intelligence to the extent of grasping what each item stood for, he was pleased to find himself equal to the effort.

Their three hundred pounds in the meantime had dwindled considerably, but, as Cleo showed no signs of anxiety, it never occurred to Morgan to feel uneasy. Cleo, who, for the sake of simplicity and also to enhance her authority over the people she should employ, was making every arrangement in her name only, had had to pay a large sum down before she had been allowed to take possession of the theatre, for she had been preceded by some other enterprising actress, with whom the lessees had been less stringent, and who had come to grief, much to their disgust. The costumers and the printers, too, were shy of unknown dames with stage ambitions, and their co-operation was not to be obtained without a show of bank notes.

Nor was Cleo unprepared in the all-important question of the play itself. She had employed some of her past leisure at Hampstead in translating many pieces from the French, and she now gave Morgan half a dozen to read, saying she had already formed her own opinion as to which one contained the best part for her and she wanted to see if his judgment would tally with hers. Morgan was glad to have this quiet task to keep him occupied for a few days. He took it, however, very solemnly, for he wished to arrive at an honest decision, but he did not wish it to be different from hers. However, he could not say he liked any of the plays. Half of them were modern, half Oriental; all artificial and stilted, and full of long-winded inanity. Eventually he selected one of the Oriental, which he thought would at any rate give Cleo an opportunity of displaying her dresses—to such Machiavellian extent had she already influenced him. To his delight, she declared that his choice was hers. He timidly ventured on a little criticism, but she laughed and assured him that the play itself signified nothing—plays were mere excuses for acting. This one provided a part which, if not the ideal one for her, would at least enable her to display herself and her genius to some advantage. Of course, she was well aware she was not making the début that befitted her genius, as that would have involved a play written specially for her in which every other part was artistically subordinated to her own, a vast theatre such as the one she had dreamed of, and a lavish expenditure; her brain, moreover, being entirely relieved of all material considerations and her spirit left unfettered. Under the present make-shift circumstances she must be content with such humble beginning as the poor funds at her disposal would allow her. And Morgan felt quite guilty at his inability to provide the ideal début she described, feeling she had quite a right to despise this mean and unworthy beginning, and that it was really generous of her to face the difficulties occasioned by their narrow means without complaint.

That there were difficulties he could not help knowing, for Cleo was at no pains to conceal the fact. Rather was she intent on showing that she was perfectly capable of vanquishing them. When the open-handed policy she had been compelled to adopt had reduced their resources to about fifty pounds, Cleo withdrew the money from the bank, saying it would be safer in her pocket. But by this time her unhesitating payments had begun to produce their effect, and it had got about that she was no mere penniless adventuress, but a wealthy stage-struck dame. As a mysterious personage, suddenly springing from nowhere into the theatrical world, she began to arouse a good deal of interest, and the flâneurs in those circles obtained kudos by pretending to precise information about her. The rumour of riches spread. Tradespeople became sweet and pliant—the plucking of a goose with golden feathers was not an every-day event.

Cleo, who could afford to pay anything out of the profits of the huge success to come, cleverly betrayed the rich amateur's ignorance of charges, varying it by the occasional query: "Isn't that rather dear?" Her delight at securing an abatement of a few shillings was so undisguised that it caused much amusement to complaisant tradesmen.

The transaction of all this preliminary business afforded Cleo an immense enjoyment. Her front to the world throughout had been the perfection of boldness.

CHAPTER II.

And now Morgan found himself doing quite a deal of work, arranging parts for typewriting, reading proofs and trying to understand something of the—to him—intricate system of theatrical accounts. He was proud when he succeeded in following business details, astonished to find they were not beyond his intelligence. He passed to and from the theatre several times a day, curiously glad to feel himself a working part of all this complex machinery. But he was never quite comfortable in the building, wandering uneasily about its corridors and almost feeling as though he ought to explain his presence to one or other of its scattered population he encountered in odd corners. Everybody about the building seemed vaguely respectful to him, as though possessed of some faint notion that he was attached to Cleo in some incomprehensible way or other.

So far Cleo had behaved with perfect sang-froid. If at home she had occasionally allowed her natural excitement to appear, it had been of a pleasurable kind and fully sympathised with by Morgan. In the mere commercial transactions that had relation to the enterprise, she had shown herself as calm and unshakable as a rock, but as soon as the actual fact of her chosen art began to be concerned, she commenced to reveal other sides of her nature that disturbed Morgan's blind worship in no little degree.

The first thing that began to stir his doubts was her method of engaging the players, for she put on the airs of a grand patron, and such pleasure did this part of the business give her that she prolonged it unduly. She made actors and actresses wait upon her time after time when she had not the slightest intention of engaging them. She liked to have a crowd waiting in her anteroom at the theatre and admitted to her august presence one at a time. It behoved her, she explained to Morgan, to impress people from the beginning, and, though this was the first time she had had a theatre of her own, she wanted to appear as if to the manner born. Moreover, when he took the opportunity, by way of expostulation, to express his sympathy with the rejected applicants, who had been kept "hanging about" in vain, she was able to make a show of justification, urging it had been necessary for her to have the widest latitude of choice.

When the company was complete she laughingly admitted it was none of the finest, but it would make an excellent foil for herself.

But it was only when the rehearsals began that Morgan discovered Cleo possessed attributes, frequently associated with genius, it is true, but by no means certain symptoms of it. Her patience was astonishingly short and she possessed a temper that was perfectly ungovernable, once it was roused. He likewise observed that there was a certain domineering spirit in the whole control of the theatre.

His eyes were first opened to this state of affairs one day when he had wandered on to the stage and stood surveying the desolate emptiness of the house, in the vague spaces of which cleaners flitted about or busied themselves amid the dim tiers of swathed seats. Orchestra practice was proceeding in the band room, and Morgan stayed to listen for awhile. A sudden high-pitched brutal comment gave him the first inkling of the conductor's bullying methods.

The discovery soon followed that the stage manager was worse than the conductor, and that, when Cleo once lost her head, which she did very easily at rehearsals, she became almost hysteric. She was, however, always ready to explain away her exhibitions of temper, saying that the stupidity of the players and the worry of making things go right were trying beyond human endurance. Which explanation he had perforce to accept.

It was in apprehension of witnessing her outbreaks that he dared not stay at the theatre during rehearsal hours for more than a few minutes at a time. He could not help knowing, however, lounging about the house as he did, that Cleo was disliked by all the company, she and the stage manager being bracketed together as a pair of bullies. He was aware he himself was better liked, for he got on very well indeed with a couple of the men and thought them "very decent fellows." Though their poverty forced them to borrow occasional half-crowns of him, that only made him sympathise with them the more.

Morgan himself would have been puzzled to tell what difference the new light in which Cleo was showing herself was making in his attitude towards her. Her personality, taken as a whole, remained fully as wonderful and impressive for him as before, and in the hours of her calm he could scarcely believe he had ever seen her worked up into such tense, nervous states. At such times there seemed possibilities of indulgent explanation, for in all else she was living up to his conception and to his expectations of her. His faith in her genius was unshaken. Nothing had occurred to make him doubt the glorious successes to come. Yet were the shortcomings she had so far displayed distinct and tormenting drawbacks to the enthusiasm with which he had begun.

CHAPTER III.

The frenzy of activity grew greater as the time of opening approached. The three weeks allotted for the rehearsal swept by for Morgan in tempestuous flight—an impression which he got from watching the feverish evolutions of his Cleo. He found himself, too, drawn into London night life, assisting at restaurant supper parties and sitting down with men in evening dress who affected cloaks and crush hats, and who were scarcely names to him. Cleo presided, sometimes as hostess, sometimes as guest; Morgan, who figured as "my husband," having the feeling that the others were just civilly tolerant to him. As for himself, he was inclined to be taciturn, being little versed in the matters on which the rest discoursed so racily. Cleo gave him to understand that these men, and others he had stumbled against in the corridors of the theatre and who seemed to have an easy entrée to her, were those whose good will it was necessary to secure—critics, journalists and the like. She further confided to him that she considered she had achieved a triumph in drawing them round her. Asked if they were of the first importance, she had to confess most of them were attached to various weekly papers, whose influence, however, she thought must be considerable. The names of the sheets were but dimly familiar to Morgan and had that equivocal ring about them that suggested vagueness of circulation. He did not quite approve of this fawning on critics and hinted as much, whereupon Cleo insisted the critics were only too glad to fawn on her.

"Do you suppose they have no insight?" she asked, "that they are incapable of recognising beauty and genius? They can read the future in my face, and for the sake of their own reputation they dare not overlook or ignore me at the outset."

The world seemed to hold its breath on the last day, and Morgan was conscious of a strange hush that seemed to hang over the crowded, grinding thoroughfares. The last of the money had been spent in advertising, and every portable effect, including his own watch, had gone to raise more. All day long he lounged about the theatre in feverish suspense. From the box office man— an incommunicative individual with an absurd mustache, who spoke with an air of resentment at being accosted—he learned that the advance booking had been very slight, that, so far, the announcements and the various odd paragraphs from the pen of Bohemian acquaintances, who had spoken very favourably of Cleo's beauty, had failed to attract more than seven or eight pounds.

But never for a moment did Cleo lose faith in the venture—that would have been to lose faith in herself. Of course she knew her name was absolutely unfamiliar to the public, she explained, in anticipation of unsatisfactory takings, and, therefore, she could not expect to draw a full house the first night. She had, however, taken steps to secure appearances by an extensive distribution of paper. But she expected the effect of her performance to be magnetic. She alone would stand forth and the play and the rest of the players would scarcely obtrude on the consciousness of the spectators. After the first evening or two they would certainly have to turn away business.

The near approach of the moment when the realisation of his panoramic visions was at last to begin, freshened again in Morgan all his sense of the romance of the situation. There had been times in the last few days when he had suffered from despondency. There were sides to theatrical life that were little to his taste. He had long since known, for instance, that the stage manager was addicted to obscene talk; and when, one day, just as in the middle of a rehearsal he was about to step from the wings on to the stage, he was arrested by a torrent of vileness that came from that same individual, he was not very much surprised at the mere fact. But he was vexed and disgusted that the fellow should not have restrained himself in the presence of Cleo. What was worse, Cleo herself seemed to be perfectly unaware of anything exceptionable, for she made not the least protest; from which Morgan gathered that the sort of thing must be quite usual and that, had he not shunned the rehearsals so persistently, he would have known it before. Thus, there were moments when he felt utterly alone in this strange life, when he longed for real, human sympathy. He yearned for some other being who was not Cleo, to whom to turn, to whom to pour out the human emotion that was in him; some being who belonged to the life from which he had cut himself off, and to which he looked back almost as from another world. Yet these were only momentary longings that mastered him. His whole interest, his whole imagination, were bound up with his present life; and the fascination exerted over him by Cleo and the wonderful future he believed was to be hers sufficed to attach him enthusiastically to her career.

Thus, as the rising of the curtain approached, so did the excitement in him overcome every other emotion; so did he become absolutely a creature of this region into which he had plunged, breathing its air with avidity and entranced by the prospect.

"I've a surprise in store for you, dear," Cleo confided to him that day at lunch. "I've arranged a special scene at the beginning of the second act, in which I alone appear. No one has any suspicion of it, but I tell you, dear, the effect will be wonderful. Coming after I shall have charmed everybody with my acting in the first act, it will carry the audience off its feet with enthusiasm."

CHAPTER IV.

Morgan, installed in a box, all by himself, was eagerly interested in the audience as it came straggling into the house, which, thanks to the paper distributed, ultimately presented a pretty compact appearance. He himself was ignorant how much real business had been done, but, so far as he could judge, the gallery and pit were being fairly well patronised. No doubt a good many had been drawn by the gorgeous poster representing Cleo, twice her natural size, and dressed in a costume somewhat like the one she had worn when he had first made her acquaintance. Appropriately huge ornamental letter-press declared her to be "The Basha's Favourite;" and it was on the first act of "The Basha's Favourite" that the audience was now waiting for the curtain to rise.

And at this moment of culminating excitement the scene impressed Morgan curiously. His mood was essentially one of romance. That the play itself was full of inanities was forgotten; but its title and Egyptian colour together with Cleo's personality had somehow got inter-blent and interwoven with the enterprise itself, making even its commercial and prosaic sides instinct with mystery and unreality. He seemed to have wandered into an Arabian Nights' tale. The figures that filled the stalls, pit, and galleries took on the aspect of a crowd that might people a dream or the visions a child seeks in its pillow. He was conscious of the shapeless totality of myriad conversations—a blur of sound, mystic and bewildering.

Now, too, the front rows of stalls, which he knew were reserved for the critics, began to fill, and a waft of unpleasantness came to him as he recognised a few of the acquaintances he had made at recent supper parties. The disturbance was fatal to his mood. He felt suddenly unstrung. A strange sense of unhappiness invaded him—a bitter, far-embracing uncertainty. He was uncertain of himself, of his life, of all life. The solid scene faded from before his eyes. He became self-centred. All his consciousness of living and having lived—his consciousness of all he had ever felt and all he had ever thought and all he had ever done—was with him as a vast bitterness that gave him a sense as of an infinite nebula. And then, as in a flash, this nebula concentred itself into a point—a point that was his whole sense of life and consciousness. He was now as in a black tomb, without past, without future, without sense of direction, without an active thought; with only a mere awareness of existing, with only the cognizance of the present time-point on the flowingness of his consciousness.

The tuning of instruments began just then, and the rasping sound tore at him, dragging him back to a consciousness of externals. Then, as his eyes rested again on the stalls, he drew right back instinctively into the shadow of his box. For he had caught sight of Lady Thiselton.

She was in the fourth row from the orchestra and by her side he recognised Mrs. Blackstone. They could only have just entered, for he was sure those two seats had been empty but the moment before. He felt tolerably certain Helen had not yet seen him, and he intended to take care she should not see him. Yet he had an intuition that she knew all.

In his altered position in the box he was fairly safe from recognition by her, even whilst he could watch her closely, noting the quick, eager glances she cast about her from time to time as if she thought it possible he might be seated amid the audience. Eventually, however, she lapsed into a sort of listless immobility.

And even though he shrank from her, her advent brought back to him a yearning wistfulness; it awakened and half-appeased a sense akin to home-sickness. In that moment he would have liked to fly to her—how much had she stood for in his life! She symbolized for him all that of humanness which is comprised in the word "comradeship;" she represented the truth, attachment and loyalty in human relations even as Margaret represented the perfume, the sweetness, and the perfection.

The rise of the curtain forced him to take his eyes off her. The background of the scene on the stage was apparently the pillared exterior of a palace, yet the foreground was a carpeted space in which a many-coloured medley of yataghaned men with baggy breeches and beautiful slave-girls in Oriental costumes kept re-forming in ever-shifting kaleidoscopic grouping. And then the audience suddenly were aware that the medley had divided into two harmonious sub-medleys, whilst, in the chasm left towards the front, Cleo stood majestically and addressed a verbose harangue to the Basha, her relation to whom was known from the title of the play. In full view and hearing of so heterogeneous a crowd did the Basha in return reproach her with coldness and indifference to him, which she vehemently denied, playing the *femme incomprise* and by her perfect self-assurance cloaking an intrigue, which Morgan knew she was carrying on with a handsome Christian, because, having read the play, he knew what was coming.

In the unfolding of the plot, Morgan was quite uninterested. In fact, he had long since lost all grasp of its movement and meaning, and, instead of taking in the dialogue, he contented himself with judging effects and their impression on the audience.

Though he had seen a little of the rehearsals, he had not yet acquired any notion of Cleo's abilities, for she had been busy directing and criticising, simply reading her part as a "fill-in." He had all along taken it for granted that she must be a great actress. At his most despondent moments he had never doubted that, simply because it had never occurred to him to doubt it. However, he was not without some notion of what good acting should be, and he felt something like a murderous bludgeon blow when, at the end of five minutes, it began to be forced on him that she had not even the least glimmer of instinct for her art.

Despite all her magnificence and the absence of any gaucherie in her movements when off the stage, all natural grace disappeared the moment she attempted to be somebody else. Her delivery was unnatural and pompous; her motions were stiff, strained, ridiculous. The whole of the first act was unsatisfying to the intelligence, but instead of dominating it by the force of her personality, Cleo, by the incompetence of her acting, set up its silliness in relief. If she had not talked as much as all the other characters put together—for every word that even the Basha managed to steal in elicited ten against it—there would have been nothing to suggest she was the leading character. At one point, indeed, her absurd strutting about the stage drew a chuckle from somewhere among the ranks of the critics. To watch her became so painful that Morgan at last turned away his eyes.

All was over. His beautiful visions had gone. His eyes were suddenly opened and he found himself transported from dreamland, not to reality—for he could not yet believe this was reality—but into what seemed a horrible nightmare.

The act ended at last and the curtain fell amid a frigid silence. Then there was a little clapping in the gallery—the colour had no doubt pleased a few of the spectators. But it died away immediately in discouragement.

There were the usual noises of shuffling and disarrangement and talking and exits. Morgan drew back as far as he could into the shadow. He was glad to be thus isolated—he could overhear no criticism or comments. Naturally his looks stole towards Helen. She had not moved. He could see that a strange, sad expression had come over her face. Then she seemed to smile as Mrs. Blackstone made some remark to her and a reply fell languidly from her lips, after which a desultory conversation sprang up between the two.

In that moment it seemed to Morgan that Helen had some wondrous power against fate and he seemed to be wishing with the intensity of prayer that she might raise her hand and release him from his nightmare.

But he knew that was only a yearning fancy!

And as the thought came to him that the curtain was to rise again in a moment, it brought back to his memory the precious confidence Cleo had whispered to him at lunch time.

"I've a surprise in store for you, dear"—the words surged up again in his ears —"I've arranged a special scene at the beginning of the second act, in which I alone appear. No one has any suspicion of it, but I tell you, dear, that the effect will be wonderful. Coming after I shall have charmed everybody with my acting in the first act, it will carry the audience off its feet with enthusiasm."

As nobody had the air of having been charmed by the first act, he wondered how the predicted effect would be altered in consequence.

CHAPTER V.

Morgan, of course, could not guess the nature of the new scene that Cleo was now going to introduce. The stage during the second act was to represent "a private apartment in the palace," and here the action assumed some dramatic semblance, taking the following course: The Christian lover manages to effect an entry into this same private apartment and to hold a long, loving discourse with the Basha's favourite, and when eventually the two are about to embrace, in comes no less a personage than the Basha himself, and advances quietly on tip-toe and listens for awhile. Suddenly he stamps his foot on the ground and the room is filled, as by magic, with eunuchs and soldiers. The audience once more get kaleidoscopic impressions, and Cleo and the Christian are seized and bound, both spitting defiance and declaring their mutual eternal love, on hearing which the Basha turns pale under his Oriental skin. The curtain falls as he bids his myrmidons put her into a sack and heave her into the Nile, and his favourite is carried off, loudly bidding her lover take heart, for she loves him and will love him always.

Morgan could not see what Cleo could possibly add to this, and his curiosity gave him some little temporary spurt of interest as the curtain rose. Up it went, slowly, slowly, and the apartment in the palace stood revealed in all the glory of gilded pillars and mirrors and rugs. In front of a huge stretch of mirror on the right was a couch, on which sat Cleo, wrapped in a sort of yellow silk cloak which fell about her in pleasing folds. Morgan was beginning to think that she must have deemed it best to omit the innovation, when Cleo rose languorously, took a step towards the great mirror, and, standing erect, inspected herself therein. "Yes, I am worthy of him," she said to herself proudly, then, with a brusque movement, she disengaged the garment from her shoulders and it slipped to the ground and lay there in a soft heap. The spectators then became aware that, save for a sort of transparent web of floating serpentine drapery, it had been her sole covering, and Cleo herself remained gazing into the mirror, regarding her gleaming reflection with evident admiration, whilst the other mirrors likewise gave back the sinuous grace and superb modelling of her body.

The silence for a moment was profound and painful. Cleo's audacity had caught the audience by the throat so that it could not breathe. Her all-consuming egotism had driven her to this device for satisfying her rage for the world's admiration. And as she stood there in statuesque pose, her rich golden-red hair falling over her shoulders and the full scarlet of her lips gleaming startlingly, awaiting a great storm of charmed applause, for which the audience seemed to be gathering its forces in the interval, again she sent that strange loose softness of her voice floating through the theatre like a hot wind: "Yes, I am worthy of him."

But she had scarcely got through the phrase when a piercing cat-call shrilled through the house from the back of the pit. Almost simultaneously a derisive howl came from the gallery; and then an appalling hissing, hooting, and groaning broke on Cleo with the force of a tempest that drove towards her from all points. She turned a defiant face to it and gave the house a blazing look of contempt. But a whole chorus of cat-calls now sprang up, dominating a sort of see-saw of dissonant disapprobation. The stalls alone sat in solemn, wondering silence, not unmixed with apprehension. And suddenly the curtain began to descend, whereupon the uproar ceased abruptly in favour of a mighty spontaneous outbreak of cheering, unmistakably ironic.

Those behind the scenes had been as much astonished as those in front, and the stage manager, as soon as he had collected his wits, had adopted the only sensible alternative the situation afforded.

A silence fell again upon the theatre. Not a person stirred. An obvious curiosity as to what was to follow possessed the house. In a minute the curtain rose again—on the same apartment in the palace. Cleo reclined on the same couch, robed in a terra-cotta gown which Morgan recognised at once. And then there came a tapping at a little window, and, after much appropriate dramatic business, this window was opened by Cleo, and her lover leaped into the room, man-like and adventurous.

But Cleo's audacious mistake had wrought a miracle on the audience, destroying the stage-illusion, and rousing its dormant light of intelligence. Its capacity for being profoundly played upon and emotionally excited by the inartistic unrealities of absurd characterisation and of absurd combinations of circumstance had been rendered unresponsive. In vain did the play appeal to its ethical sense, striving to enlist its hope for the ultimate triumph of the Good, the True, and the Wronged. It had begun to view "The Basha's Favourite" in an extremely critical mood, and to manifest its keen sense of the utter impossibility of a play, which in years gone by had enchanted and moved to tears average audiences, not only in its native land, but in London as well, where it had been a sort of fountain-head for multitudinous adaptation.

Cleo, however, went straight on with the performance, carrying it through with an indomitable defiance, caring not at all that the intensest passages, which otherwise would have thrilled, were received with scorn and laughter and ironical cheers and cries of "Go it, old girl!" Each time a servant made an entry he was received with an enormous ovation. Single voices were heard again and again in sarcastic comment, now from the top of the house, now from the back. As the curtain fell at the end of each act, the disorder became volcanic, but the stage manager knew better than to allow the curtain to go up again in response to the continued applause.

Certain it was that the audience thoroughly enjoyed its evening, and, when the curtain fell for the last time, surpassed itself in a great demonstration of its frolicsome mood. It had been obvious throughout that the house had been quite conscious of its own superior intellectuality, of its immeasurable elevation above the fare offered. But Morgan derived his sense of the ghastly failure of the whole business, not so much from the demeanour of the audience as from that of one of the critics, who somehow summed it up for him. This critic, whose bald pate had fascinated his eye, had a curiously irritating, spasmodic chuckle, and Morgan in vain tried to be unaware of him.

In the intervals of the acts he had remained numbed and dazed, only gathering to himself a grain of sympathy from the piteous look in Helen's face. Her demeanour confirmed his intuition, that she must know everything. She had sat rigid and mournfully attentive in contrast to Mrs. Blackstone, who had laughed with decorous unrestraint the whole evening. But he could not prevail upon himself to let her discover him, and at once plunged behind the scenes to get to Cleo.

He found her in her dressing-room with her maid, who had come to the theatre to help her, and he had a thrill of disgust as he watched her rub the cleansing grease over her painted cheeks. It now struck him as horrible—this pollution of the human face night after night with filthy cosmetics that could only be removed by a filthier grease. He felt that all she had so far restrained was going to break forth and he stood by with subdued mien. Such shattering as had befallen himself he was strong enough not to consider for the moment. His immediate feeling was one of pity for her. He fancied he saw her now, not as the heroine of his fantasy, but just as she was. Sympathy in him there was none, and he could not make a hypocritical show of any. But he soon understood that she took it for granted his faith in her was as unshaken as her own; that she really believed her performance had been a great one. Her self- illusion was pitiable. She burst forth into bitter invective against the public, he listening without being able to find his tongue, but with the consciousness that, even if she had behaved madly that evening, the audience deserved at least some of her censure. Why had it sat there, so determined to have its evening's fun out, cruelly hounding and torturing a creature who, from her very temperament, must have found the punishment a hellish one? Why, if people had really been shocked, had they not quietly left the theatre? That surely would have been sufficient indication of their disapproval. "I am not beaten yet!" cried Cleo, with frenzy. "The day will come when these people will fight and trample over one another's bodies to catch the least glimpse of me. To-day they have rejected me with scorn, as they have always rejected the greatest. Read the early careers of the actresses the world now worships! But I am a hundred times more determined than before. The public shall treasure the dust my feet have trod on. They shall look back on to-night as a blot on their lives. My genius shall triumph! My genius shall force them to submission!"

However, he induced her to come and have a little supper alone with him. As they passed out through the stage door the man handed him a twisted note, which Cleo was too absorbed to notice. A glance sufficed to enable him to recognize Helen's writing, though it was but hastily scrawled in lead. The fact that it was addressed to him in his newly-assumed name was the final confirmation of her knowledge of his fate. He put it away till he could read it, trying not to wonder at its contents.

Meanwhile, he was shutting his eyes as to what was to follow. He knew very well that even if he opened them he would equally see nothing, but it gave him some comfort to imagine he was shutting out a view it were better not to look at. He managed to get Cleo to eat and drink a little, and when she was calmer she told him the theatre was to open the next evening just as if they had scored a great success. He knew better than to make any show of opposition or disapproval just then, though his heart became still heavier at this announcement of hers. He mentally vowed, however, he would take care to remain behind the scenes. He did not venture to ask her whether she intended to repeat "the innovation" that had done the mischief, because he feared her pride might force her to defiant assertion that she would most certainly repeat it; whereas, if no reference were made to it, she would, in all probability, quietly omit it.

She ended by a great fit of hysteric weeping that lasted half the night.

CHAPTER VI.

"My poor, dear Morgan," read Lady Thiselton's note. "My heart is a-bleeding. The moment I saw her appear I understood everything. Of course, I don't know how you came to meet her, but such a creature was bound to be fatal to you. Your marriage to her can only be considered as the veriest mockery. It would be a crime against Heaven—observe that this crisis has made me religious—to look upon it seriously at all. Won't you come to see me, Morgan? You must need a friend and surely I have the right to be that friend. Why not come to-morrow afternoon; or when you will, if you will send me a message. H. T."

"P. S.—I hope she'll see this so that she quarrels with you and casts you off."

He knew he must go to her, but he shrank from doing so as yet, though he did not try to explain to himself the shrinking. So he sent her a line saying he would come one afternoon when he felt he had the courage. After posting the letter he had a great longing to cry.

He realised the ugliness of the position now, his terrible relation to this strange, hysteric woman, and the thought kept darting through his mind like a whizzing shaft of flame: "I am married to her, I am married to her!"

To weave poetry out of life! That was simply to attempt what poets and philosophers and even imaginative men of affairs, seduced by the apparent novelty of the notion, had attempted before him. At a certain point of existence, such men find it easy to tell themselves—as if in unsuspecting answer to some dim foresight of what the experiment might lead to—that it does not matter much what happens to one in life, so long as it is a series of interesting happenings; interesting, that is, to each according to his temperament. But poems woven of reality are not the same detached products as poems written on paper. They are an integral part of life, and, as such, related to its great forward sweep. All the consequences that attach to human action must attach to the particular weaving, however fantastic and pleasing the immediate pattern.

Morgan was now face to face with the consequences of this attitude he had taken towards existence, though it had been forced on him by his temperament. And they were consequences that were not goodly to look upon.

Cleo had gone early to the theatre to go into the accounts and to show everybody she was not in the least disconcerted. When he himself arrived some time later she informed him that last night's takings were about twenty- five pounds, but she had already paid away the bulk of it for fresh advertising.

She was once more calm and business-like, despite that their funds were exhausted, and besides various liabilities there were the salaries and wages to be paid at the end of the week. As yet, however, nobody about the house had any suspicion of the emptiness of the treasury.

The newspapers, he was glad to find, had dealt with Cleo very gently. The notices were short and cold, just giving an outline of the play, which, they said, was indifferently acted and practically a failure. No mention was made of her indiscretion and it was perfectly obvious from the tone of these notices that the writers had felt she had been sufficiently punished, and that, for the rest, she was not to be taken seriously. There came, too, a message from the censor, to whom, somehow, last night's occurrence had got known, to the effect that the beginning of the second act must be omitted, else he must forbid the play to be repeated. From his letter it was clear the censor was taking the same charitable view as the critics, and that he foresaw the piece would very soon die a natural death. Cleo shrugged her shoulders and wrote the necessary undertaking. Morgan understood that her "innovation" might have got her into serious trouble, had not the entire hopelessness of her acting proclaimed her as a person to be pitied.

That same day Morgan could not help broaching the subject of the finances. The money side of the enterprise had by now got stamped on his brain. He had a grasp of the various items of their liabilities, and he felt the responsibility for them to rest upon him. No longer might he repose at ease in the secure shade of her mighty presence. She, however, refused to bow her head under the weight of business difficulties.

"We have till the week's end," she said. "There is nothing to worry about now."

He did not find this reply reassuring and felt impelled to make out for himself a list of the debts, including the salaries and wages that would have to be provided for by the Saturday. The total amount was about three hundred pounds, the same as the sum already expended. He carefully put the list away in his pocket-book, with what end he knew not.

In the evening the house presented a rather more than half-filled appearance, a result which had been mainly achieved by paper. At the box office the takings were only about seven pounds. It was quite clear that Cleo, whatever gossip she might have caused in professional circles, had created no profound sensation in the town, so that not even a *succès de scandale* was decreed to her. The play itself went very fairly indeed this second time, though it was acted scarcely a whit better than the evening before. Cleo perhaps put a trifle more ornamentation into her part, but the audience showed no critical tendencies.

On the third evening the theatre was two-thirds empty, and two pounds four and sixpence represented the seats actually paid for. On the fourth evening they played almost to empty benches, the takings amounting to seventeen shillings and sixpence. This ended the experiment.

The fifth day—Friday—was an eventful one, for duns began to arrive early in the morning. The creditors had suddenly become assailed with doubts, which were now deepened by the return of their emissaries, who not only had been unable to obtain access to Cleo, but who had furtively been warned by the traitorous stage manager "to look sharp after their money." The *camaraderie* that had hitherto subsisted between that gentleman and Cleo had come to an abrupt end, she cutting him short impatiently in the course of some discussion and bidding him not to argue. In further token of his annoyance he had worded a notice she had told him to put up as follows:

"The curtain will not rise to-night. Treasury to-morrow at mid-day, if possible."

The actors and actresses looked very sad, indeed, as their eye stumbled on the last two words. Cleo, in ignorance that the stage manager had exceeded her directions, for he had inserted the "treasury" part of the announcement on his own responsibility, was invaded by the company in a body. Being pressed by the ladies and gentlemen for some definite statement about their salaries—for several of them were in great need, having long been out of an engagement— she turned on them in towering fury and asked how they dared insult her by questioning her *bona fides* in that way. But as soon as she learned what had dictated their action, she at once sent for the stage manager and, in presence of all assembled, curtly ordered him to leave "her theatre" immediately. At first he stood dumfounded, and, on her repeating her injunction more vehemently, he began to bluster back at her. A pretty scene ensued, he, with much Billingsgate, lustily demanding his money, she insisting he must come for it at the right time and place. In the end, she sent for the police, and the astonished stage manager found himself forcibly ejected. She next proceeded to tear down the offensive notice, and soon afterwards the company departed, leaving Cleo and Morgan in sole possession.

"What's going to happen to-morrow?" he could not help saying, when Cleo had at length finished telling him her estimate of the stage manager's character.

"When mid-day comes, the salaries shall be paid without fail," replied Cleo unhesitatingly. "You just don't trouble your mind," she added. "Leave me to arrange everything."

He pressed her for details. But beyond a general assurance, conveyed with an air of mystery that on the morrow he would find their coffers quite replete, she would tell him nothing. They went to lunch together, for there was always some small silver at the bottom of Cleo's purse, and she then gave him to understand she had business to transact here and there during the afternoon, and that he must amuse himself alone as best he could.

Vaguely supposing that this secret business had reference to the raising of funds, Morgan separated from her and went back to their rooms, where, at least, he felt he was hidden away from the world. A little later he had an idea. He would go and see Helen.

CHAPTER VII.

Helen looked wonderfully sweet to-day and an atmosphere of quiet calm seemed to pervade the room. It seemed to Morgan as if he had entered into a haven. Helen wore a simple grey gown that went well with her subdued demeanour. The sanity and soundness that underlay her occasional frolicsomeness and high spirits became in that moment accentuated for him; and the almost superstitious feeling he had experienced at seeing her at the theatre now returned to him, the feeling that she was possessed of some magic power to redeem him.

"I have been too shame-faced to come before," he began. "I knew I did not deserve to see you again."

"Don't, please," said Helen. "If you make speeches of that kind you will force me to be flippant, quite against my sense of the fitness of things at this moment. Not that I want to be too tragic, but my state of mind is rather a complex one. What's yours?"

"Mine is a very simple one. I am just conscious of mere existence and of a heavy weight on my head."

"I don't like your symptoms, Morgan. If I diagnose correctly, they mean nascent 'desperation.' Now, so long as I am in the world, you ought never to develop that disease."

"But I omitted one important factor of my state of mind," he confessed; "and that is the knowledge that you *are* in the world."

"And does it take your attention off the weight of the load—just a little?"

"It is the one pleasant fact I have to dwell upon. But please talk a little about yourself. It will do me good."

She, however, had little to tell him. His letter had dealt her a heavy blow. His silence about the details of his sudden action had made her the prey of her imagination, which had created frightful possibilities. Her favourite theory had been—an indiscretion committed by him in some moment of depression and a remorse that had resulted in a marriage with some vile person. But she had been somewhat reassured at seeing him go into the theatre one day in company with Cleo. That had been a pure accident, of course, but it had enabled her to divine a good deal. Cleo's appearance—she had taken particular notice of her face—had at least narrowed that vast dreadfulness which had till then tortured her. But it was a face that by no means pleased her.

"However," continued Helen, "it seems I've been talking about you instead of about myself. I have been living, I suppose, in the usual conventional routine. My conduct has been really most exemplary and the austerest chaperon would have patted me on the head approvingly. Oh, no, I forget. There's one little matter over which I should have got lectured and that is my rejection of so eligible a bachelor as Mr. Ingram, on the mere ground that I couldn't overlook his past life. Anyhow, he hasn't committed suicide, though I fancy he has done something worse."

"You mean he has followed my example?" suggested Morgan.

"Not anything as bad as that. You know I'm only the daughter of a country gentleman and the widow of a baronet. Well, he has consoled himself by marrying the genuine brand of aristocracy, though she's a *divorçée*. Her income's double mine; her intelligence one-tenth of mine."

"She must be a very brilliant woman, indeed."

"You have developed courtly qualities, I perceive. But I am quite ready to concede, on re-consideration, that her intellect is only the hundredth part of mine. You know I am frightfully conceited about my brains. But now tell me how everything came to happen? Where did you meet her?"

He recollected that Ingram was implicated in the recital and could not be kept out. But he was in a mood when he could no longer keep back anything. He hungered for every crumb of sympathy he could get, and, besides, he looked upon things now with such changed eyes that such reservations relating to his personal life as he had before set up seemed futile and meaningless. Very soon Helen had learned how his connection with Ingram had begun and developed, by what strange chance the letter he had written to him had spun the first thread of the web in which he was now floundering, and how he had sought to lose himself in the apparent dreamland before him. Helen's eyes were fixed on him as her quick brain seized on every point. The narration came to her as a complete revelation.

"And if I hadn't insisted on your dining that evening," she cried, "you would never have got into this purgatory of a dreamland."

"I think I should have got there all the same," he answered, smiling, conscious of how much good it was doing him to talk to his dear friend again. "I must have met Ingram sooner or later and then the same thing would have happened."

"Ingram is a blackguard!" said Helen severely. "With all his thick-headed cleverness, he had yet insight enough to know that you would be taken with that creature. Probably he knew already how your letter had impressed her and that she was curious about you. And so he reckoned to play on your temperament, hoping that might prove an easy method of ending his connection with her. Why, he must have jumped at the idea of taking you to her."

Morgan was rather apologetic on Ingram's behalf, pleading that he must have yielded to the sudden temptation and was not really such a Machiavellian fellow.

"There have been times when, I feel sure, he spoke to me from his heart. But I do not feel revengeful against him, so let him be dead and buried, so far as we are concerned."

"With all my heart," said Helen. "But I confess," she went on laughingly, "it annoys me to think you saw more of the game than I that evening. That is a fact that wounds my vanity. And now about this theatre business. You must be in a terrible plight. Was there ever such a man as you, Morgan, for getting into scrapes?"

"When a man is born into the wrong world—" he began.

"He must be a very interesting sort of person to know," concluded Helen.

When Morgan went on to relate the history of the enterprise he seemed to get a saner adjustment of his mental focus. In the telling he had sight of the whole business as a lamentable, real piece of his personal life, even perceiving as he described the stormy incidents of that morning—more dramatic than anything in "The Basha's Favourite"—that it had not been without its humorous elements. He understood quite well, of course, that unless Cleo now found the requisite money, she would be hopelessly bankrupt.

"And so she's confident of finding it," observed Helen.

"I am quite in the dark," said Morgan.

"Perhaps she intends opening the theatre again."

"Heaven forbid!"

"You don't expect she'd take any notice of the prohibition! Now Morgan, dear, I think you've treated her handsomely and she has cause to be grateful to you. You offered her the incense of a profound faith in her genius and a profound admiration of her person. Not content with that, she needs must have the same incense—compounded of the same two essentials, observe you —from the world at large. For this purpose you made her a nice little money present and enabled her to realise her dreams of a theatre. You gave her the greatest joy of her life. In return—what has she given you? A few kisses, a pretence of love, and a heavy burden on your poor head! If the madcap hadn't tied you to her, the worst criticism to be made would have been that you could have got the kisses and the rest very much cheaper. But as it is—well, I think you'd better say good-bye to her."

Morgan shook his head. "Impossible!" he said.

"She wouldn't grieve very much," insisted Helen. "She certainly couldn't go on doing anything for long except thinking of herself. You may be sure that once she realises your present estimate of her, she will not wish to keep you longer. She is not wicked—as I am, you know—she is simply an exaggerated incarnation of the most unsatisfactory sides of feminine nature. All women have something of her in them, but the less of her they have the more charming you'll find them. In the sham, tawdry world of the footlights she feels something akin to her whole being. It calls to such a woman almost from her very cradle, and fly to it she must. It is true that, in her case, this stage-infatuation was a real misfortune, for in some other walk she might have made a furore. That nude scene, in fact, was symbolic of the temperament, and, had she taken to writing, would have come out as an autobiographic novel. There are women who cannot make themselves interesting to men without the confidence-trick, who cannot even talk to a man for the first time without laying bare their whole souls. Should a woman you scarcely know try the trick on you—shun her. She also is afflicted with the same disease as your Cleo, with the same rage for displaying her interesting self; though it may find a more refined—and certainly a more decent—expression. I am giving you so long a lecture because you sadly need it. I am giving away my sisters to you, because you must be protected against them. If I had given you a few such sermons in the past, you would not have had to undergo the punishment of listening to this one now. Now, having well lectured you, let us proceed to be practical. I am going to pay the debts she has incurred and after that she ought to leave you free."

"No, Helen!" exclaimed Morgan. "You have paid enough already. I feel utterly contemptible when I think of the use to which I have put your money."

"Why will you persist in taking such unphilosophic views? For a poet, you have a singular grip on the world. To me money is not such a reality. And if it were, what is it between you and me? If the position were reversed, Morgan —it may be a shocking admission to make—I should not hesitate to take money from you, you conventional Philistine. I thought you were above such petty considerations—to say nothing of their coarseness."

"It's unkind of you to overload me with debt and employ specious arguments to persuade me the load doesn't weigh."

"How can there be such a thing as a debt between us? I don't really believe you're going to punish me by not behaving sensibly."

And so the battle continued, each fighting doggedly. He kept dragging in the five hundred pounds he had already had, and she insisting that mustn't count, even if regarded from a strict business point of view. For she claimed that he had caused her unspeakable torture of late, at least as great as that of a lady plaintiff in a breach of promise case, and she was, therefore, entitled to damages. The pleasure he would give her by his agreeing to the cancelling of the old debt would only be fair compensation. Then, since this old debt had been wiped out, there was no reason why she should not help now.

He ended by compromising on both points. The repayment of the five hundred pounds was to be deferred indefinitely, the debt itself being absolutely cancelled in the meanwhile, but it was to revive if he should ever have the means to satisfy it. And also Helen was to be allowed to pay the theatrical liabilities, provided Cleo agreed to her doing so, though her identity was not to be divulged.

"And now that we have at last come to an understanding, I think we deserve some tea after our exertions," she declared, rising to ring for it. "Practically I have gained my points, though not verbally. I have profound faith in woman's dogged persistence. It can achieve anything—even win your love, Morgan. Let me see. How far had we got? You were to kiss me on the forehead once each time? And this stage has four months to run before any advance can be made."

Her reference to her love for him chilled him. Somehow he now believed in it as real, though he had always taken it as a toying pretence. He had come to her to-day as to a comrade—to feel himself in shelter for a little while, and for the luxury of opening his heart to her. And now there came upon him a great sense of guilt towards Helen, perhaps accentuated at that moment when his consciousness of her worth had arrived at its fullest and had endeared her to him more than ever before. He was filled with remorse as he remembered he had taken pleasure in keeping from her the knowledge of Margaret's very existence, when Margaret was for him all that Helen aspired to be.

His habit of keeping the various threads of his life distinct had led him to omit the consideration of what might be involved in their subtle relation, for they were all necessarily related since they were merged in the wholeness of his life; and it seemed to him now, all a-thrill as he was with Helen's sympathy, he had behaved abominably in not telling her that his spirit vibrated only for Margaret, that the thought of Margaret brought him all the magic emotion that floats and palpitates, like some wondrous sweet perfume, and that the elect who love true alone may know.

He had already told her to-day much of what he had hidden from her. Let him complete the confession and reveal even what was most sacred to him. Even now he was conscious of certain instincts that made for reservation, but he fought against them.

"Helen," he called, "I wonder whether you would care to listen to the sentimental chapters."

She had been watching his face whilst he had hesitated and she now grew white.

"You know we used to talk quite a deal about those sentimental chapters," he went on. "There was a sweet little girl, too, whose existence you suspected."

"I remember," said Helen faintly. "We did talk about those chapters, but you would never let me get a glimpse of what was inside them. And then I could never really learn whether they were real or imaginary. As a woman of the world, I believed there must be such chapters in the biography of a young man who had lived twenty-eight whole years; as a woman in love with the young man of twenty-eight, I longed to disbelieve in them. Which shows that the real nature of the individual is finer than life is. Life would make us all cynics if the noble in some of us did not find truth too plebeian a fellow to keep company with. I have long since suspected that truth is not that beautiful nude young person one sees rising out of wells at Academy Exhibitions. Illusion, at any rate, is every whit as real a factor of the universe, and it is far more agreeable to live with. So, naturally, Morgan, I chose it to live with, hoping, of course, it was not illusion. However, there *was* a sweet, little girl?"

"Your inference from my poem was perfectly correct."

"Farewell, my fine dreams," said Helen, in mock-heroic declamation, which did not blind him to the pain beneath. "But you'll introduce me to her, won't you?"

"It's the sweet little girl's sister," he corrected; "but I can't introduce you to her, because I shall never see her again."

"You *shall* see her again," said Helen. "Don't be such a faint heart."

"Even if I were free, I am not fit even to look at her."

"The sooner you get a more appreciative conception of yourself, the better."

"Truth has too great a hold over me for that."

"How fine it must be to be loved by you," half-mused Helen. "With you it is first love and everlasting."

"Yes, it is everlasting. It is a quality of my fibre, divinely inwoven like mind in matter. It is something immortal, so that even if Margaret change and forget me wholly, she can never take away the living fragrance that came to me in the first times. I have loved her and shall love her always."

"What nice things you say. If they could only have been inspired by me! But all that is over now. So her name's Margaret. I am sure she will never change, nor even begin to forget you, Morgan. But won't you begin to read those chapters now? I do so want to hear them."

He placed them before her unreservedly and she at length had his life complete. But when he had finished he was alarmed at her pallor.

"You are not well, Helen," he cried impulsively.

"'Tis nothing. I shall be all right in a moment." She drew her breath heavily. "It feels like pins and needles," she added. "I want to get the transition over now, though it is rather an abrupt one."

"The transition!" he repeated, only half-comprehending.

"Yes. It is attended with queer sensations. Pins and needles, thousands of them—and something feels tight. But I shall emerge all the better for it. So far I have only loved you; henceforth I want to love you and Margaret as well."

"How I have made you suffer!" he murmured brokenly. His hand sought hers. "My good angel!"

She drew her hand back.

"No—not angel, but only a simple prophet; and as a prophet I tell you you were born to be happy."

He shook his head, bethinking himself he must go back to his Cleo.

"Now I hope you won't make me miserable again," said Helen, as he rose to go, "by leaving me in the dark about you. And mind you let me know at once if you have need of me to-morrow. A special messenger will be sure to find me, as I shall not be leaving the house till four o'clock. Keep a stout heart and let the light of hope vanquish the vapours and fogs. Above all, bear my prophecy in mind."

CHAPTER VIII.

When Morgan got back to their lodgings he had the sensation of entering the atmosphere of a charnel house. Cleo had not come home yet, and he had leisure to ponder on Helen's attitude towards him and her bearing when she had learned all. Of course, he told himself, he must not take any notice of her wild suggestion that he and Cleo must part and that their marriage didn't count; nor did he permit himself to be allured by her optimistic pre-perception of the future. Noble heart that she was, she had been striving to lessen his pain. He felt he understood what had prompted her every word. And the readiness with which she had bowed her head in acceptance of the emotional position as soon as she knew about Margaret compelled his admiration. Not a word of rebellion, but only a quick gasp of breath; and then he was conscious he had won a sturdy ally.

Ally! When there was to be no battle, was not the word an empty one? Yet no; surely it was a blessed thing to know of a ready and willing heart, even if its services could not avail one! That which signified naught in practical light signified much humanly.

He was awake now, could see the exact bearings of things, and he felt a desperate courage to stand his ground. All his sense of suffering, of the shipwreck he had made, and of what he might have to face in the next few days, had become fused into one large poignant emotion. It was an extra poignancy to be aware that Helen would continue to suffer because of his determination to face the consequences. But he was married to Cleo, and, unless she expressly left him, he must stand by her.

Cleo returned about half-past five and ordered some tea. She said she was just a little tired, but her face was jubilant as she handed him two weekly papers that had appeared that day containing laudatory notices of "The Basha's Favourite." In spite of her attempting to appear calm, he could see she was very much excited about them, and when he had read the strings of unblushing falsehood and handed them back to her in silence, she lovingly let her eye run over them again. Over the tea, she grew eloquent once more, especially drawing his attention to the truth of particular phrases and to the admirable insight and appreciation of the writers. But she volunteered no information about the business which had occupied her afternoon. Morgan was somewhat puzzled. He was still inclined to hold to his belief that she had gone on some harum-scarum chase after money, but as she did not manifest the least sign of disappointment or dejection, it was hard to think that her pockets were as empty as before. He refrained from questioning her, however, for in a grim way he had begun to derive entertainment from watching her, and he, therefore, did not wish to interfere with her. He preferred to wait and see what coup it was she was now preparing.

After tea, Cleo suggested it would be a good idea if she had her effects removed from the theatre. Her costumes, in particular, she was eager to have safe at home. So Morgan accompanied her to the theatre. She had already packed everything in a large trunk, which she now had carried down. But in the corridor the two commissionaires attached to the house sternly blocked the way. They were very sorry, but the lessees' orders were that nothing was to be allowed to pass out, having regard to the amount still due under the contract for the theatre.

Cleo passionately ordered them to stand aside. The men insisted that though the obligation of paying their wages rested on her, they were still the lessees' servants, and had to obey their orders. Morgan argued with them quietly, but found them obdurate. He did not know if this action of the lessees was legal or not, but anyhow money was owing to them and there seemed to be a show of justice on their side. He took Cleo aside and besought her to let the matter rest for the moment, pointing out that, as the men were so determined, there was nothing else to be done, short of a physical set-to. "Besides," he added, "if you are quite confident of settling everything to-morrow, the trunk may just as well stay here over night."

To this Cleo ultimately agreed, won over by Morgan's last argument. But none the less did she give loud expression to all that was in her mind anent the lessees and the commissionaires. She went home again with Morgan in the worst of humours at having been thus baffled. But later in the evening she attired herself gaily and carried him off to a little restaurant supper party, given by a gentleman he had met before, but about whose occupation he possessed no information, though he had gathered that the theatre was his chief interest. There was one other lady, plentifully powdered, and two other men of the party, but the host was the most garrulous of all, pouring out the most fulsome flattery of Cleo's acting and assuring her the critics hadn't treated her fairly and that all artistic aspiration was wasted on the British public. The same ground was traversed again and again, the bulk of the conversation centering round Cleo.

To Morgan it seemed that Cleo had made an enormous number of acquaintances in the few weeks that had elapsed since their marriage, and with many of them she appeared to be on terms of easy *camaraderie*. Every day during the week scores of visitors had dropped in to see her and to chat familiarly—all sorts of strange men and women that seemed to flock round her, anomalous citizens of Bohemia, vague hangers-on of the theatrical cosmos; all that strange melange of the happy-go-lucky, the eccentric, the ill-balanced, the blackguardly, the unprincipled, the hapless, the shiftless, the unclassed, the sensual and the besotted that shoulder and hustle one another in the world of the theatre; all the riff-raff recruited from the greater world without by the fascinating glare of the footlights.

The supper was a gay one, and Cleo, drawing new life from the stream of adulation, strolled home on Morgan's arm, overflowing with the wonder of her own personality, was it in regard to her genius as an actress, or was it in regard to the magnetism of her beauty. Her step seemed to have recovered all its old springiness; her defeat was as if it had not been. She was very optimistic about her career and again spoke of Morgan one day writing the play of her life. That would be, of course, after they had travelled in Egypt and the East. He was sufficiently taken off his guard by her demeanour to begin to think it was impossible she should not have some mysterious financial resource to fall back upon for the morrow.

"We shall not want to be very long at the theatre," were her last words to him that night. "Let us try and get there by ten. I shall pay the salaries at twelve o'clock and we can leave the house soon after."

CHAPTER IX.

Morgan's attitude in the morning was one of interested expectancy. Cleo was as full of vitality as ever. Perhaps it was that, as she entered the theatre, the sight of her trunk, waiting in the corridor for redemption, stimulated her masterfulness afresh, for she found pretext for asserting her authority over everybody on the premises. Up to the last moment she revelled in the enjoyment of all the powers and privileges that one acquires over other human beings by engaging to pay them a wage.

As the time went by and Morgan saw no sign of the appearance of the requisite cash, he ventured at last to broach the subject to her, and she replied firmly and clearly:

"At twelve o'clock the salaries shall be paid."

But at the time specified, Cleo, who was sitting with him in her private room, hid her face in her hands and began to sob hysterically. Then he was able to elicit the truth. She had passed the last afternoon interviewing moneylenders, but they had all laughed in her face—which had simply called forth her contempt for them. As a matter of fact, she had been expecting a miracle to happen!

A conviction had come to her that, when the moment for making payment arrived, she would have the necessary money. How or whence it was to come she had not considered; her belief was simply a blind one. Though she had not found it waiting for her on her arrival at the theatre, her faith that the powers that worked the universe could not possibly allow her to undergo the great humiliation of being a defaulter towards those she had employed, was still unshaken. In her the sense of the Ego was so great that, if rightly interpreted, her feeling about the world would have been found to be that it was created specially for her and carefully shaped and subordinated to suit the needs of her existence. She could not understand her being so utterly beaten as she really was. Her half-crazy, superstitious notion could only have been combatted by its non-realisation. At her hesitating confession that she had been expecting the money to come somehow, Morgan had at once grasped the whole working of her mind, for he understood now what manner of woman it was that he had made his wife.

He knew that the company and employés were assembled, expecting to be called momentarily.

"Cleo," he said, "I have had the offer of enough money to pay all that is owing. You must decide whether I am to avail myself of it. If you say 'yes,' it shall be here within an hour."

But she scarcely heeded, for in that moment she rose as if following up some train of thought, and pulled out every drawer of the bureau, looking carefully into each as though in search of something. When at last the perception was forced on her that the miracle had still not happened, she sat down again with a sigh.

He repeated his statement and she wanted to know from whom the offer came.

"A friend," he answered.

"It is some woman who loves you," she flashed at him.

He could not repress a start.

"It is! It is!" she exclaimed excitedly, her eyes ablaze. "Do not attempt to deny it; I can read it in your face. Ah, I understand now; it is the same friend who helped you before. And you led me to believe it was a man."

"I made no mention of the sex."

"But you knew I was deceived all the same. How dared you conceal from me that you had had the money from a woman you had loved? Did I not return Mr. Ingram all he had given me, because I felt it would be a desecration to use a penny of it? And I thought you were fine, Morgan, I thought you were fine."

Scorn rang in her tones, but he did not answer, because he wished to avoid a scene. It were better, he thought, to let the storm exhaust itself. The unassuming introduction of the "woman you had loved," in place of the reverse, did not, however, escape him.

"Had I suspected the truth," she went on, admirably dramatic now that she was not on the stage, "I should rather have taken some deadly poison than have touched this filthy money of hers. Did you take me for some vile creature? I shall pay back every farthing. Oh, to throw it all in her face! No, no! this is my affair. How dare you suggest that I, your wife, should accept more of her money! As if I could fall so low! These debts are mine. You are not to interfere."

He could only bow to her will. In the first moment of disillusion he had not been without a certain apprehension that she might wish to take advantage of the fact that he belonged to a wealthy family. But he saw now the thought had done her an injustice. Creature of rich, luscious sentiment, of gorgeous emotions, she scorned to be untrue to the equatorial magnificence of her nature. Nor had she yet finished expressing her resentment. All the untamable tiger in her had been roused, all the fiery, indomitable pride that was as essentially a part of her as her fixed conception of her genius. She was not to be browbeaten by adverse fortune into whining and accepting charity from her husband's mistresses—she had slipped into using the plural now. She turned at bay against the whole situation. Let these people go unpaid for the present—she would pay them when she could. She wanted to go out at once and make a speech to them, but Morgan, fearful of some great uproar, managed to prevail on her to let him make the announcement that money engagements could not be kept.

Very much to his astonishment, everybody took the news quietly enough. "Is there no chance of getting anything?" he was asked, and sad indeed were all faces when he assured them every penny had been lost, and that, though his wife had been confident of raising some more money—he mentioned this possibly with the idea of softening the bitterness against Cleo—her hope had been quite disappointed. Morgan himself almost trembled with emotion, for he knew how eagerly some of them had sought the engagement. Three weeks of rehearsal and a week of acting under most trying and disheartening circumstances, and then to receive nothing! And all that time they had submitted to be bullied and blustered at. If the whole affair had not been so piteous it would have seemed grotesque.

The stage manager, arriving just then, was less tractable, and Morgan feared his vehemence would excite the others.

"And she had the——impudence to chuck me out of her——theatre," he screamed; "and now I can't get a——penny out of her!"

He announced his intention of breaking her head forthwith, and threatened "to do for" Morgan, who barred his way.

Cleo left the theatre a little later, followed by abuse from the stage manager, who was forcibly held back by some of the company. She looked longingly at the trunk in the hall, but had apparently resigned herself to the loss of her costumes, for she passed by in silence.

In the afternoon, Morgan was astonished at being served at their rooms with a writ, which concerned both him and Cleo, and which had been taken out on behalf of one of the creditors. Though Cleo had run the theatre on her own responsibility only, it had been thought possible that he might possess resources, with the result that he had been made co-defendant.

Cleo seized the paper and calmly tore it up.

Then followed a long consultation, Cleo manifesting some signs of depression at the sum total of the results of her efforts, beside which her unshaken belief in the future contrasted curiously. Everything had been against her. She had had a bad company and a stupid first-night audience, and had from the first been crippled by want of money. She recapitulated all her disadvantages, dwelling on each and making the most of it. But this was only by way of beginning a long wail of lament. The undisguised coldness of his demeanour towards her ever since the night of her début had wounded her deeply, though she had been too proud to say anything. Her indictment against him was bitter and severe. The discontinuance of his slavish admiration for her and of his blind belief in her genius was in her eyes an unpardonable sin. As soon as the public had turned against her, she averred, he sheep-like, had followed their example. And he was the one human being in the whole world whom she had trusted and believed in, the one she would have looked to for sympathy and comfort. She had shown her trust in him by marrying him—a privilege she would not lightly have accorded to another—and he should have stood by her in her misfortunes. Why, so-and-so had told her her acting had never been surpassed on the English stage; and he had seen every piece played in London during the last thirty years. She repeated the flattery and fawning that had been bestowed upon her by the men who had been fluttering around her, accepting all as the natural outpour of their sincerity; she quoted with unction the lying notices she had shown him the day before.

Morgan knew better than to expect her to have one thought of sympathy for him, to utter one word of sorrow for the plight into which her stage-madness had brought him. She seemed to think that his dominating sentiment should be, throughout all and despite all, one of gratitude to her for having married him. In proof of which she now mentioned that she had won the admiration of millionaires, of foreign counts by the score, of Indian princes and Eastern potentates, all of whom had written her letters of sympathy at her shameful treatment by the public, had declared their love for her, and had offered to place their whole fortunes at her disposal. She had indignantly destroyed these letters without showing them to him, and would not have thought of claiming any credit for this had he not forced her to do so by his brutality towards her. The Indian prince, in particular, had proved persistent, and even now it was open to her to become mistress of a gorgeous palace and a regiment of servants.

By way of contrasting the fineness of her own conduct with the coarseness of his, she did her best to exasperate him about Helen, applying terrible epithets to her and vowing, in a burst of tiger-like tragedy, she would destroy the beauty of this woman he had loved with vitriol, should their paths ever cross. In addition to Helen, there were general allusions to his mistresses, for Cleo, having begun by converting singular into plural, now retained both singular and plural. Lastly, quieting down somewhat amid a flood of tears, she claimed that Ingram would not have acted in so dastardly a fashion—he, at least, had always valued her at her true worth. It was his misfortune, not his fault, that his money affairs had not turned out well and that he had been unable to build for her the promised theatre. It was his very sense of the dignity of her genius that made him object to giving her a less impressive début. Ingram, too, had had no thought but for her, and he had been undoubtedly heartbroken at her leaving him.

And when, in the end, he prevailed upon her to say what she purposed doing, she informed him that to mark her sense of the degradation that would be involved in the acceptance of the aid offered by her rival, she had preferred to borrow five pounds of her maid, who was at least an old and faithful servant —she had taken her with her from Hampstead—and who stood by her loyally. Out of these five pounds she intended to pay the landlady's bill for the week, and the balance would bring them within the shelter of her parents' home.

Whatever feeling of humiliation Morgan might have had at the confession of this loan was all but lost in his surprise at her sudden mention of parents. He had never thought of her at all in relation to parents or in relation to other human beings whose blood flowed in her veins. She had pre-eminently struck him as a figure to be taken as "detached"; his feeling about her, though he had never precisely formulated it, was that she had not come into existence as other people, but that, in her case, there had been a special act of creation. Her parents had got impasted into the vagueness of that background, out of which she had come floating into his life.

The position, however, was a difficult one for him. He could scarcely chide her for borrowing, grotesque as the borrowing was. The maid, he learnt, was leaving her that same afternoon and was to be married soon. What helped him to decide was the great curiosity that had come upon him to make the acquaintance of the people who had given her to the world. Something of his old attitude came back to him. The desire to see what strange thing was to follow next stirred in him again. But this time a greater bitterness was mixed with it, a better grip on the wholeness of life, an active consciousness that, though he might now derive a grim sort of enjoyment from watching the unfolding of circumstance, the experience would be nevertheless real, would represent so much of his personal life. No longer would it be a mere desperate submission to idle drifting amid the scenes of a dreamland; though the same temperament as before was at the back of his decision. Of course, his general determination to face the full responsibility of his relation to Cleo likewise counted for a good deal in his assenting to accompany her on this visit she purposed to her parents.

He questioned her about her family, and she told him that her father was a printer at Dover; that her mother was simply her mother; that she had a brother and two sisters, all unmarried, all living at home. She was barely eighteen when she had left Dover, but she had ceased communicating with her family as soon as she had made Ingram's acquaintance. However, in anticipation of a great success, she had written to them again a few weeks back, informing them of her marriage and of the theatre of her own which she was to have immediately. Her father, in reply, had written her a cordial letter, and had, in fact, suggested she should bring her husband to see them if she should ever find a suitable opportunity. They would therefore be likely to meet with a warm welcome, and they could stay at Dover till her plans were mature, which would be very shortly. What these plans were likely to be he could not elicit, though he gathered some vague millionaire was connected with them, and that they would enable her to clear off all the debts almost immediately. But since, at the moment, they were entirely without resources, it would be useless, she pointed out, for them to take any notice of the writ that had been served. Creditors would obviously be putting themselves to vain expense in suing them now, and it was therefore best for them to go for a little while where at least they would be free from being worried.

During the evening Morgan managed to find an opportunity of writing to Helen a brief account of the day, saying he would look for her answer at the Dover post-office.

And he and Cleo left London by an early train in the morning.

END OF BOOK III.

BOOK IV.

CHAPTER I.

The son and daughters of the Kettering family were out taking the air, as the Sunday morning was a fine one, and Morgan sat talking with his father-in-law in a front room, that was depressing with horse-hair upholstery and wax fruit under glass shades and a series of prints representing certain emotional moments in the life of a young blue-jacket. Cleo was in some distant region of the house with her mother, who had beamed on Morgan with a most unaccountable friendliness.

Mr. Simon Kettering himself was a mild-featured little man, whose Sunday broad-cloth was but a thin disguise of the fact that all the week he worked amid his journeymen in apron and shirt-sleeves. He wore spectacles with light steel frames that seemed to cut deep into his flesh; his hair was fast greying and his face was much lined, which, however, interfered little with the benevolence of his expression. His hands were large and coarse-grained and of a tint that no longer yields to ablutions.

On their arrival, about a quarter of an hour previously, Cleo had left Morgan in the hall and had gone up to see her parents, returning for him some five minutes later and introducing him to them in the room in which he now sat. As he was not present at the actual meeting of Cleo and the old people, he now asked Mr. Kettering if the sudden appearance of his daughter after all these years hadn't startled him.

"Me!" exclaimed his father-in-law. "Why, not a bit! When she was only that big, I soon found out it wasn't any use taking notice of her goings and comings. The missus has been worrying about her a good deal. But I always said to her: 'Selina's a girl who can take care of herself, and sure enough she'll turn up all right one of these fine days.' It was very wrong of her, though, not to let us have a line from her for nigh on six years. But I fancy she was always a bit ashamed of us. Her notions were always so grand, and plain, hard-working people weren't good enough for her. I'm very sorry indeed that things have turned out so disastrously. My Selina, to tell the truth, is a queer creature, sir, and, if I may take the liberty of saying so, I think you were a fool to marry her."

Cleo, at her first interview with her parents, had made a clean breast of the fact that her theatre had been a failure and that they had lost all their money, though she did not omit to mention she was conducting negotiations which would soon put them on their feet again. Morgan smiled at Mr. Kettering's bluntness, and he somehow divined that there was a shrewd pair of eyes behind those spectacles that took in far more than they appeared to do.

"I'm hanged if *I'd* ever have married her," pursued the master-printer, "and that's telling you the plain truth, sir. You see what she has done for you already. Why did you give her all that money? You should have let her go on acting and drawing a regular salary, instead of risking all that capital in that monstrously foolish way. You'll excuse my freedom, I know, sir."

From which Morgan deduced that Cleo's version of the whole affair had not been entirely coloured by truth. From the way Mr. Kettering dropped his voice and looked reverential as he mentioned "all that money," it was quite clear Cleo's imagination had magnified the loss to accord with her sense of the fitness of things. A great loss of money was the next glorious thing to a great success.

Mr. Kettering proceeded to lay it down as a general maxim that there was nothing in life like drawing a regular salary. Ever since he had been a master-printer on his own account, he had been regretting the fact. A workman knew exactly how much he had to spend and how to spend it. But in these days when competition was so severe and trade so uncertain, the master had much to be thankful for if he could pay his way at all. Not that he himself was not perfectly able to earn a living at all times, he added in some haste, as if to reassure his son-in-law; and certainly his daughter and her husband were quite welcome to be his guests as long as they chose to stay under his roof.

Morgan felt drawn towards the old man, though he perceived that Simon Kettering's soul could not take wing out of the atmosphere of his workshop, and that whosoever wished to commune with him must descend into it. But it was from this very atmosphere that Cleo had emerged—Cleo, with her vitriolic notions and her pretentious scents! This, then, was that mystic past against which her figure had stood out!

Cleo and her mother returned a few minutes later, interrupting Mr. Kettering's account of the many vexations that preyed on him—his troubles with his men, the heavy expense of constantly renewing the composition on his machine rollers, the idleness and wantonness of the apprentice, the perpetual ordering of "sorts" from the type-founder, the inconsiderateness of customers who kept his type locked up, and the carelessness of everybody but himself in the handling of his material.

"We've been getting along capitally, Mr. Druce and I," he broke off to explain to the two women. "It's well on towards dinner-time, and the children ought to be coming in soon."

Cleo seemed relieved to find that Morgan hadn't been bored. Her mother, in whose strange, deep-cut features was suggested something of the spirit of

Cleo's face, was a brisk-looking, homely matron of fifty.

"So Cleo is really married!" she repeated for the tenth time, her face aglow with satisfaction. And her eyes rested wonderingly on Morgan till he almost fancied he could hear her mental exclamation: "A real live husband!"

Soon the other members of the family arrived, Mary and Alice and their brother Mark, a young man of thirty, who looked hard-working and reticent, and had large moustachios. They stopped almost on the threshold as they perceived there were strangers in the parlour, then they recognised their long- lost sister; but, embarrassed by the presence of the strange gentleman, as well as by the startling fact of her presence, they stood hesitant and rather shame- faced. Cleo smiled at them encouragingly, whereupon her sisters came tripping over and smothered her with kisses. Their expressions of love were so loud and so flowery that Morgan began to recognise the family blood. When, a moment later, he was introduced to them as Cleo's husband, their faces became of a fiery red, as though there were something discreditable in the fact of matrimony, and they exhibited a stiff shyness that was almost stupid. The introduction completed, they stood looking at him, giggling and giggling. But Mark now came forward with outstretched hand, saying quietly: "I am glad to know you, sir."

"Let us go in to dinner, children," said Mr. Kettering.

They dined in the back room on the same floor, for the ground floor and the basement were devoted to the trade. It was a long, narrow room, lighted by one window at the end, and almost filled by the table. Morgan found himself between Alice and Mark, whilst Mary sat opposite him. Both the girls were young, Mary about twenty, whilst Alice did not seem more than seventeen. In appearance they struck him as inferior imitations of their sister. They were much shorter and far less well-proportioned than Cleo, their red hair was coarser than hers, and their features were duller. Their voices, too, were reminiscent of hers. Altogether, though it was abundantly evident that they were Cleo's sisters, they were perfectly unarrestive. Nature had made a success of Cleo, but had egregiously failed to repeat the performance.

The one servant of the house waited at table, prim, sedate, formal. A corresponding air of restraint seemed to prevail during the whole meal. It was not till afterwards that he realised that they were somewhat in awe of him as being obviously a "fine gentleman," and that they were feeling they had to live up to him. Cleo showed no inclination to speak, and the other women would not venture to begin. Mr. Kettering, on whom lay the onus of entertaining, at length strove to face his responsibilities, and, addressing himself to Morgan, discussed the comparative fineness of the weather at London and Dover. Morgan, in return, asked questions about the town and the harbour and the boats, managing to keep up some sort of a conversation with him. Eventually the situation began to depress him, so terribly stiff were they all in their attempt to be genteel. Besides, his appetite was of the poorest, though he was somewhat astonished to find the fare so plentiful. Mrs. Kettering kept pressing him to eat more and more, and apparently found it hard to understand that his refusals were final. "Are you sure?" she asked him each time; and once she plucked up courage to assure him he must not stand on ceremony with them, and that he need not hesitate to eat his fill. Morgan thought it extraordinary she should so persistently refuse to believe in the sincerity of his small consumption of food, but, attributing her solicitude to sheer good-nature, he was sorry to cause her such evident dissatisfaction.

He was glad when the meal was over, for he was beginning to feel stifled. The family did not disperse, coffee now being served, of so curious a flavour that Morgan could not get further than the first sip.

"Don't you like coffee, sir?" asked Mrs. Kettering.

He began to feel a little bit persecuted. He did not hesitate to reply in the negative, since the question was put from Mrs. Kettering's point of view and the answer had only to apply to her conception of the beverage.

At length Cleo said she was going to take him for a stroll, and he willingly fell in with the idea. But they did not go far, taking possession of a seat as soon as they arrived on the sea-front. They seemed to have nothing to say to each other. Cleo appeared lost in thought, and he, after gazing idly at the few promenaders and the children playing on the shingle and at the white cliffs of France gleaming across the straits, relapsed into a half reverie. He had somewhat of a sense of physical relief at being able to breathe here at his ease; of temporary respite and security from being hunted by creditors. But he was intensely miserable all the same, the one immediate gleam of light being the hope of a letter from Helen.

As yet the Kettering family was a new experience to him, and though the stiff gentility and aggressive hospitality so far exhibited had made him somewhat uncomfortable, his judgment of these people was favourable enough. Still, he was possessed of the idea that he was not going to stay in that house more than a few days. Not that he had the least conception of what else he was going to do, but events had been following each other in such quick succession that he could not believe in a cessation of them. The last two days, in particular, had seemed very crowded. Yesterday all those dramatic events in the theatre—though not on its stage; to-day their departure from London and their incursion into the reality of that poetic nebulousness from which Cleo had originally emerged.

He was glad that Kettering had not addressed to him any personal questions, for he wished to tell neither truth nor falsehood about himself. The anticipation of the topic arising was not an agreeable one, and it was likewise unpleasant to dwell upon the possibility of embarrassment arising from Cleo's habit of embellishment. He wondered what her schemes were, though he could not take them seriously. And this train of thought ultimately brought back to him the fear that perhaps after all pressure might be brought to bear on him to make him avail himself of his father's purse. The thought of his father gave him now—as it had given him throughout all this time of trial—an uncontrollable emotion, but he would not let his mind speculate about the grief and attitude of his family, forcibly interposing a veil between himself and them. Tired out at length, he let his reverie merge into mere uncritical perception. He was conscious of afternoon sunshine, of a great stretch of sky, with a continent of white cloud containing big blue lakes; his eye took in the expanse of sea, glistening, streaked, patched, lined, and shaded, with the pier in his centre of vision, a mass of kiosks, pole-lamps, and conventional iron- work. And in the foreground parasols dotted here and there made spots of black, brown, green, and red against the yellowish shingle.

Commonplace as the scene was, he found it restful to dwell upon in a lazy fashion. He forgot for a while that Cleo was by his side, and when he awoke again to the consciousness of her presence he found she had been engaged in reading again the two favourable notices of her performance, which she had carefully carried about with her.

Soon Alice and Mary appeared, and all four went home together. Tea was laid in the same room, the table being set out as for a heavy meal.

"Did you enjoy your walk, sir?" asked Mr. Kettering, while the trim servant, waiting at table with the same solemn gravity as before, put before him a huge cup of very strong tea, of which no milk or sugar could alleviate the astringency. He now found he was expected to eat large quantities of boiled fish, plum-cake and sweets; and Mrs. Kettering, perceiving that he didn't do justice to the fare, enumerated to him other things that were in the larder, with the suggestion that he might perhaps prefer a choice of them. Some of the stiffness that had characterised the former meal had vanished—Morgan could see now that had been due to shyness at his presence—and, though Mark still showed little willingness to converse, the girls were evidently beginning to find themselves again, occasional gigglings heralding their return to normality. But the concentration of the united attention of the family for Morgan's benefit was somewhat disconcerting. The girls vied with each other in pressing plum-cake upon him, and seemed to view his refusal as a personal rebuff. He did not understand just then that each considered a bit of her own niceness went into the cake when held towards him with her own hand, and that it was this niceness he was rejecting. As for the cake, they took it for granted that there could be no difficulty about disposing of that. Before the end, Morgan got the sensation of having the food rammed down his throat with a pole.

They tried to flirt with him, too, but here again he unconsciously annoyed them by his unresponsiveness. In fact, being entirely unacquainted with the game as they were in the habit of playing it, he set down the strange attempts of Cleo's sisters to provoke him to banter as rather silly. He did not know that they had thrown off their first unquestioning acceptance of his impressiveness and were now subjecting him to sharp criticism. They had their own notion— and a very definite one it was—of what a perfect gentleman should be, and they were not disposed lightly to accept a substitute. What, however, struck him particularly was their unbounded affection for their father and mother, for Cleo and Mark, and last, though not least, for each other.

During the evening Mary grew so bold as to offer to show him the harbour by night, and he welcomed the suggestion as likely to afford him a little quiet distraction. He had sat amid the family for several hours, and it had not occurred to anybody he might like to be just alone. The day had seemed interminable, and as they had been behaving more freely among themselves, once the restraint had worn off, he had begun to get a somewhat revised perception of them. Their peculiar atmosphere was beginning to enter into his being, and his vision of them, therefore, to lose its first impersonality.

Though the sky was clear, there was no moon that evening, which elicited the remark from Mary that it was a pity. Morgan presumed that moonlight made the harbour look much more poetic, whereupon Mary admitted that she wasn't thinking of the harbour, but of the fact that it made walking with a girl much more poetic. She wanted him to say that walking with her was so heavenly, absence of moonlight notwithstanding, that he couldn't possibly imagine any improvement. But he didn't say it. He only just gave the faintest indication of a laugh.

When he happened to admire the far-stretching, soft shadow of the sea, with its gentle, irregular line of white where it met the shore, she asked him if he wouldn't like to be rowing just then with a girl on a lovely lake. She wanted him to say—yes, if the girl were she. But he did not say it, and he had no idea that she was getting angry.

They walked on a little in silence, passing a girl talking to a man under the full light of a lamp. Mary remarked that the girl was exquisitely pretty. She wanted him to say that she herself was a thousandfold prettier. But he did not say it; and she led him off the front rather sulkily, taking him over a drawbridge and on to the quay that bisected the harbour. They strolled about amid the piles of timber and along more quays and drawbridges, now and again encountering other promenaders in the soft darkness. For awhile Morgan found the stillness delicious, almost forgetting the existence of his companion. But very soon she recommenced her tactics, making statements that credited him— by implication—with flirtations galore, and hinting at vast experience on her own part and lovers by the score. Certainly she laid pitfalls by the score, but she was so invariably unsuccessful that she could not help at last giving expression to her vexation.

"You're the first man I've ever known," she said frankly, "who didn't think me beautiful."

He recognised he had got a whiff of his Cleo there, but, just as he was about to deliver the polite reply to which she had forced him, they happened to turn round the side of a great wood-stack and, at the same moment, an impressive chorus of voices floated softly across the night. They were now on a quay that ran across the harbour, parallel with the cliffs that rose at the back of it. To right and left were the massed silhouettes of shipping and small craft, of odd superannuated sailing vessels and huge-funnelled steamers, and in the intervening waters were moored half a dozen Russian gun-boats. On the largest of these a sailors' service was being held. They could hear the priest's sweet voice raised in exhortation, and then again rose the sailors' chant.

Morgan listened enraptured. The velvety surface of the water, traversed here and there by glistering bars, the subdued stars above, the profound silence of the night, the strange whiteness of the cliff beyond, rising in marked contrast to the dark line of dwellings at its foot, save where the patches of green on its face showed as grey stains in the darkness, the looming hulls and intertangled masts and rigging, the mystic scattered lights of the harbour—the enchantment of all entered into his spirit, attuned to this beautiful singing of the vespers.

And then, of a sudden, a bugle-call rang out, clear and far-reaching, from the great barracks of the Western heights; instinct in its rhythm with discipline, valour, and martial fire; thrilling into the spaces of the night in strange contrast to the spirit of peace that breathed in the sweet concord of the sailors' chanting of evening hymns.

"What a funny lingo!" said Alice, as the chaplain's voice was again heard in prayer. Her laugh rang out, loud and scornful, insulting the solemnity and beauty of the scene. Morgan instinctively began to move on, pained to think that these sojourners in English waters might deem they were being scoffed at.

"It wasn't at them I was laughing," she explained, as if aware she had offended him. "Something came into my mind that happened just at that spot. It's so funny that I can't help laughing every time I think of it. If you're very, very good, perhaps I may tell you."

She looked up at him, wagging her head about to indicate her last sentence had been intended playfully. Morgan expressed a desire to hear it, in a sort of indifferent murmur.

"Well, there was a fellow I let dance with me three or four times, and I went for a walk with him twice or so. Then he began to get a bit cheeky, and so I thought I'd put him in his place. I wouldn't take any notice of him for a long time, and when we passed him in the street I pretended not to know him. At last one day he comes up to me and he says: 'Mary, I can't stand it any longer. If you won't speak to me again I'll go and drown myself.' And then he begged so hard that at last I promised to go for a walk with him in the evening. Well, I kept my promise, and we strolled along here. And just at that very spot we stood still to look at the harbour. 'John,' said I, 'there's the water; now drown yourself.'"

Again she laughed immoderately at the recollection of this brilliant *jeu d'esprit* and her admirer's discomfiture.

But the *jeu d'esprit* kept echoing oddly through Morgan's brain.

"There's the water. Now drown yourself!"

CHAPTER II.

Morgan found the Monday infinitely easier to get through. For the members of the family were absorbed in the duties of life, so that he was left much to himself. Alice and Mary kept the accounts and served behind the counter in the stationery shop. In a workshop at the back Simon Kettering, Mark, four journeymen and one apprentice stood "at case," whilst in the basement two antiquated printing machines rumbled on, worked by a small gas-engine. There was also a Columbian press for pulling posters and a platen machine for small work. Mr. Kettering devoted a few odd minutes to showing Morgan over the establishment. As he observed, it was not a magnificent concern; but he had it all under his eye and by hard work made it yield him a living. Still, times were hard and—and Mr. Kettering, having once begun to enlarge on the subject of his disadvantages, proceeded to pour forth all the accumulated vexations of his spirit.

Cleo remained in the parlour during the morning writing letters, but she did not offer to enlighten Morgan as to their nature. He was rather glad of this incommunicativeness of hers, for he felt in too restless a mood to talk to her. Impatiently as he was awaiting Helen's letter, he would not inquire at the post-office till the evening. He could not bear the idea of coming away empty-handed.

Meanwhile he amused himself rummaging leisurely amid the contents of an old mahogany book-case. He found rather a medley of worn school-books— old-fashioned geographies and histories and foreign conversation grammars; of mouldy novels, many in French and Italian; of illustrated lives of actresses, prime donne, and celebrated courtezans. Most of the novels and non- scholastic books were of a shoddy, sensational type. Here, then, he had evidently stumbled across the source of Cleo's early mental nourishment; this was the literature with which her nature had found affinity. In nearly every book he took down he came across passages underlined, with occasionally a note in the margin in her own handwriting. The rich manner and false, pompous sublimity of these passages brought a smile to his lips, though making his heart contract painfully. He called to mind the books he had seen lying about on the occasion of his memorable visit to her in company with Ingram, and he now had an intuition that the slumbering of her fierce activity for so many years had been facilitated by a plentiful provision of literature of the same kind. Her imagination had found some compensating stimulation and satisfaction in the luscious scenes amid which it had wandered.

And suddenly he had a startled flash of memory anent a paper-covered novel he was holding in his hands. The lithographed wrapper, with its illuminated veiled figure and its seven mystic stars, he had seen before; and he now recognised the book as an older copy of the very one he had found her reading the first time he had ventured to call on her by himself. It was the work of a lurid lady novelist, popular some ten years before. He turned its pages with bitter interest. Passage after passage was marked and underlined. And at length he lighted on one that seemed to jump from the page and strike him in the face. It was doubly underlined in red ink, as well as thickly marked down the margin.

"In me is reincarnated the spirit of the ancient East, and it is my mission to interpret that spirit to the modern world."

And lower down on the same page, indicated with the like emphasis:

"By sitting in this temple each day and meditating herein I have ministered to my sacred moods, and I have kept pure the essence of the ages, which I am to revive for the modern world."

Morgan remembered only too well by whom and on what occasion such words had been addressed to him. He put back the volume and shut the book-case.

At the one o'clock dinner they all came together again. There was the same profuse solidity of fare as on the previous day, and the same insistence that Morgan must do justice to it. The girls seemed in high spirits, mysterious signs and words passing between them, accompanied by much laughter, of which Morgan dimly suspected he was the cause.

When the clerk at the post-office, looking through a little heap of letters, picked out one and put it aside, Morgan could scarcely restrain his emotion. He chafed at having to wait whilst the man satisfied himself there were no others for him, and the quiet way he took the letter revealed little of his almost overmastering impulse to snatch at it as a wild beast might snatch at meat. Blessed writing on the envelope! Tears were streaming down his cheeks as he stepped again into the street! And when at last he began to read, all that he had suppressed surged up and almost choked him.

"My very dear friend," said Helen, "I want to write to you such a great deal because I know how welcome a long letter will be, and yet I fear that I cannot make this one very long for the simple reason that I am feeling serious. Moods are like dresses. Some of them do not suit me at all. Seriousness not only spoils me, it makes me absolutely idiotic. Most people I know, however, prefer me like that because then I express my agreement with their opinions so very readily. But to be serious. I don't quite understand what you are going to do at Dover. Still, I am glad you've gone, for I'm dying to know what her sisters are like. By the way, I mean to make the acquaintance of the Medhursts. I have an idea I shan't find that a very difficult task. Then perhaps my letters may be more agreeable reading for you, for of course we shall continue corresponding unless you are back in town before long. Morgan, don't lose faith! I told you I was a prophet—or should it be prophetess? When I looked you in the face last I read therein that you were born to be happy.

"In the meanwhile I don't want you to be uncomfortable. And I now come to a point I hate to mention because I am afraid of you. You fly at one so savagely. I don't think you ought to allow a question of mere money to poison such sweet human relation as ours. Won't you look at it in the right spirit? I implore you, do. I want you to believe that I understand and sympathise with your feelings, but recollect now I am writing to you as your best friend, without any admixture of anything else, and it is as my best friend I want you to respond to me. Forget that I am only a woman. Let my purse be yours. Take only a trifle if you will, but still take it. It will make me happy, for I want to feel sure that you are bearing up. Meanwhile I am in dreadful suspense to hear from you.

"Yours

affectionately,

"H

"P. S. In the name of Heaven, write me quickly to tell me what the sisters are like. I have bought a map of London in sections, and I spend hours wandering with you in some of the strange places. What funny shapes the Thames has in some of the sections, and how nicely the pieces underneath it fit into it. Alas! the days, the days that are no more! What a sob re-echoes from those simple words!"

Blessed writing! In what an impasse were his life without it!

CHAPTER III.

Though in his reply to Helen he promised to accept her money in case of need, he could not prevail on himself to begin just then. His instinct was against that course as strongly as ever, and he was precisely like a proud, obstinate child that continues in its fixed attitude long after being convinced. He gave her an account of the Kettering family in as gay a note as he could strike from his leaden mood, for he wished to allay her anxiety about him. He had read in her letter far more than the mere words; her heart beat through every line.

There were still five shillings in his pocket—enough to pay the postage on sixty letters, he grimly reflected. So far he had had no occasion to spend money for anything else, and no beggar had crossed his path to tempt from him the little he had. He needed nothing beyond his food, and of that the Ketterings' hospitality provided a sufficiency, though by the third day the over-profusion of plain dishes was no longer maintained.

Cleo seemed to be getting mysterious letters from town, and she gave him to understand she would be able to put her new scheme before him very soon now, but in the meantime he must be patient. The memory of her defeat had already almost gone from her mind, as did all things which were disagreeable to it and which, therefore, it could not assimilate; and, if she conversed with him at all, it was only on the subject of her genius, her imagination making, if possible, still more gorgeous flights than in the first days he had known her.

But this bluster about her genius only made him smile bitterly now, for he knew but too well that the foundations of any scheme of hers could not be laid in the good, solid earth. He could not guess the nature of the negotiations she had apparently begun, though he had a suspicion she was offering her genius to moneylenders as a security for some gigantic advance. The thought made him feel some impatience. She could not expect him, interested as he might be in her evolutions, to stay here indefinitely, eating the bread of hard- working Simon Kettering, even if that were not becoming daily unpleasanter. He was already thinking that, in his next letter to Helen, he must tell her to send him a little money, so that, even if he did not leave the town, he could either live elsewhere or arrange to pay Kettering for his board and lodging, thus giving Cleo a fair time in which to reveal her hand. He would be as patient as possible with her, so that she should not have any real ground for the least reproach to him.

By the fourth day a fuller comprehension of the family had come to Morgan, and a growing unhappiness at living with it. His perception of the Ketterings, at first of the same nature as a traveller's perception of people among whom he is sojourning for the first time, had ceased to be art. Their spirit had begun to act on his, and he now not only saw them as a full reality, but he likewise felt them as a full reality. His first impression of them had merged gradually into his present one, though there had been well-marked stages on the route.

At the beginning, the Ketterings' interpretation of hospitality had been indicated by the quantity of food provided; the incessant pressing him to eat had been a special attention to him, and his refusal had been taken first as mere ceremony—natural on the part of a gentleman—and next as somewhat of a slight. And in proportion as he became less of a novelty to them, so did they resume their normal mode of life. By the time the fact of his being their guest had ceased to occupy the centre of their consciousness breakfast had become reduced to coffee—of the same curious flavour—and thick bread and butter, tea to the same astringent beverage as before and thin bread and butter, the two other repasts of the day being likewise administered with a due regard for economy. Mrs. Kettering, too, no longer enumerated the contents of the larder in the hope of tempting him with some delicacy that was not on the table. The trim servant girl who had waited so staidly and respectfully at table had now developed into a perfect slattern who had the habit of answering her mistress back, sometimes in a way that almost amounted to bullying, and who seemed to have as much to say in the concerns of the family as any one of its members. The kitchen, too, obtruded and occupied the foreground of life.

Morgan did not, on account of this change, which he knew did not signify any falling off in hospitable feeling, and which, indeed, he rather appreciated so far as the reduced fare was concerned, reverse his judgment that he had fallen among kind-hearted folk. It had been a strain on them to maintain an appearance of gentility, and their recoil had been merely that of a stretched piece of elastic. He had lost his importance as a special person, and was now only just one of them. He understood that the family was exactly what it had to be, that its temperament and mode of life were perfectly attuned; yet, for him, there were a thousand unseizable roughnesses that depressed his spirit. Though the Ketterings and he spoke the same mother-tongue, words bore different values for him, and full communion was impossible.

But his estimation of them was more of the nature of passive mental apprehension than of active criticism. He himself, however, had been criticised and he knew it, for Alice and Mary had at length made him feel that he did not satisfy their conception of a gentleman. The simplicity of his manners did not convince them. They seemed to hold by some complicated code of etiquette for ladies and gentlemen—Heaven knew how they had become possessed of it—of which he fell sadly short. He did not understand in the least their shibboleth of flirtation, their particular methods of banter, the precise shade of significance of their facial expressions and movements, the exact values of their phrases and catch-words; all of which was knowledge that, according to their notion, was the common stock-in-trade of breeding. Their atmosphere of coquetry did not appeal to him; and, as a rule, he remained supremely ignorant of the fact that they *were* coquetting with him. Thus it was they giggled and laughed and made fun of him, having attained to a vast feeling of superiority over him, and a not less vast pity for their poor, dear sister, who had married him!

He could see that nature had made precisely the same failure with their personalities as with their bodies. Each was a bundle of traits that individually made "Cleo" echo through his brain, yet the total effect lacked convincingness. In Cleo all such characteristics were fused into her general magnificence; in Mary and Alice they seemed to exist at random, failing to give any sense of harmony, but only one of irritation. The airs and graces they assumed did but emphasise their crudity. It was, indeed, an illumining perception when it struck Morgan that their absurd movements and struttings and the queen-like way in which they tried to hold their heads bore a singular resemblance to the stage-gestures of "The Basha's Favourite." At the same time they possessed a large fund of animal spirits. They talked a good deal about dancing and sitting with young men in hidden corners, or going a- rowing with them; though when or where they did any of these things he could not quite make out.

Then again, the ostentatious love for the rest of the family and for each other they had exhibited the first day turned out to be a dependent variable that often approached vanishing-point. If the girls showed a certain uncouth good-humour in their calm moments, they certainly had violent tempers which they made no effort to restrain. If Alice, attempting to pass along the narrow dining-room, caught her dress on Mary's chair: "If anybody else were to sit like that——" she would commence angrily, and then a nice quarrel would ensue. Quarrels, indeed, seemed to be evolved from incredible beginnings, and the evenings bristled with them. Mrs. Kettering was easily drawn into these disagreements and took a leading part in no few of them. Simon and Mark, however, would remain impassive, the first reading his paper and uttering now and again a facetious, mild protest, the second smoking his eternal pipe in unyielding taciturnity. Mrs. Kettering likewise annoyed her daughters by constantly talking to Morgan in their presence of the difficulty of finding husbands for them.

One morning Cleo, who was down early, pounced upon a letter for him and wanted to read it. But as he recognised his father's writing—the envelope had had much redirection in varying scripts—and as her letters were always sealed to him, he refused to open it in her presence. He was not in the mood for a squabble with her. The fact that his father had managed to pierce his inaccessibility had unnerved him, the mere sight of the letter almost making him tremble. He put it in his pocket; it was imperative he should be alone when reading it. Cleo grew sulky and looked it. Alice and Mary, being in a particularly affectionate mood that morning, came hovering round her, entwining her waist with their long arms, pressing their faces gently against hers, and kissing her with ostentatious sympathy. "What has the naughty man been doing to our darling?" they asked in a sort of playful, mincing lisp. "Has he made our dear, dear sister miserable? Naughty, naughty man!"

That made a beginning. As a continuation Mrs. Kettering took it into her head once more to lament the scarcity of possible husbands for Alice and Mary over the breakfast table. They retorted that no doubt there were plenty of husbands to be picked up without a penny, who'd be glad to come and stay at the house and idle about and eat their fill. Evidently they had overheard talk between their parents, for it had been represented to them that Cleo and her husband were only in Dover on a friendly visit to the family.

Before the others had realised it Morgan had risen and left the house. His every nerve was a-tingle with pain. He was finished with the Ketterings, he told himself; it was impossible for him ever to set foot in that house again.

CHAPTER IV.

The sense that a final rupture had occurred between him and the Ketterings was so strong in Morgan that for the moment he omitted to consider the difficulties that might arise as regards Cleo. He saw now that by becoming their guest under circumstances such as his he had exposed himself to the possibility of insult from the first. But he did not condemn them; he simply felt he could not live in contact with them.

He was too unstrung to read his father's letter yet, though, as he thought of it again, the reflection occurred to him that old relations were intruding into the new life that had begun with Cleo. First Helen and then his father had overtaken him!

He started to walk briskly through the town, which he soon cleared. The movement helped to calm his excitement, though it did not diminish his bitterness. All the morning he tramped through the country, deriving some little comfort from the feeling that he was all alone. He lunched on bread and cheese at a wayside inn, partaking of the meal in an old room with rough tables and benches. Near him lay four huge potatoes, newly broiled in their skins. Through the window he looked out on to a yard where poultry strutted about amid straw, dung, and rubbish, in the shadow of a hay-rick. Not till then had he the heart to take the letter from his pocket. An examination of the redirections proved interesting. It had been first sent to the address where he had lived with Cleo, whence it had been redirected care of Cleo's maid, who, in turn, had forwarded it to Dover. He understood now how those first mysterious letters had come for Cleo so quickly, though he did not quite see why she should have concealed from him this arrangement with the maid.

As he broke the envelope a labourer in corduroys came into the room, and seemed taken aback at finding a gentleman there. He was the owner of the broiled potatoes, but apologised for taking possession of them. Morgan bade him sit down and have his meal, but the man, his face shining with good-humour, insisted he must not disturb him, but would go and stand at the bar. He took only two of the potatoes, his good-nature impelling him to leave the other two for Morgan, with the hearty, encouraging remark: "Pull into them, sir!"

"My Dear Son:

"I am writing this only with the faintest hope of its ever reaching you. If by any chance it does, I beg of you to inform me of your whereabouts at once. Your letter came upon us like a bombshell. I do not wish to reproach you for the hurt we have suffered. I only want you to believe now in my desire to stand by you, however terrible the mistake you have made.

"Of course, we put the worst interpretation on your silence about the person you had made your wife. I hurried up to town at once, but you had gone from your old rooms and left not a trace. I learnt, however, that you had a sister who used to come to see you sometimes. I suppose that is your wife. Naturally I assumed you had acted towards me as you had because you thought I should reproach you for having spoilt your life. How little you seem to know me, Morgan! *That* is what I have to reproach you with. Why was I so little in your confidence? Did you think me incapable of sympathising with you because you are a young man and I an old? How little you seem to know me, Morgan, I must repeat again.

"I do not want to indulge in useless retrospect. I do not want to exercise my imagination and yours in tracing out some more desirable course of events that might have resulted from your acting otherwise. But I cannot help giving expression to my deep sorrow at the plight in which you now must be. I do not know how the whole thing came about—what led to your acquaintance with the lady who is now your wife; but I do wish that, instead of writing me that curt letter, you had had sufficient belief in my love and sympathy to come to me despite all. My pen is powerless to express all that is in my heart. I can only just tell you that this is the worst heart-ache I have had in my life.

"If this reaches you, dear Morgan, don't be too proud to let me hear from you at once. I am an old man now, remember, and this suspense is killing. Especially as I have come so near to finding you and have only just missed you by a day or two. On coming up to town I at once called at Mr. Ingram's flat, and then I learnt for the first time he had married a great society lady. The commissionaire gave me his new address in Grosvenor Gardens, and there I was fortunate enough to find him. He seemed astonished to hear you had got married and disappeared. I asked him about your quarrel with him, and then he told me what he knew—that you had run through all the six thousand pounds, had been afraid to tell me, and had behaved abominably rudely to him because he made to you certain suggestions for your own benefit. He was sorry he could not help me to find you. He seemed, indeed, quite distressed about you and sympathised with me in my trouble.

"My poor Morgan! How could a genius like you be bothered with having to manage money? What is the use of a man like you having a rich father if his riches are not for you to enjoy! If you had only said a word! It was hopelessly foolish of me to imagine you had suddenly developed the ability to husband your resources. But you seemed so comfortable and cheerful when I last saw you that I did not suspect anything. And then my attention was so concentrated on my book that I scarcely had a thought for anything else.

"You must forgive me for having called a private detective to my aid. What else could I do? The anxiety was terrible, and I hadn't slept for nights. He was a long time about it, and he ought to have done it sooner, for I gave him a very good photo of you to work with. But he assumed you had gone further afield, and sought to find you in the provinces. So your wife is an actress! The detective assures me she stood naked on the stage before a whole theatre full of people. That isn't true, I hope.

"As I have already said, I was too late when I called at your address, and the landlady said she couldn't forward letters, as no new address had been left with her. But it struck me that perhaps she had her reasons for making that statement, and so now I write in the hope that my letter may be forwarded after all. If it is, then write at once to your dear father, who, if you have made a mistake, will help you to live it down. I implore you not to keep away from me any longer.

"Of course, I have seen the Medhursts several times. John and Kate feel the blow quite as much as I do, though they have done their best to console me. Margaret, too, poor girl, is very pale. She shuts herself up in her studio and pretends to be working. But I'm hanged if I can make out what she's at. There is just a mass of blackfish wax, and, though I always find her shaping it with her fingers, it always seems to look the same. The composition of my book has progressed fairly well, but I am looking forward to your helping me with it a tremendous lot."

Though he was twenty-eight, Morgan felt he still had in him a child's fresh spring of emotion, and he had no more than a child's strength to struggle against it. He hurried from the inn, suppressing his sobs for a moment with one grand effort.

He walked back to the town and found an expected letter from Helen awaiting him at the post-office. He had asked for ten pounds, and she had sent him a bank-note. She had written him only just a few lines to accompany it, but promised to make amends as regards length next time. She said he had made her happy by giving her so practical a proof of his belief in her friendship, and added she was very glad indeed he was thinking of lodging elsewhere, instead of staying with that horrid and amusing family. She hoped he would make up his mind on the point very soon; and the sooner he had a terrific quarrel with his Cleo the better. As soon as she should hear of it she would execute a war-dance, adequately complicated for the occasion.

How good to him were those he had fled from! How endless was the morass

161

into which he had floundered!

And yet the very touch of the bank-note stung him. It represented the fact of his degradation; it summed up the hopelessness of his position. The sympathy poured upon him, welcome though it was, but emphasised his sense of the pitiable failure of his existence. He still burned under the terrible insult of the morning; he smarted from the friction of living amid the petty, squabbling vulgarity of the Kettering household. He remembered, too, he must come to some understanding with Cleo; he must give her an opportunity of joining him wherever he should be staying. And, of course, he must also write to thank Mr. and Mrs. Kettering for their hospitality.

The afternoon passed by. He dined modestly at a sort of coffee-house at the back of the harbour and arranged for a bed-room there. Later in the evening he found himself forced to go out again, for it suffocated him to stay within four walls. And even as he walked at random, the blackest fit of his life came upon him. He thought of those first years of enthusiastic striving, and those following years of half-hearted striving; he thought of the long stretches of time dissipated in mental lounging, in lethargic inaction he had been unable to combat, so paralysing had been his sense of the futility of effort. Looking back now, his whole inner life seemed to have been a long, increasing bitterness. But he did not pity himself; his attitude was one of cruel self- criticism. If only he had been an isolated soul he would not have felt so keenly. But the course of his life had reacted on others and embittered their existence. It seemed as if he could not take a step without wounding those who loved him. He was not fit to breathe the same air with them, he told himself.

Of Margaret he scarce dared think, so great was his sense of his unworthiness; but the light of her face, as it swam up before him, thrilled him with the consciousness that his love for her was abiding, that this affair on which he had embarked was a grotesque nightmare in which his true being had not been concerned at all, though it had become irredeemably involved in it. Once or twice it had given him pleasure to imagine that it was in Helen's power to do more than just sympathise with him, but then he had never forgotten that was only a wistful fancy. It brought the tears to his eyes to think of her attempt to cheer him with her prophecy of happiness for him. Happiness for him! Dream as vain as his Cleo's lust for glory!

It was past ten o'clock, and the sea-front was already deserted. He strolled eastward, following the roadway to where the houses ended, when it swept round the foot of the cliff, on whose top rose the ancient castle, and eventually degenerated into an ascending foot-path protected by a wooden rail. He stayed awhile at the bend, gazing into the immense darkness, in which, here and there, glimmered a light from a passing vessel, and listening to the swish of the water lapping the foot of the sea-wall. A fisherman preparing his bait hailed him "Good-night!" from the glooms of a small, primitive jetty. He returned the salute civilly, but, as he was not in the mood for human intercourse, he sang out and wished the man a good haul and then moved on. Up, up the incline he went, the rugged cliff-front towering above him, clothed with great grey patches. The path narrowed as it wound its way up the side and at length ran into the cliff, through which a long gallery had been hewn. But the solid blackness that faced him at its mouth did not give him pause. He felt his way along, stumbling up the rough incline, and turned down another gallery which intersected this one at right angles, and which led to the face of the cliff where its opening, high above the water, was barred by a tall iron rail. Here he stood and looked out to sea.

The nocturne was beautiful in its largeness and silence. The sublimity of the great spaces emphasised his own existence just then as petty, crabbed, and sordid. The discords within him were so harsh that he could not respond to the sweet mystery of the night, or to the music that called from sea and sky, from the shadows and the spaces.

Again that bitter sense of his whole life became concentred in one moment. And then, as the sound of the soft-flowing tide came up to him again, it seemed to bring with it words that echoed strangely through his being. And his being seized upon them and gripped them. The voice of Mary Kettering seemed to be commanding him, as if her hostile spirit were hovering near, and he could hear her vulgar laugh disgracing the solitudes.

"There's the water. Now drown yourself!"

The consciousness of his personal unimportance to the world was accentuated against the free vastness on which he gazed. The mission that alone had had power to stir his blood, of being a voice to the spell of which all men should yield, had been decreed against. His hope of winning the right to live amid and breathe an atmosphere in harmony with his being, an atmosphere in which his individuality, as he conceived it, should ripen and expand and yield all the fragrance that was in it, was utterly dead.

He could not detach his dead hope from his life; its rotting carcass weighed it down and poisoned it. The love, too, that Margaret had inspired in him but remained as an exquisite bitterness. And as for those who loved him, better they should bear the blow at once than that he should torture them constantly. Let them mourn for him now; let them, in the years that were to come, sometimes feel his presence with them and think of him as one who had had good in him, but whose life had proved piteously futile. For them much pain now and an occasional pang in the future; for him, the sweetness of unending rest, for was there not sweetness in death?

He looked again out to sea, striving to pierce the darkness that floated over the world like a spirit, and divining the far-off line where the sky touched the water.

One last, glorious swim to reach it! And out there, in the infinitudes, amid the silence and the loneness, with all the still music of the universe lulling him to sleep, should his being gently merge into the all-pervasive essence; there, in the large freedom of the airs, under the full spread of Heaven's stars, and in the soft embrace of the velvet waters, should he feel his blood beat to an end; there, in the heart of those mysterious spaces, were fitting place for a poet to die!

CHAPTER V.

He turned to go back and descend to the shore below, but just then he heard a strange whispering that reechoed through the passages. A flash of light seemed to fly down the long gallery, driving the darkness before it, and then a young man and a girl passed by, the former holding a lighted match. He waited a moment, half-startled, half-annoyed at their intrusion, then groped his way after them, eventually stumbling out of the tunnel's mouth. And, as he descended the incline again, he became aware of other couples standing about in the shadows, within alcoves of the cliff, or seated on the grassy slope just outside the wooden hand-rail. In his first abstraction he had overlooked these.

He could not begin his swim here with the consciousness of all these human beings so near at hand. He wanted the complete sense of isolation from his fellow-creatures, the feeling that he and the infinite were alone face to face. An idea came to him. On the other side of the town stretched some miles of shingle at the foot of the cliffs. Here he would seek the aloneness he felt to be imperative.

He started to walk briskly the length of the town, and his way took him through the harbour again. Here again he caught glimpses of isolated couples, leaning against the stacks of wood or half-lost in the shade of some black hull rising high alongside the footways.

His perception of externals seemed to have grown keener; his glance seemed to pierce where the shadows were thickest.

And all these couples gave him just then a sense of the vast, futile movement of life on the planet, of the infinite succession of human generations, each appearing and blossoming and mating and dying. He seemed in that moment to feel a hideous meaninglessness in this tidal wave of life travelling through the ages.

He crossed the railway line and passed on to the broad shingle that sloped to the water's edge. The air was almost still, the water was smooth and gentle. He set his face westward and trudged along, seeking the place where his foot should stand on the solid shore for the last time. He calculated to go about a mile, so as to be free from any sense of the proximity of the town; but he was somewhat dismayed to pass another couple after he had gone about a hundred yards. Couples—couples everywhere! Should he never escape from them? How crude seemed all this love-making when one caught a glimpse of it from the outside as a large, collective fact!

That, however, proved to be the last encounter, but as he tramped on over the grey shingle, amid which shone the white sprinkling of chalky pebbles, a sudden screech pierced the night and a train came rushing along the track that ran alongside the beach, its engine vomiting a lurid smoke that showed ghastly in the dark and that disappeared within the tunnel under the cliff like a giant flame snuffed out. And soon he had ceased to hear its roaring.

The incident seemed to him symbolic. His flame, too, was to be snuffed out; but he had the thought, with a grim smile, that he wasn't going to make so much noise about it.

Now and again he floundered into a puddle or rivulet that flowed seaward across the expanse of shelving shore, but he felt his sense of aloneness amid nature increase at each step gained. The pieces of chalk, scattered on all hands, grew larger and larger, evidently fallen from above and rounded by the wash of the waves. The patched whiteness of the cliffs rose high on his right; a tiny, solitary light shone far out at sea. Clouds were beginning to gather, and some of the stars were hidden. The night grew darker; the stillness disturbed by his footsteps alone and the low melody of the gently-breaking waters. The sea itself stretched before him, a vast, soft shadow, but the eye had to look at it determinedly to separate it from the sky. And now "Shakespeare's Cliff" towered up, its side gashed and scarred as by a giant's axe. The fallen masses lay heaped at its foot, grotesque yet solemn. Then there were larger masses, piles of enormous boulders on his right, as if a whole cliff had crashed to fragments; and a great expanse of them, mossy and weed-covered, stretching on his left to the water's edge. He was aware of them, too, ahead of him, extending in the gloom indefinitely. And soon he had to pick out a tortuous way between the mighty heaps on one hand and the far-spread belt of rock on the other.

On and on he passed, and stayed at length by a chalk rock, tall as himself, wrought by the tides into the semblance of a head, a veritable giant's head, with masses of long, intertangled weeds on its top and sides, like the strange, wild unkempt locks of a sea-god; its front showing blurred features like a carven face eaten away by the slow gnaw of a thousand centuries.

"If you had but a tongue, what secrets of the deep you could tell!" he could not help saying aloud.

And then, as he stood listening, his wish seemed to be answered. The face before him seemed to glow with a light as of life in the mystic gloom that wrapped it. And it spoke to him through the silence with a voice that was as a golden bell sounding from the heart of the universe. It spoke a language that his being comprehended; it sang to him a song of peace and sweetness and wonders. And he knew that the melody that beat through it was but a murmur of the great essence calling to him; the essence that was fragrance, that was light, that was music; the essence that sometimes showed through the grossness of things and that he himself had striven to capture as it flashed here and there for those in whom burned an intenser spark of itself than was allotted to the generality of men—for the bard, the painter, the seer—towards whom it leapt as flame leaps to flame, yet who saw it but as the seekers of visions see an elusive gleam flash and half die within the blur of a magic crystal.

Here, then, was the spot!

CHAPTER VI.

He proceeded to disrobe himself, for he wished to feel the embrace of the waters on his bare flesh. But he was not so absorbed in his self and his purpose as to extrude all thoughts of those who were dear to him. Nay, such thoughts, perhaps, were part of his very self. Eyes that till now were dry became blinded with tears, so that the shaded, floating night-world seemed to palpitate before him in a strange blur that was like a despairing mood externalised. It were best so, he reassured himself again; better that he should now plunge into the sweet mystery, of which the little he knew was by a dim, exquisite divination, better that he should live only as a sad memory than as an evil-causing reality.

Then, too, it occurred to him, it was right that his clothes should be left on shore. He would put them out of the reach of the tide, and the weight of a boulder should defy the wind. The letters of his father and Helen would serve to identify the owner of the clothes; he would not destroy them, since there was nothing in them save what the writers might be proud of having written. They would then know the worst at once, instead of having to endure the long-drawn, vain hope that is worse than despair. Even if his body were not washed ashore there could be no mistaking his fate.

He picked his way to the water's edge and strode in unhesitatingly. The tide was just on the turn, and the touch of the light-swelling waves was at first cold and gentle. But soon he was breasting them with steady stroke, moving out to some indefinite point where should be the full mystery of the night and the spaces, and whence the shore should be swallowed up in the darkness. His sense of the world passed into a large vagueness; the blood pulsed through his veins exquisitely; the kiss of the water was warm and sweet. Steadily, steadily his hands cleft it, the activity of his brain dwindling and dwindling and lapsing at length into a mere self-abandonment to the sensuousness of the motion. He was scarcely conscious of controlling his muscles; his arms seemed to work of themselves in rhythmical sweep. Onward, onward! with only a fused feeling of warmth and exhilaration and a drowsy sense of vague far-spreadingness.

The consciousness of time had passed away, and that of space was a mere intensity of feeling. Once or twice he was dreamily aware of a strange halo of light haunting his universe.

But at last the vibrating hoot of some great passing steamship drove suddenly across the waters, a keen note that thrilled through him startlingly, dispelling the delicious languor that possessed him. He had a sense as of awakening from slumber, and then he knew that the vague halo was a long beam, flying round at some distance from him, that came from the light-house at the end of the great stone pier. His mind leapt again to full activity, shaking off the medley of sensation that had been flowing against his passive consciousness with such dull uniformity.

His blood glowed with the full glory of the sea; he was conscious of a clear sanity, for the brooding mists had vanished from his spirit. And even as he heard and felt the throb of mighty engines that came to him from afar, and considered what mastery over the deeps they represented, the thought occurred to him that he, too, was master of the boundless water, buoyant at his will. An exaltation sprang up in him as he realised throughout all his fibre its sensuous vastness, its elastic massiveness.

And with this exultant sense of mastery, with this feeling of the good red blood coursing through him, there seemed to have awakened in him an invincible something that held him to existence with a grip that could know no loosening, that made his whole being cohere with a strength that not all the forces of dissolution could relax.

On and on he swam; on and on. What an ecstacy it was to live!

CHAPTER VII.

Once more a vision of his life passed before him as a single flash, and this time it drew from him a scornful anger.

Fool! Should he who rode abreast the ocean in absolute mastery not be master of his own existence? Fool! The universe before had sung to him of life, not of death; its essence had called to him not to take him into itself, but to remind him that within him was some of its own glorious fire that might yet make his life glorious. That, too, had now leapt up, had burnt away all the vapours and purged his spirit; that, too, sang and joined in the universal chant. He recognised its clear melody, inspiring him to place faith in it and to be true to himself.

Action must be the key to the redemption of his life; a flourishing, masterful Will-To-Live the force behind it. He had made mistakes; it was for him to convert them into a good, to make of them a solid pedestal on which his manhood should stand firm.

Back to the shore again! Back to human beings and human love and human duties!

And just then an odd thought intruded on him, grotesque yet touching; one of those incongruous memories that invade one's solemnest moments. He had a vision of a labourer in soiled corduroys leaving him half his dinner at the wayside inn that morning.

He turned on his back to rest awhile, but he found he could not endure the changed position. For the reality of the world was lost to him again, and he had a sense of floating alone in the immensity of strange, dark places; the cloud-stained sky seeming to rest on his face. The night, too, had grown darker, and the throb of the steam-vessel came to him now more faintly. He was conscious of being left behind. A momentary fear invaded him.

And in that moment he seemed to see the shapes of those who loved him imploring him with streaming eyes, now beckoning him, now holding their arms to him.

He set his face landwards and thrust all uncertainty from him. He could just distinguish the softly-gleaming cliffs, but he felt strong and pure and stout-hearted. Back! Back! Back to land, to work, to love! A rougher tide rolling in helped him. He knew the spot whence he had started; it was just beyond the point where the cliff rose to its highest. The sense of distance annihilated gave him new strength, and at last he stood again amid the fallen boulders and shook the water from him. He sacrificed an undergarment as a towel, then dressed himself quickly; and, suffused by the new, living spirit, he turned his steps townward again.

But he could not go home to his lodgings and sleep. It was a small confined bed-room he had taken, whereas he felt the need of breathing deep of the full wind that had by now sprung up. He felt that the open night brought inspiration, and he wished, too, to yield to all the activity that urged within him. He passed again by the harbour, plunged into the town and through the streets that ran up the hill-side to the castle.

Action, action, action! He had come through the crisis with miraculous strength, with inexhaustible energy. On, on, through the grey night, exulting in the wind even as he had exulted in the sea!

Meanwhile his plans were coming to him.

He had often, in his bitter moments, envied the bricklayer and the cobbler. Why should *he* not begin to learn a trade even now?

He was conscious of intelligence, of patience, of the desire to labour. Why should not Kettering give him a chance in his workshop? The old man had shown him real kindness and was evidently well-disposed towards him. He felt sure he could enlist his sympathy, for, despite the apparent limitation of his interests, Simon Kettering had impressed him as having, in a general way, a keen understanding of things. The vulgarity of life in that household was but a small consideration to him now. His vow never to return to it had been made when he had taken the old vision of things. His new and saner vision made him see that vow was a mistake. Was he not strong enough to defy the corrosiveness of a mean, vulgar atmosphere? Nay, his life, by its own inner force, would flow impervious to such influence.

To labour, and by the work of his own hands to pay those whom Cleo had wronged!

Not till he had done this would he feel true to himself; not till then would he deem himself worthy of the love of those who were dear to him.

It were easy to fall back on his father's generosity, to live an empty life of indolence; but that would not give him that respect of self which alone could keep him attuned to the harmonies of being, and thus bring him the longed-for peace of spirit. For his sense of life was the sum of his inner moods, and no mere superficial remedy could inform them with that pure flowingness that constitutes happiness.

To go though the discipline he had set himself, to labour hard and achieve a fixed, worthy end by his own unaided efforts, no matter what stretch of his life it consumed, were to vindicate himself, were to vindicate his Will-To-Live!

He had arrived at a culminating point in existence. The understanding of what his life had lacked had come to him at last, and with it a recognition of that by which it was to be guided in future. Life, to be true, must involve all the functions of the soul—thought, emotion and will; must be lived with a healthy fulness. He had not so lived it. His error had lain in detachment, which had well-nigh brought him to the verge of destruction. And now it was with him a time of reconstruction.

He desired to face that full actuality of things from which he had always shrunk as from a terrifying chaos, wilfully shutting out from his vision all but its superficial forms and tones. He wished to open his spirit to the feeling and throb of the living world.

Discipline, self-discipline! On that basis alone could the human soul develop and attain to Individuality and Freedom.

He seemed to recognise some Force working in him like a Redeemer; he fancied he saw some strange Necessity in his life, working through all its dark moments, its action eventually forcing upon him a true estimation of existence, of his relation to things.

His being should assimilate from the living world all that should serve to build it up; even as a plant wonderfully drew from the earth just that which its fibre needed. But for that end he must move through the living world—not shun it. More and more of its essence would he take into himself, more and more would he defy the mean, the ugly, the evil; till at last he should be strong enough to walk unscathed even through the fire.

That thought which had come to him a short time before about the meaninglessness of life, and of the perpetual mating that carried it on, now recurred to him again; but this time he had an accompanying sense of its utter falsity. He had been wrong in his thought, he told himself, because to view life in that large way from an apparently outside point of view was in reality to lose all sight of the meaning under quest. It was the point of view which was unsuitable, not the meaning which was absent! The error was the same fatal one of detachment. If man projected a critical mind, a mere isolated bit of himself, to which adhered nothing of his essential nature, into a boundless space and bade it look from thence on the march of humanity and deliver judgment thereon, surely that judgment could not be a true one.

The true judgment of life was only to be made by the help of the full humanness of the observer. Life had to be felt within; not viewed from without from an imagined cosmic standpoint.

Not then in the long parade of history must the meaning of life be sought, nor in its massed manifestations, the sum total resulting from its activities; not amid the buried relics in geologic strata, not in the large sweep of scientific law. But each human being might find it for himself in his own limited span; for the individual life, lived true with the fulness of the human spirit, was its own end, its own meaning. And whosoever lived true to himself felt and knew the meaning of life. Living and mating might be foreshortened to mere dry facts in the great stretch of a cosmic outlook; by the emotion of the individual they were touched to divinity.

Let him, then, since he wished to live true, not seek to escape from himself, but to accept his own human outlook and be true to the fulness of his being. Let him recognise the eternal principles of humanness underlying man's varying attempts to express them in binding rules of conduct, and let him take his place in man's world—a world, both of facts and relations, selected by man's innate nature from the swirling, chaotic continuity of which man was a part—facing the fulness of life with the fulness of character.

He had climbed the long, ascending road. Above him sat the dark castle on the top of a grey slope; and, looking downwards on his left, he saw the town sleeping in its valley, its many points of light gleaming through a palpitating mist. He could just discern the other hill beyond as a tone that was lost in the dark sky, a faint luminous spot showing here and there on the top.

He stayed a moment to admire the nocturne and was glad that he had lived to see all this beauty. Yes, everything called to him for life, not for death. He continued his wandering, heedless whither; and, when at last he became conscious of fatigue, he had covered many miles and had strayed through many by-paths. The first frenzy of restlessness had worn itself out, and he sat for awhile on a barred gate, previous to turning back to the town.

His only guide now was the general sense that he must keep the sea on his left. He was but a few hundred feet from it. Once or twice he divined the water, almost indistinguishable from cloud, when a great indentation in the cliff made its edge sweep in towards him; and once a ship's light flashed out of it for half a second. He swung along steadily, and after a time found himself traversing a great, dusky stretch of land. He had the feeling of crawling over it like an insect, so vast was his sense of this flat earth; he seemed just a bit of it moving on it and thinking about it, as if it had attained through him to consciousness of itself!

He fell into a slow saunter, philosophic fancies coming to interweave themselves with his thoughts; and, when he awoke again from a long reverie, the road had grown narrow, rough and stony. He stumbled along till at length he again made out the castle in the distance, perched on its sombre eminence, just a flat silhouette against a lighter greyish sky.

The road dipped between two slopes that cut off the view, and, when he had passed them, the battlemented silhouette seemed to show deeper and the sky lighter. The morn was approaching.

Imperceptibly the darkness thinned. A quiet feeling of holiness was in the air. The stretch of common on either hand began to take on a shade of brown, though the rare clumps of scattered bushes still showed dark and solid. A fresh morning breeze came to him, scent-laden.

In some parts the clouds were lightening, melting, and as he came again into full view of the sea, he saw its whole surface glistening and of an indefinite colour. Sometimes it struck him as a sort of steely grey, sometimes it flashed upon him as a vague, elusive green. It was almost light now, and he could see the landscape distinct and wonderfully sharp-cut. A minute later he was almost sure that the sea was green, and, to his surprise, he became aware of luminous blue bars among the clouds. There was a lovely piece of green, too, with orange streaks in it. Then there came a full flood of mystic pink, and the water was one laughing sparkle. He drew deep breaths of the air and gloried in the dawn.

The pure, sweet dawn, to him symbolic of Resurrection and Life!

Though tired now, he still lingered, strolling at ease down to the town again and lounging on the beach and in the harbour. When, in the end, he arrived at the coffee-house where he had taken his lodging he found it already open, and porters and sailors were taking their early-morning coffee.

He threw himself across his bed and slept soundly till mid-day.

END OF BOOK IV.

BOOK V.

CHAPTER I.

Morgan waited till half-past one before calling again at the Ketterings, for by then, as he knew, the printer had about finished his lunch, and usually had some few minutes to spare.

He did not ring at the side entrance, but walked through the shop, where only a boy was in charge at this hour, and into the workshop at the back. Here, to his satisfaction, he found Mr. Kettering himself busy measuring up galleys with a long piece of string. The old man was startled to see him, but said he was glad he had come, as he had been anxious about him and had wanted to talk to him. Morgan noticed that he seemed a little excited. His face, too, seemed a trifle more worn and lined than usual behind his spectacles, and his beard had a scraggy appearance.

"I'm afraid, sir, my daughters were very rude to you yesterday morning," he continued, "and I want you to accept my sincere apology for their conduct. They are hard-working girls enough, but they haven't much sense, and I'm afraid not much consideration for other folks' feelings. I only hope you'll overlook it this time. However, there's something else I must tell you at once. Selina has gone away."

"Gone away!" echoed Morgan.

"Yes," said Mr. Kettering, sadly. "Altogether we've had a nice upset. Mother's ill in bed to-day. It was this way: Of course I spoke a bit sharply to those scatter-brained girls, and they answered me back in a way it makes my blood boil to think about. Women-folk are all a bit crazy. That's the opinion I've been forced to, sir, and if I had my days over again, I'd never so much as look at one of them. Then Selina—she joined in and said it stifled her to live here. It was worse than living in a mud-hovel. Then the mother said she'd better go and live in a mud-hovel. And after that they all four fell a-screaming and I couldn't do anything to stop them. As soon as I could get a word in edgeways I begged them to be quiet, but Selina was excited and disowned us all. She said she never believed she was our child; she could never possibly have come from such filth as us, and then she lost her head and cursed us—I never heard the like in my life. My heart bled for you, sir, for I said to myself: this can't be the first exhibition she has made of herself since her marriage, especially as things went wrong. However, business had to be attended to, which put an end to the scene. But when I went up to dinner, Selina told me she had packed up and was going away that afternoon, and that we needn't expect ever to see her again. Of course I tried to talk her over, and asked her not to be foolish, but to stop till she had her arrangements properly made. Then she told me sharply not to mind about *her* arrangements, and that she had no need of my charity. She pulled out and showed me fifty pounds in bank-notes. They came the day before, she said, and she had any number of thousands waiting for her. 'But what about your husband?' I asked. 'My husband?' she snorted. 'I'll make you a present of him if you like. There's another woman in love with him, who's ready to give him as much money as he cares to take from her. And he has any number of mistresses besides. So you don't expect I'm going to trouble my head about him. Besides, he hasn't said six words to me since we've been here. If he had cared about me he'd have shown it.' And, sure enough, she went off by the afternoon train. 'Tell him he's rid of me now, as soon as he gets over his fit of the sulks and comes back,' was the last she said. Yes, women-folk are all crazy. You'll excuse me repeating the remark, I know, sir; but you remember what I told you when you came on Sunday. I don't mean any disrespect by it, but I can't help thinking you were a fool to marry her."

And Kettering took up his cord again as if to continue his measuring.

Morgan's brain was for an instant full of a whirling mass of thought. He could not hide from himself that he had not the slightest sense of sorrow or regret. He knew perfectly well that Cleo esteemed him no more than a dead twig, that, by his abstention from offering up to her daily an incense and a sweet savour of gross flattery, he had destroyed all possibility of her continuing to imagine he counted for something in her life. And, of course, she was not the kind of woman to stay in so sordid and narrow a household with a penniless man, who was nothing to her beyond her husband—she with her gorgeous demands upon life! No doubt her departure had been already arranged with the person who had sent her the money she had shown her father and she had been glad to seize upon any pretext. However, he thought it right to assure Mr. Kettering that Cleo's accusations against him were entirely false and that, as regards his conduct towards her, no reproach could be made to him.

"You've no need to tell me that," said Mr. Kettering, "I never for a moment doubted you. You know, sir," he added, "you're quite welcome to make my home yours so long as it suits your convenience."

Morgan replied that, as Kettering was probably aware, he had no money, but that he was anxious to earn some, however little. Could he not do so by learning to set up type?

Kettering looked hard at him, and Morgan bore the gaze without flinching.

"I can see you mean it," he said, "so we won't waste time discussing whether you're serious. Now, Mr. Druce, I don't know who you are, and I'm not going to ask you any questions. I flatter myself I've got some little skill in reading faces, and I knew from the first that you were a gentleman, and one with his heart in the right place. Now don't think I'm taking liberties, sir, but I should like you to think the matter over again and see whether you would not do better to communicate with your family and friends. I don't want to know how you came to have the misfortune to marry my girl, but I feel that as a fellow-man I ought to ask you to reconsider your position. Maybe your folk are fretting and anxious about you. I'm only a plain man, but I think I can lay some claim to common sense, and believe me I only venture to speak to you like this because I respect you."

"I do intend communicating with my people," said Morgan, touched by the old man's sincerity and thoughtfulness, "but I want to earn my bread all the same. That is essential."

"I understand," said Kettering. "You want to feel yourself stand on your own legs. Yes, that's a fine thing to feel. Well, as I said, I like your face and I trust you. I hope you're not vexed at what I ventured to say."

"On the contrary," said Morgan, "I am sincerely grateful to you for having said it."

Kettering's face beamed, and its benevolent quality grew more marked.

"A boy apprentice is supposed to take seven years learning the trade, sir, but we needn't get discouraged about that. A man anxious to learn, with his wits about him—"

"I am anxious, and I have my wits about me," put in Morgan.

"Well, after three months he could make himself deuced handy."

Kettering's mild oath was simply intended by way of encouragement.

"You see," he went on, "once you'd learnt the lay of the case, you'd soon get your hand in for straightforward setting, and then if you didn't mind exercising your muscles, you could do a bit of pulling at press. And a man of your education, sir, might turn his knowledge to account in proof-reading. Not that there's much scope for that sort of thing, sir, in my little business. But it's just an idea we might keep in mind. There's no knowing what might come of it. Now I'm not going to omit the business part, sir. I know you must be wanting to hear about that, and I know you'd prefer to make a bargain on a strict business basis. Perhaps you care to make a suggestion."

"I am too ignorant for that. I want you to give me just what I am worth and no more. Of course, I know that I shall not be worth anything for some time."

In a few minutes they had arranged everything in such a way that there should be no obligation on either side. Morgan was to live in the house. A wage was to be put to his credit from the beginning for all work done by him that was of use, at the regular "piece rates," and such work as "pulling at press" and "clearing," which could only be estimated by time, was to be entered at time rates. Of course his earnings at first would be very small, but they would increase from week to week. On the other hand, an agreed weekly value was put on his board and lodging, which from the first would be charged against his earnings. And when eventually the wages due to him had overtaken the amount thus due by him, he should get the weekly balance in cash, or he might then, if he preferred, board and lodge where it pleased him.

Morgan was touched by old Kettering's sympathetic comprehension of his needs, but when he sought to give expression to his thanks, the old man would not listen.

Mark entered just then, and, the situation having been made clear to him in a few words, readily agreed to have Morgan by his side in the workshop, and to make of him a sort of protégé.

The whole interview had consumed barely half an hour, and Morgan went out just as the journeymen were returning for their afternoon's work. He had arranged to begin in the morning, since they had a heavy job to get finished that afternoon, and could not spare a moment to initiate him. Mark, however, said he would teach him the lay of the case that evening from a diagram. Kettering, before he left, said he would make it his business to give the girls to understand that they must treat him with respect, but begged him to ignore them in case they should misbehave, winding up with his oft-expressed conviction that all women-folk were crazy, and it was a mistake to take them seriously.

However, Morgan troubled himself little about the girls; they had no terrors for him now. An exquisite peace came upon him. It was many years since he had had the feeling.

CHAPTER II.

He was not sorry to have the afternoon free, for it gave him the opportunity of writing long letters to Helen and to his father. He felt he owed it to both to make them understand his changed attitude.

"One real critical moment in a life," he went on to write to Helen, after narrating all that had occurred up to that very moment, "suffices to work changes that may seem almost miraculous. I am not going to say that the prophecy you made just to encourage me a little is going to be fulfilled. Happiness is not for me—I have lost the essential factors of that. But a cheerful acceptance of life, a full use of each day, a consciousness of submission to a healthy self-discipline, must bring me a healthy sense of worthiness.

"Of course you will see that my making the payment of Cleo's debts a sort of goal will enable me to test my strength. Once I arrive at the goal, I shall be able to hold my head high. I have done the one and only thing, and it was good for me that the means were so near at hand. And so I hope to have your approval both of my determination and of my returning you this bank-note. I have still eighteen-pence in my pocket, and Mr. Kettering says I can draw a few shillings whenever I feel in need of them.

"I dare say my donning an apron and holding a composing-stick must at moments seem quite comic to you. Viewed by itself, it no doubt *is* comic. But it isn't a fact to be looked at by itself. It is a fact which has a relation to my whole existence—in the past, present, and future—and must be strictly viewed in such relation.

"I don't know why I should mention this except that I caught a sudden glimpse of myself as a workman and found myself smiling. Every life must have its critical moments, and I feel that I have just passed through mine. I have come out with different conceptions of things; moreover, I seem to have found the key to the scheme of my existence, and, though as yet only in a haunting way, to understand the underlying principle, working through all my dreamings, my failures, my mistakes, and my folly, towards my redemption."

In the letter to his father he necessarily had to condense a good deal, as the ground to be covered was so extensive. And some instinct urged him to be silent about his attempt at suicide. He told briefly of his marriage, which he described as a sort of a jump with his eyes open he had suddenly been impelled to take. He had fallen on a place astonishingly different from what it had appeared to him, for he had been the victim of a mirage, through which the force of his impulse had taken him into underlying abysses. He went on to describe Cleo's failure and his own awakening; how they had gone to Dover, how Cleo had left him, and why he was remaining there now. He likewise included a message for the Medhursts, but asked his father not to tell them his whereabouts. It would be sufficient if they were assured all was well with him. It was an odd fancy, but he wanted to have the feeling that he was hiding from them.

He had been too touched by his father's letter not to be frank and sincere, as indeed he would have been in any case, and he only omitted to say how close he had been to his end because he shrank from giving pain.

"There is one thing in particular I want to ask you," he concluded, "and that is not to be tempted to come here to see me. If you really do sympathise with my motives for the life I have chosen, you will understand my fear that a meeting between us now might unnerve me. I know it is a great thing to ask you to be satisfied with the knowledge that I am well and cheerful, and that, my wife having left me of her own accord, I have nothing to reproach myself with in my conduct to her from beginning to end. But I want to begin my new work and submit myself to the new discipline. So much for me depends upon it that, though I am strong and confident, I must not run the risk of being distracted from my purpose by forces that are stronger than I. Where the issue is so great—as it is, according to my conception of things—it is but natural I should distrust myself a little. The year is just half gone. Give me the opportunity of testing myself and of inuring myself to the discipline with no other encouragement save the knowledge of the worthiness of my purpose and the goodwill and approval of whoever understands me. I want to stand alone for the present—isolation brings out every atom of strength in me. Then, perhaps, when the new year comes and I shall have had the strength to stand firm, I may be able to look you in the face."

Helen, in her reply, would not agree with him that he had lost the essential factors of happiness. She still stood by her prophecy. She understood and entered into his every feeling, and approved of his plans unreservedly. The ten pounds she had given to a starving man.

"I wanted to celebrate your choice between life and death, and the dawn of your new era, by making a human being happy, if only for a little while. You should have seen his face when he understood all that lump of money was really his. What emotions must have stirred in him! He must have thought that the age of miracles had come again. It gave me the sensation of drinking some ethereal brand of champagne—it was to your happiness, of course, I drank.

"I was aware, from the beginning, that you were beset with dangers from your own temperament and disposition. But perhaps, after all, it is best that your temperament should have worked itself out its own way. You will emerge the better and the stronger for it in the end, and then, when you do come into your happiness, you will be able to appreciate it with your whole being. But I must own to a sense of guilt—I might have been a truer friend to you had it not been for my selfish love for you. You have yet to forgive me for that.

"It rather vexes me that I cannot do more than just look on and see events shape themselves inevitably, like a spring uncoiling. I should so much have loved to be the good fairy of your life. But, alas! that cannot be, since its very inner force is its own good fairy.

"P. S. I have managed to write you a whole letter without one flippant phrase. Which is certainly a proof that your admonition to me not to look upon you, in apron and shirt-sleeves, picking up type, as a comic picture has made a due impression on me. I am seeing you the whole time as a sort of glorified, idealised workman, enveloped in a mystic halo, and standing for the dignity of labor and the nobility of man. By the way, I have met Miss Medhurst. I had quite a thrill as we shook hands! And she had not the slightest idea I was of any special interest, more than any other casual person she might meet. Strange dramatic position, was it not? Of course, I never want her to know about me. Which reminds me, I am rather alarmed lest your mood of confession should have led you to make me known to your sire—I hope not. And please don't. May I come to Dover for a day now and again in order to see you for ten minutes each time? I have decided to cut Scotland and pass August at Folkestone instead, just lounging on the beach and reading novels. Please say 'yes.'

"P. P. S. I don't like the idea of my rôle being limited to writing you amusing letters. Won't you allot me a more active and satisfying part? Would it not be a good idea for you to appoint me your 'London agent?' Suppose you give me the list of your creditors and remit me your money as soon as you have a decent instalment put by. You could leave the distribution to me. The workmen should be paid first, of course. I shall arrange to ferret them out, which, I think, will not be difficult, as most of them are, no doubt, attached to the theatre. It would make me so happy if you said 'yes.' After all, one's life, when once its conditions are settled, and its allotted tasks performed, really reduces itself to inter-relations with a few chosen personalities, and everything else becomes a mere background against which one lives. It is the few who occupy one's central consciousness and make one happy or miserable. You will see, therefore, how important to me this apparently little thing will be."

His father's reply was brief and to the point. He thanked his dear son for listening to his prayer, and was happy to hear that everything was now well. As to the irreparable mistake, that, of course, must be faced and lived down. He would respect Morgan's wishes and not seek to see him for the present. Directly he had received Morgan's letter he had sent a long telegram to the Medhursts, which he was now supplementing by a letter. They had telegraphed back, asking him to convey to Morgan their love and hoping they might hear about him from time to time. "You have made me understand a good deal to which I have been blind," he went on. "You were never an ordinary lad; you had special needs, as has every lad of any individuality. I should have sought to comprehend them, instead of trying to drive you along the ordinary lines. No wonder there was a discord—a jarring and a clashing. God speed you, my dear son, and with all my heart do I wish you success in doing that which you feel to be right. For the present, good-bye!"

When Morgan wrote again to Helen he prayed her not to come just yet. His mood was desperately set on isolation, till he could feel he had tackled the task before him and made substantial progress. He hoped she would not alter her plans, as she had meditated, but he gladly accepted her services as "London agent." There was little chance, though, of his being able to send her the first remittance for several months, by which time she would probably be back in town.

CHAPTER III.

Meanwhile Morgan had settled down "at case" and was patiently learning to pick up the "stamps." He was initiated into the mysteries of ems and ens, of leading and spacing and making-up. Racks and galleys and wooden and metal "furniture" played a large part in his dreams; turpentine, paraffin and machine-oil, roller composition and inks became the breath of his nostrils. By an effort of concentration he would never before have been capable of, he made rapid advance, Kettering generously letting him do such work as he could do most effectively, so that his wages' account mounted week by week. The close attention his work demanded made mind-wandering and aimless thinking impossible; but as time went by and he found himself acquiring skill, his enthusiasm grew, and he threw himself into his new occupation almost with frenzy, taking a sort of savage satisfaction in the grey grime of the workshop with its soiled wooden fittings, and in the silent companionship of his aproned co-workers.

He filled up his time at every department of the trade, learning—besides type-setting and proof-correcting—to take the gas-engine to pieces and to clean it, to help to make ready "formes" on the machine, to mix inks, to clean rollers and to work at press, either as inker or puller. But the grime had no power to enter into his spirit, though some slight suggestion of his occupation began eventually to show itself in his face. His hands, too, suffered severely, for soft white hands get quickly ill-used in a printer's workshop.

Still smarting under a long lecture from their father, Alice and Mary had at first taken care to confine conversation with him to trade exigencies; but after a few days they had grown to accept him as part of the household, and were civil to him again. Mrs. Kettering liked to get him to herself of an evening and talk to him for two hours at a time. Kettering himself would fidget a good deal at such times, but scarcely ventured to intrude, though apparently his greatest delight was also to converse with Morgan. But Mrs. Kettering showed no such scruples about entering into the conversation and eventually taking Morgan captive, being entirely without respect for the fact that her husband was in legal possession. In either case Morgan's contribution to the conversation rarely exceeded one-fourth of the whole.

Mark continued taciturn as ever, though his enormous mustachios seemed to grow constantly, as if benefitting by the energy that should have gone into speech. Sometimes he would accompany Morgan on a long walk, and on such occasions Morgan would try to discover the secret of his personality. He learnt after some difficulty that Mark regarded women pretty well as so many demons put on this earth to entrap men's souls. He however had to confess he hadn't formed this opinion from outside experience, but then, he added, he had taken good care to steer free of the sex. He was satisfied to do his work and smoke his pipe—a veritable pipe of peace.

This philosophy, however, only represented one-half of him, though its few simple facts had had to be elicited in little bits, buried in irrelevances, and as there were apparently numbers of such little bits, the process of extrication had been a somewhat painful one. Nor did the other half come as a single revelation. It was also conveyed in little bits, which Morgan had to dig out and piece together and these bits were more difficult to find than the others, for they were infinitely tinier. Mark had once been in love, but had been too shy to let the object of it suspect it, or, rather, he had not known which way to set to work, and the prize had been snapped up by another.

Of course, Morgan's thought sometimes indulged in flights that had little relation to the workshop or to the processes of printing, but only within strict and narrow limits. These he further narrowed by giving up a great part of his leisure to the perusal of such technical books as Kettering possessed. Cleo still figured largely for him. She had been too big and important a fact in his life to lose her place as yet in the centre of his consciousness. But even had he the power, he would not have attempted to gather any intelligence as to her movements, though he could not help speculating somewhat on the very point. Should she ever return into his life again—and he could not make up his mind as to the probability of her doing so—then would be time enough for him to concern himself with her practically.

And amid all his toil, he had ever a sense of something light and dainty, something he was aware of as a haunting, unseen presence. And then at moments there gleamed upon him the wistful fancy that, beneath all the phrases and arguments with which he had equipped himself for the battle, it was really his love for Margaret was helping him to be strong, that it was the hope of his one day attaining to be worthy of her friendship was aiding his self-purification, that it was the flame she had lit in him had now sprung up again, defying all the mean elements by which he was surrounded to eat into his spirit.

And once the fancy had come to him, he nurtured it, so that it grew and grew and became part of his very self. If, indeed, it had not been truth when it had first come to him, it was truth now.

CHAPTER IV.

Strolling out one evening, about the end of August, to cool after the heated atmosphere of the workshop, Morgan was dreaming a beautiful vain dream. He had gone half way down the shorter St. Margaret's road, and in the distance rose the square church-tower. For the last two or three minutes he had been conscious of people a few yards ahead of him, and, as their slow stroll was yet slower than his, he had been getting nearer and nearer to them. Now his eye rested half vacantly on their backs, and the perception forced itself upon him that the three backs were those of ladies; and the next thing that dawned upon him was that there was something familiar as well as pleasing about the carriage, the curves, and the movements of those backs, still some twenty paces ahead of him. But he was still dreaming of Margaret, and these perceptions from the outer world were not strong enough to destroy the images in possession of his mind. He was quite close on them before he became aware that he had stumbled on Mrs. Medhurst, Margaret, and Diana.

Though conscious of them, he had, in his abstraction, almost walked on them in the narrow road, making them turn instinctively. He knew he was trembling visibly as he stood face to face with Margaret, her figure flashing on him for a moment like a divine vision; then he saw nothing and felt a fire burning at his temples.

"Morgan," said Mrs. Medhurst's sweet voice, and the cloud of things passed away, and he became aware her arm was supporting him.

"So we know your hiding-place now," sang out Diana. "Why wouldn't you let my old sweetheart tell me? I'm sure I'd have got it out of him all the same had he been in London."

"Morgan doesn't even offer to shake hands with us," said Margaret in soft suggestion.

Now that the encounter had been made, he pulled himself together to face it. He felt shame-faced and altogether unstrung, and he knew that the instinct that had made him insist on isolation had been fully justified. He was over-conscious, too, of the stains on his hands as he held it out. And yet beneath all his discomfort there was a full tide of immeasurable happiness. He could not speak yet. His throat swelled—the emotion was too overpowering. Here again was Margaret, the real Margaret, by his side, talking to him!

His eyes took her in greedily. Under the large straw hat, with its poppies and corn, her face showed exquisite, a face that might float tantalisingly across a painter's vision, and vanish after but allowing him the merest glimpse. Though she was clad in a simple dark blue serge dress, the grace of her figure seemed to him a revelation, and a ravishing sprig of cornflower peeped from her waistband. There was a repose, too, and a gentleness in her bearing that made him think, by contrast, of his Cleo, and of the uncouthness of Alice and Mary when they attempted to be stately.

Perhaps the very thought seemed to call out to him in warning, for, suppressing a sigh, he tore his eyes away from her.

"Why couldn't you let us know?" persisted Diana, who had been evidently much put out by the failure of her artful letters to seduce Archibald into giving away the secret of Morgan's whereabouts.

Mrs. Medhurst and Margaret both looked at Morgan and smiled, as if to convey to him that *they* understood his motives, and to indicate that Diana was not in the secret. Diana's quick eyes, however, noted the movement, though she said nothing just then.

"I had reasons," said Morgan, vaguely, feeling he must make some sort of an answer to so definite a question.

"We are staying at St. Margaret's," explained Mrs. Medhurst, "and we have been taking a stroll along the cliff-path. It began to get too dangerous, so we climbed a fence and cut across somebody's ploughed field, and then through a common, till at last we got on to this road. And now we're wending our steps homeward. You, Morgan, I suppose, are wandering after the labours of the day?"

He felt they were talking to him in as simple and natural a manner as if they had but parted the day before, under normal circumstances; and he was grateful for this delicacy that abstained from embarrassing him and made the meeting an easy one for him.

"The beauty of the evening tempted me," he said, growing more at his ease.

"And shall not our beauty tempt you as well," suggested Mrs. Medhurst laughingly, "to come and see our humble cottage. It is a quaint place. Mr. Medhurst bought it and we furnished it ourselves."

"Do come, Morgan," put in Margaret persuasively, as if some instinct told her he was going to hesitate.

He knew that battling against the temptation would be hopeless. He seemed to be walking with angels in the last flood of the evening sunlight, and something of the divine calm of evening came over his spirit. He was borne along, gently, gently, till all the sense of the day's toil behind him fell away.

The cool air breathed on him, and fluttered the blades of grass on the common, and shook the purple wild-flowers that grew along the wayside. It was laden with the odour of the sheaves that were spread over the fields amid the brown stubble, and seemed to waft to him something of the elemental poetry of the great mother Earth, of the informing spirit of religions of antiquity, of the human joy in the harvest festival, of the symbolic cornucopia, of the grateful offerings of first-fruits.

With a rare understanding of his emotions, they referred no more to him or his work, but plunged at once into their holiday adventures, so that he also was carried away from himself. Diana was learning to swim, and was as full of the subject as she had once or twice, according to her own account, been of sea-water. Margaret's enthusiasms were all for boating, and she took the others out whenever the sea was smooth enough to soothe her mother's fears. The cottage, too, was such fun that they never grew tired of it. And then there was a field near at hand where they had a tennis-court marked out, and where Diana and Margaret kept the ball going between them.

It did not take them long to reach St. Margaret's, and they entered their cottage just as the sun was on the point of sinking. Morgan, now abandoned to his adventure, was delighted with the curiously-built place, with its tiny hall, on one side of which was the little drawing-room, and on the other the dining-room. The walls were boarded and the ceilings were low, rough and whitewashed. Sketches and prints were hung in profusion, nooks were draped, and wicker and quaint chairs and knick-knacks were arranged in a charming disorder, whilst books were scattered everywhere. A piano loomed huge in the crowded little drawing-room. And all this had been achieved, whispered Mrs. Medhurst confidentially in his ear, by the outlay of an incredibly few pounds.

Morgan had an enchanted couple of hours, handling the books, listening to Margaret's playing, and admiring Diana's skill with the mandoline, which her many-sided caprice had taken up of late. He joined them in their evening meal for, according to their rural regime, they dined at two and supped about nine. The dining-room opened direct into a third inner room, which mysterious place Morgan judged to be a kitchen; for the cottage was built long and low.

When eventually he rose to go, they bade him good-night with the same implication of normality. It almost seemed they were taking it for granted he would come again on the morrow. But he knew their omission to give him a definite invitation was dictated by their feeling for him; that they did not wish to seem to intrude on the life he had chosen, but were leaving it to him to decide.

He strode off through the gathering darkness on the hour's walk that would take him back to Dover. The colour had not quite died out of the west, and, as he watched the violets and the cold blues and the pearl greys fading with the strange, lingering light on the distant horizon, his feeling of the evening just passed brought back to him the echo of some lines in the poem, from which Helen had once quoted to him:

"It lies in heaven, across the flood
Of ether, as a bridge.
Beneath, the tides of day and night
With flame and darkness ridge
The void..."

He had the sensation of being in the middle spaces now, floating down towards earth again from some rare ethereal region, to which his spirit had mounted.

Perhaps, too, of Margaret might it be true, as of the Blessed Damozel:

"... she cast her arms along
The golden barriers,
And laid her face between her hands
And wept."

He recalled now what his father had written in his first letter about her shutting herself up in her studio and her pretence of being at work on a mass of wax. The hint of her suffering had been almost intolerable to him then; and he knew that, in spite of all her gaiety to-night, the wound had not healed. He pictured the four of them sitting in the shaded lamp-light of the little drawing- room, and, as the echo of the music she had played surged again in his ears, he seemed to feel behind it a strange, ineffable sadness, as one might be conscious of the dark depths of a moon-lit stream. Her every movement rose before him again, giving him the sense of pain suppressed for his sake.

He had abandoned himself to the charm of the evening—it had been so wonderful to him! But now his vision seemed to have grown keener, to be piercing deeper. His memory of each moment was marvellously clear. How vivid still was the picture of Mrs. Medhurst bending down into the light, when he had noticed how the gold was fading out of the still beautiful hair. In the haunting memory of her sweet face he seemed to see now an under- expression of anxious pity and love.

Perhaps now that the pressure was relaxed, Margaret had stolen up to her room and was sobbing passionately to a silent world.

They seemed to beat through him, these sobs! And then Mrs. Medhurst's face again seemed to be with him, and the knowledge that his father had loved her in the olden days seemed to bring her closer to his heart. He stood still and threw out his arms in the darkness, with the vain yearning fancy that perhaps she might be there, that perhaps she might take him to her.

"Morgan," sang out a voice by his side.

His arms dropped and his heart beat painfully, and, though in a moment he had perceived it was Diana had overtaken him in the gloom, he could not recover himself.

"Why, you're crying!" she exclaimed, as her hand stole into his. "And so is she. That makes a pair of you. I'm sure I don't know what it's all about, but it's enough to vex a saint. Something mysterious has happened and nobody will tell me a word about it. And I dare not ask Margaret. I tried it once, and it just started her off crying—I thought she'd never stop!"

He did not answer her. He but held her little hand tighter, aware that the contact made his own seem coarser. They moved on together.

Suddenly he checked himself. "You must not come any further," he began. "I must see you back."

"Tell me first what has happened," she persisted; "Why have you become a workman?"

"I cannot and must not tell you. Besides, you could never understand."

"I understand a good deal more than you grown-up people think I do. Why can't you leave off being a workman? And why don't you come and marry Margaret? She's awfully in love with you, and so are you with her—you know you are!"

"Yes Diana, I know I am," fell from his lips, and immediately he regretted the words.

"Then come back now and tell her," said Diana, tugging at him as if to make him turn.

"But look at my hands," he said, half in jest, half in earnest. "See how rough and stained they are! I shall always be a workman, and I shall always be very poor."

"Margaret doesn't care anything about that," she protested. "She's not that sort of girl. Do come back, please, Morgan. Mamma's reading downstairs. I'll steal up to Marjy and tell her you're waiting for her. If you stand under the window, I'm sure you'll hear her crying. Come along, Morgan, you can take ever such a nice walk together, and——"

193

"And,"—he echoed stupidly.

"Oh, I was going to say I'll be glad to get the pair of you off my hands."

"I'm afraid that pleasure will have to be postponed indefinitely," he observed. "And now, Diana," he added, as sternly as he could, "you must be going back home without me—that is, I'll see you safe to where the houses begin."

"Morgan, you're a brute!" she answered with equal sternness. "But I mean to get to the bottom of this mystery all the same. I'll make a bet with you. How long do you give me to find out?"

"Ten years," said Morgan. He had now turned back with her.

"Ten years!" she echoed mockingly. "Why there'll be any number of olive-branches by then. Yours, of course, I mean."

"Diana! You are a very wicked girl."

"Well, I'm fourteen. That's quite old enough to be wicked, isn't it? Good-night, Morgan." And she suddenly sped ahead, and before he could recover from his astonishment she had become a shadow amid the darkness.

He strode after her, though he had not the least anxiety for her, as they were not yet a mile distant from the cottage. From the speed with which she kept ahead of him, it was clear she was determined to elude him; seeing which he contented himself with keeping within range of her.

When, eventually, he turned towards Dover again, it was with a feeling of half-sorrow that he should have happened to take that walk. Strong and firm as he was, he was not strong enough to endure such ordeals. He had winced most whilst Diana had been speaking to him. And then the figure of Cleo came up again. Cleo, to whom he was married!

In the depression that now came upon him, a friendship with Margaret, even years hence, seemed an impossibility to him. She might remain with him as an ideal figure, but the real living Margaret was too dazzling for him to look upon.

CHAPTER V.

Morgan did not venture again to take any walks to the east of the town, though he dwelt with pain on the possibility of the Medhursts hoping to fall in with him again. He could only trust that they would understand, though from their point of view there might perhaps seem no reason why he should avoid them so utterly. Had not the last encounter been a success, they might argue, and had he not been perfectly cheerful and, to all appearance, happy in their company?

Once or twice he thought of writing to Mrs. Medhurst, but he could not get down a word, and the pen dropped from his hand.

He felt the effects for several days, a vision of that lamp-lit room continuing to obtrude between him and his work, and the stream of music still flowing from Margaret's fingers. His proofs were dirty and needed much correction; and he even found himself setting up his thoughts in type, instead of following his copy.

However, he toiled on, almost with desperation, and Mr. Kettering's respect for him and his abilities advanced greatly. He and Mark had never ceased to call him "sir"; and Morgan, on his part, could never cease wondering how such sterling character could exist side by side in the same family with the general instability that characterised the women. As for Alice and Mary, he had been so long now in the house that an occasional quarrel with them signified nothing; in fact, that was part of the routine of the life.

About the end of the year he got his first chance in life. Mr. Kettering had been very proud, indeed, of employing him, especially as he had proved so apt a learner, and the experiment had entirely been crowned with success. The old man had enlarged on Morgan's superior culture to the traveller of a great London paper firm—himself a man of some education—who had for many years been going abroad regularly on the business of his firm, and who as regularly looked in for Kettering's order. This Mr. Brett thus came to make Morgan's acquaintance, discovered he knew Greek and Latin, and divined some mystery was at the back of Morgan's present position.

The direct result of this acquaintance was that, on the first day of the next year, Morgan found himself installed as "reader" in a large firm of printers in Upper Thames street, London, in which a brother of Mr. Brett was the junior partner. He had thoroughly mastered the business of proof-reading under Kettering's tuition, and his Greek and Latin and general culture had done the rest for him, for there was now scope for all of it in his new position. His salary at starting was two pounds fifteen shillings per week, the same as that of his predecessor, who had left the firm voluntarily.

But even before leaving Dover he had had the satisfaction of being able to send Helen a few pounds to pay some of the workmen, and she had been able to make a satisfactory report to him. While she had been in Scotland a couple of letters had passed between them which sufficed for all they had to say to each other; and to his father as well he had reported progress from time to time. Simon and Mark Kettering both exhibited signs of emotion when the moment for parting came, and, though they were sorry to lose him, rejoiced with him at his promotion.

"And I can only hope," were Simon's last words, "that my daughter will never turn up to worry you, and that, even if you forget her, you'll sometimes think of us folk here at Dover. And, be sure, if you ever find yourself in the town again, there's a hearty welcome waiting for you at my house."

In London, Morgan took a large, airy garret in Southwark, to get from which to his work he had only to cross the bridge, and fitted it with a narrow folding-bed and the few things he needed. He made his own breakfast, had his dinner sent into the works at one o'clock from a neighboring coffee-shop, had tea made for him by one of the girl folders, and supped at home on bread and cheese. In this way he managed to live and to dress neatly—patronising a very different sort of tailor from his old London one—on a pound a week. Every penny of the rest he put by rigorously.

About this time he learnt that his father could not come to town yet, as the winter was a severe one, and he had had a touch of rheumatism. As Morgan had come to look forward to seeing him now, this was a disappointment. Moreover, he had grown to take a keener interest now in the affairs of the home. At one time it had occupied little part of his thoughts, but now a finer sensibility to his domestic ties seemed to have arisen in him. He was very much concerned about this illness of his father's, the full extent of which, he had an idea, had been concealed from him. Helen, too, he saw but once during his first month in London, on which occasion he donned his best garments and went to take tea with her. Though their friendship had been so long passive, it was not less intense than heretofore. By some mutual instinct they seemed to avoid discussing his personal concerns now, Helen receiving him just as an old friend and as if there had been nothing in their lives to make a special link between them. She seemed to have grown somewhat graver in expression, and he was not sure that he did not like her face better like that. She amused and cheered him, and, once they had come together again, she insisted there was no reason now why he should not come oftener. And so, on a rare Saturday afternoon, when he was free, he would come in for an hour and listen to her pleasant chatting. Only when he brought her money would she permit herself any reference to his progress in life.

Of Cleo he heard nothing. She had not made another appearance on the boards, or, if she had, it had been in some obscure way. She intruded into his thoughts often enough, and was still a reality to him when he specially dwelt on her. But he was quite startled one day at suddenly realising the rapidity with which she was becoming a far-off shadow. There were moments now when he could almost believe that the whole episode of his marriage had been the veriest product of his fancy.

Frequently in the evenings and on rest days he would employ his leisure wandering amid the regions in which his lot was now cast. For the first time now he felt the mammoth city as a reality; for the first time he seemed to comprehend it—what it was and what it represented. In the days when he had trodden these same pavements with Helen its aspect had been merely panoramic. Now he himself was of it, a living and breathing unit of the multitude of toilers that peopled these vast industrial quarters. His vision pierced the swarming surface, the great grimy thoroughfares with their tramlines, their miles of sordid shops, their windowed expanse of brick, dingy and far-stretching, their serried lines of narrow houses.

And then he would feel that a great sense of the spirit of human life was passing into his blood. Leaping flashes of light came to him at times, as he sat in his garret with the fused murmur of the world surging in his ears, illumining for him abysses that had appeared to him once dark and bottomless.

CHAPTER VI.

It was early in March before Archibald Druce was well enough to come to town. Morgan's working day ended at seven o'clock, and at that hour Archibald called at the printing establishment, and the two went off together.

Morgan was excited, and he could see his father was. Neither had any "news," since, in their exchange of letters, everything had already been told. Still, they talked a little about the home, and then there were further details of Archibald's illness. Both perhaps felt the meeting was a trifle cold, but they knew the constraint would melt away presently.

"I haven't yet thought how we're going to spend the evening," said the old man. "We must dine together somewhere. After that we might perhaps look in at a theatre; it won't matter if we are late."

Morgan, who had no alternative suggestion to offer, readily fell in with this one, remarking that the dinner for him would be a rather magnificent kind of supper.

They eventually settled on a restaurant and ordered their repast. Then, somehow, as they sat facing each other, their tongue-strings seemed to get loosened.

It was a long time since they had last met, and Archibald, who had been full of his book then, now confessed he had put it aside for the present. For several months past his mind had not been in sufficiently fresh condition to enable him to work on it. Morgan remembered now how he had suggested a title for it half in scorn, and even such small remembrance was painful to him. He felt he had had something very like contempt for his father's literary scheme, forgetting, in the self-castigation of the moment, that at the time it had merely struck him humourously, and that his sin had not been quite so heinous as it now appeared to him. If the element of humour now coloured his vision of things but very slightly, that was only natural to his present stage of development.

They lingered over their coffee, not rising till about half-past eight.

"Suppose you just come and sit with me in my room, father," said Morgan. "If we have to decide on a theatre now, I am afraid we shall be quarrelling the rest of the evening. Besides, I do not want to acquire the habits of a young man about town. We can have a quiet talk for the rest of the evening."

"Yes, I should like to see your place," said his father. "It will enable me to judge of your powers of graphic description."

He was beginning to be more cheerful already and to show it. He took Morgan's arm affectionately, and they went back to Upper Thames street and crossed Southwark Bridge.

"I hope the woman hasn't forgotten to lay the fire," said Morgan, as he turned the key.

A moment later he had lighted the cheap lamp and the room stood revealed in all its bareness. A small table, three wooden chairs, the little bed, a trunk in the corner, and a washstand, were insufficient to make it look furnished, garret as it was.

"I recognise the place," said Archibald, depositing his things on the trunk. "It's quite large and airy. You are lucky to have only the front walls sloping. But the window gives you a back view, so perhaps I ought to have said 'back walls.'"

Morgan lighted the fire, and the two sat down before it.

"What have you in that cupboard just by you?" asked Archibald. "I feel inquisitive. I must get up and poke about.... Coals and crockery," he enumerated with slow unction, "a saucepan, a coffee-pot, a tea-pot, a broom, and some exceedingly dirty dusters. My dear Morgan, what a wonderfully compact place you have here; it's a miracle of completeness."

"I've given up coffee at night, but I make excellent cocoa. You shall have some before you go."

"Capital!" said the old fellow. "I'm enjoying myself immensely. This is quite a picnic."

"I am quite comfortable here," said Morgan, half to himself.

"There's only one suggestion I have to make," said his progenitor, "and that is you ought to have just a strip of carpet under your feet, or a small rug would do just as well. Last year at home, now, I had the carpet taken out of the drawing-room, in favour of a polished floor, but, Lord bless you, I found myself doing nothing else but sneezing, in spite of the odd rugs, for in a drawing-room you don't just happen to think where you're standing. But here when you just sit down at your table or by your fire it would be so easy to take care you've got the thing underfoot. I must send you a rug to-morrow— you know I owe you a birthday present."

"Birthday present! I had forgotten there were such things in the world. Thank you for reminding me, father. Such gifts, when they are sincere, add sweetness to life. And it will be nice to have something of yours here."

The fire blazed up cheerfully. They sat a little while in silence.

"When do you calculate you will get those debts paid off?" asked Archibald at length.

"Within three years, if all goes well," said Morgan. "I make a lot extra sometimes, now. I did a little article for a magazine we print and a little work for another journal. I am friendly with both editors. Besides, my salary may improve. In fact, my hopes at starting have been far exceeded."

"And after that?" asked Archibald, looking at him with unconcealed anxiety. It was evident it was a question he had been wanting to ask. Morgan hesitated a moment, though his answer was ready.

"After that I see no reason why I should not follow along the same lines. I shall be on the high road to build up a career for myself, and I have a feeling that I shall eventually branch off into journalism, where all the knowledge and experience I shall have gained will be of use to me."

"Tell me, Morgan," said Archibald. "Have you abandoned your first ambition entirely?"

Morgan leaned forward towards the fire and rested his head on his hands. For a moment he seemed lost in meditation, and then at last spoke slowly.

"There are times," he said, "when poetry still beats in my blood, when melody comes to me hauntingly. Often, as I sit here brooding, there surges up a full flood of I know not what, save that it is exquisitely beautiful. And, as I walk through these long, grey streets, lined with flaring market-stalls and massed thick with people, I seem to feel a great throb, a living heart-beat, that speaks to me of humanity; and what these bustling streets hold of humanness, of the warmth and energy of life, comes to me like a flowing tide. The pain, too, I feel; for there are odd, pathetic episodes. One catches sight of faces pinched, starved, unrebellious, large-eyed children of six a-marketing shrewdly with slender purses; and now and then a figure detaches itself from the crowd and speaks a whole history. If there is much pain and privation, much foulness and wickedness, there is also much of the joy of life, of the ecstacy of overflowing animal spirits. There are plague-spots, there are besotted critical jeerers at the wayside with an aggressive sense of superiority to all unlike themselves; there are half-grown lads and girls boisterously foul- mouthed. But probe beneath the large, vigorous unrestraint, the rollicking vagabondage of the streets, and you will find the far-spread, steady—if colourless—respectability of the industrial family. And at moments something grand, rugged, and passionate, a roaring harmonic discord, seems to sweep though the reeking grime, through the swarming boisterousness, through the magnificent brutality, through the utterance of putrid tongues, through the grey, lamp-lit atmospheres, as though man and his activities were but the swirled symbols of a music played in high Heaven. And as I stand listening, terrified yet thrilled, there seems to come a sudden lull; and then I perceive a goodness showing through the rough-and-readiness, sometimes blurred in the individual lives, sometimes inspired to a full glow. Often its leaps and flickerings are irregular, inconsistent, unpredictable. In the ruffian the spark is scarcely alive, but in some rare moment it will quicken and show through tremblingly.

"And all these perceptions to which I was blind before have wrought their effect on me. They have fused into and strengthened the better part of me. They make poetry in me, not such as I once wrote, but a full-blooded, living poetry. You see, father, I have drawn inspiration from all this reality. I have felt the true spirit of the universe in this dense-packed encampment on the march of civilisation, this living pattern in Time's kaleidoscope; the same spirit that lies behind the green country and the sweet airs, behind a great idea, a noble deed, a gracious woman.

"And so I feel that I am fortified enough to defy all external sordidness. The soiled lime-washed walls, the heavy grind of machinery, and the tinged breath of the printing-house I am insensible to; and with this result I am satisfied. I will not take up my harp wherewith to gather harmonies from amid the discords of things, as I feel it is in me to do. If such dream comes to me at times I know it must remain a dream, for I must continue with my shoulder to the wheel and do my full share of human labour!"

He broke off. An almost sacred stillness followed his half-mused speech, to which Archibald had listened with bent head.

"Will you forgive me, dear Morgan, if I remind you of something?" said the old man, breaking the long silence. "I feel you are the best judge of your own life, and I do not mean to say a word that should make you imagine I am trying to interfere with you. I only want to ask you not to forget that we at home have claims upon you as well. We want to have you near us a little, too. Your mother has been fretting about you of late."

"My mother!" said Morgan. "Is she aware of my existence? She never cared about me."

"But she cares about you now. Won't you come home to us when you are through this—in three years' time, say?" pleaded the old man. "Your end will have been achieved, you will feel sure of yourself by then. And, to tell the truth, Morgan, I've set my heart on—your being a great poet."

Archibald looked down almost guiltily as he spoke.

Morgan had a consciousness of the strange, complete reversion of the position the years had brought about.

"I could never, never consent not to live by my own labour," he said, giving utterance to what, at the moment, he intensely felt to be the one essential condition of existence for him.

"Come now, surely we can get over that difficulty," said Archibald eagerly. "I take it it is immaterial to you what work you do, so long as it is of a kind in which you can employ your faculties. After all, the principal point in your present occupation is the discipline it affords and the habits of mind it is forming in you; all of which could be employed in some other direction. It would simply be a matter of your mastering a different set of facts for the different employment, which you could do very quickly. Why not accept a position in the bank? That would afford you an honorable livelihood, and it would help you to be near us. Then perhaps some day, when you feel you have lived down the old mistakes, you may be inspired to take up your pen again. Mistakes! Why should they kill for ever the first fresh ambition of your life? Mistakes! I made them, too, when I was young. So has every man who is worth his salt. Of course, there's one mistake you can't undo—you don't mind my alluding to it, Morgan. But if you continue to face it as you are doing now— my God, Morgan! you are suffering!"

Archibald groaned heavily, then checked himself and put on as cheerful a face as he could muster.

"I meant to have proved to you," he continued, "that you scarcely take a scientific—I had almost said an intelligent—view of your function in life. The desire to live by your own labour is actuated by the very proper feeling that you ought to be doing your duty in the social organism. Your present work is equal to, say, three respectable pairs of boots a week. That, you will admit, is a fair measure of your utility. Now, if by becoming a great poet, you could give pleasure and delight to thousands of your fellow-men, it seems to me your utility would be fairly represented by quite a considerable number of pairs of boots, and very respectable ones, too."

"How it would have delighted me to hear you argue like that when I was a boy," almost whispered Morgan. "Forgive me, father," he added immediately. "I did not mean any reproach."

"I admit my not arguing in that way at the time was one of my mistakes. But I am sure you will yet be a great man. For the present, however, I shall be content with your assurance that you'll come back to the bank eventually. Gradually, perhaps, you'll fall thence into the vocation you were born for."

"I think I can promise so far as the bank is concerned," said Morgan, slowly.

"Thank you," said his father and bent down to warm his hands in the flames, so that the light shone on his face.

There was a silence. Scarcely a sound came to them here in this lonely, bare garret. Morgan studied his father's face anxiously. How silvery was the hair in places; and there were lines that had not been there a year before. Both these signs seemed to accuse him louder than any words.

"Father," he cried, "let me come closer to you."

CHAPTER VII.

The next evening Morgan sat pretending to be reading a book, his feet sedulously planted on a new Turkey rug, which struck a startling note of colour and decoration amid the bleakness of the attic. At last he closed the volume and let it fall wearily on his knee. The visit of his father had tried him severely. He had been shaken by a storm of emotion, and it had left him somewhat shattered. And now that Archibald had departed, an aching sense of loneliness had come to him such as only comes to the man who lives thus isolated. He had been able to leave his work for an hour in the middle of the day, so that, including his usual dinner interval, he had passed two hours in his father's company and seen him to his train. The old man had been miserable in town; he couldn't bear to be so near Morgan yet cut off from him all day, and, since he was far from well and needed the comforts of his own home, it was decided between them he should go at once.

At last Morgan threw down the book impatiently. He walked round the room for a time, but could not rid himself of his restlessness. "My soul is sick," he repeated again and again. "I need my friends." He poked the fire and threw more coal on; he looked for awhile through the panes of the window into the vague blackness of the March night. And at last he bethought himself of getting ready his evening meal, merely for the sake of concentrating himself on something. Just as he was on the point of opening the cupboard, into which his father had pried so jocularly, there came a timid tap at the door.

"Come in!" he cried, not quite certain that there *was* anybody there.

As his invitation seemed to be complied with, he instinctively turned his head to view his visitor, who stood just within the door smiling at him.

"What! Margaret!" he cried, as his head almost swam.

She closed the door softly and advanced into the room.

"I've just come to pay you a visit, Morgan," she said laughingly. "Please say it was nice of me to come. What! Aren't you going to shake hands with one of your oldest friends?"

He was not quite sure that his brain hadn't given way, and that her presence was not a mere manifestation of the fact. He had never been able to trust himself sufficiently to go near the Medhursts. Sedulously keeping to the London south of the river and to the immediate vicinity of his work—save on his rare visits to Belgrave Square—he had run but little risk of encountering any of them or, indeed, any other acquaintances. He was aware the Medhursts knew he was in London and employed by a large firm, but they had never been told the exact details of his whereabouts. However, he found himself shaking hands with Margaret but too bewildered to say anything.

"What a strange expression in your face, Morgan! It seems to ask any number of questions, but I can't make out whether it looks pleased or angry. At least be polite enough to make me welcome. It's nice and warm in here, so I think I'd better take my jacket off."

"You don't give me time to recover my breath, Margaret. Of course, you are more than welcome, but I am not good enough for you to visit. Come, take a chair by the fire."

"You not good enough! It is simply wicked of you to talk like that. But why are you rubbing your eyes? I believe you think I'm a phantom."

She removed her jacket and also her hat, instinctively throwing them, as Archibald had done the evening before, across the trunk. Then she smiled at him again in lovely reassurance that she was real flesh and blood. She had on a soft woollen dress of that favourite silver-blue in which she always looked her best. She wore a bunch of forget-me-nots at her waist, and a little knot of the same flowers at her throat was fastened with a small, lyre-shaped brooch, set with pearls. There was just a touch of creamy lace at her wrists and throat, and what dainty little tendrils of golden hair lay on her forehead!

"Your chair is very hard," she exclaimed, jumping up almost immediately. "I think I'll sit on the bed instead."

"You won't find that much better," he said, drawn into good humour by her briskness, and charmed that so exquisite a presence should grace his attic.

"It's miles better," said Margaret. "But you still look puzzled. Isn't your ingenuity equal to the task of guessing how I found you out?"

"I don't know, unless Diana's old sweetheart paid you a visit yesterday," he answered smiling, as he spread the new rug under her feet. "But he certainly said nothing to me about it this afternoon when I saw him off."

"He was probably afraid to let you know he'd been weak enough to yield to our blandishments. I had an idea you were living in a garret—the garret always seems to put a sort of hall-mark on genius. It's a very nice garret, too. I like mine better, though—it's a lump larger."

If the pure pleasure of being near her began to predominate, it was certainly not unaccompanied by the pain that was always with him because of his vain love for her; so that his entire feeling was a rather mixed and undecided one. He could not quite abandon himself to gladness at her coming, and perhaps the very unexpectedness of it aided this emotional embarrassment.

"Have you been working much of late?" he asked, that being a natural question to follow her reference to her studio. He was, indeed, relieved that the conversation had got on so definite a tack and that she had not alluded to his avoidance of her family or reproached him for it.

"I'm just doing a little group of greyhounds. I'm going to exhibit them at the Academy. It's such a bother and such fun, too! I've got over the worst part now. The big mother and two little ones playing at the side of her make twelve legs and three tails—quite a forest of them. I had no end of trouble to get a good composition. But the chief bother was with the models. The dog would never keep still, and I had to keep on moving my wax figure just as it moved. Sometimes it would turn upside down, and then I had to turn my work upside down as well. Do you know what I should like to do, Morgan?"

"I don't, but I should like to."

"I wonder if you'd let me make a bust of you! I want to very much."

"Why?" he asked, without meaning that exactly, but only by way of surprised exclamation.

"Well," she smiled, "I just want to. I could have an old bench brought up here and a lot of clay. If you sat to me, say, for a couple of hours every Sunday morning, you'd begin to recognise yourself after a time."

He was powerless to refuse. With her speaking to him, he became as passive as the clay she moulded. He knew her power; perhaps that was why his instinct had led him to elude it.

"That is really good of you, dear Morgan," she exclaimed, while her eyes sparkled with honest delight.

Time was, perhaps, when seeing her thus he might have taken her hand.

"But don't look as if you already regretted making the promise," she went on to protest. "I assure you it won't hurt a bit; not any more than having your hair cut. By the way, why do you wear your hair so short? Oughtn't a poet to have long, noble locks? They come out very effectively in clay, those long, noble locks. I hope I'm not making your bed too hard. Come now, Morgan, are you still so heavy-hearted? What can I do to make you merry?"

"Take supper with me," he responded quickly, with an atoning flash of briskness, the while he upbraided himself for oppressing her with his dejection. "It will be a real Bohemian supper."

"How nice! I'm dying with hunger."

"In here, I mean," he explained. "I make my own supper."

"I know. We heard all about the inside of that cupboard."

"You won't mind sitting on the hard chair?"

"No. What's the menu?"

"Bread and cheese and——"

"Not beer, I hope," she interrupted hastily.

"And cocoa," he finished. "Do you mind keeping house here for two minutes whilst I run down to get the milk. We have a dairy two doors away."

He returned in a moment and she helped him to set out the table, for which there was no cloth.

"This chair *is* hard," she said again later, when she had been seated on it some little time. "I must send you a soft chair, Morgan. I haven't given you a birthday present this year."

"Indeed, you must not. Such luxuries are out of place here, and you ought not to try to spoil me."

"But, dear Morgan, you've a lovely rug, and I'm sure you ought to have a nice chair to keep it company. You've your guests to think of now. I must have something to sit on when I come and so must your papa. I'm willing to admit my suggestion was not quite a disinterested one; in fact, I'm prepared to be perfectly unscrupulous so long as I carry my point."

"I'd better yield before you get so far as that. Only, of course, the chair shall be used exclusively for my visitors."

"Oh, you must sit on it sometimes, as well."

"Well, let us not quarrel about it."

"Of course we're not going to quarrel about it. We're going to be the best of friends now, aren't we?"

"I never dared dream——" he began.

"Dreaming hasn't anything to do with it. It really isn't at all necessary, so the omission need not count. All along I've had the feeling as if you were thrusting me back away from your life, and I have always wanted to count for something in it, if ever so little. Won't you let me now be of some help to you? It is wicked of you to continue in this terrible solitude. I feel that you've promised to let me come here and model you really against your will; don't deny it, Morgan— your face spoke only too plainly. I should be standing here and talking to you, but you would be as solitary as if I had never come. I want to break down that stupid barrier between us; I want you to believe in me, to trust me and to show me you trust me."

"It is myself I dare not trust. Such a friendship needs strength, and I am not strong enough, Margaret."

"Then you must find the strength, Morgan. Weakness is an unmanly excuse, and you are a man."

"You talk like that because you still do not realise what it means for me to— to——"

He hesitated.

"Go on," she said. "I am strong enough to listen."

There was a silence, but she knew he was collecting his scattered forces.

"To be friends with you," he went on determinedly. "You say that I kept you at arm's length. That is true. But then you don't know what my life has been —you never did really know even when we were close together."

"Tell me then, Morgan. Make me understand why you kept me at arm's length. I do not know how you came to marry so suddenly, what woman you married, or why she left you. I want to know all about her. Tell me, if it doesn't hurt you too much. Perhaps it will hurt you less after you have told me."

"I have kept you at arm's length, Margaret, because I loved you. I am struggling now to keep you at arm's length because I still love you. Dare you stay here and listen to me after that?"

She looked him straight in the face.

"I dare, Morgan. I want you to know me as well as to love me. If you had understood me, you would neither have thrust me back nor would you be struggling to do so now. You no doubt always considered me just a pretty girl, who thought and acted always as becomes what it called a young lady; a colourless, conventional creature, without any judgment or emotions of her own; just a white sheet of paper with a name written across in beautiful lettering; a simpering thing in petticoats who must smile and blush just at the right moments and be perfectly proper at all times; who must never act unless she has a fixed rule to guide her; who is supposed to understand nothing at all of real life; for whom human beings are reduced to a strange uniformity, the men in their evening dress so simple, so nice, so attentive, so easy to understand, the women—but then such a young person is not supposed to concern herself with the women. That, I'm sure, is the sort of girl I appeared to you, Morgan. I am sorry that, so far, I cannot take your love for me as a compliment. You saw me as a painter might see a model, and perhaps you enshrined my image as a sort of poetic fancy. You loved me as an unreal spirit. But I am not what you thought me; I am a real person. I can think and judge for myself, and I can be myself. That is why I have had the courage to come here to you, and had I known earlier where you were I should have forced this interview on you long ago. And this despite the fact that you are married, that you love me and that I—love you. I have the courage to face the occasion, to outrage convention where convention makes no provision for the needs of the particular occasion. I know that, despite all, we can be very dear friends. Only trust me a little, Morgan, learn to know me better, and I am sure you will trust me altogether. Make an effort to be strong and perhaps I may help you."

And so Morgan poured himself out to her, told her all; and, if at times he faltered, she bade him go on, she would not blush.

The recital was a long one. Interruptions and discussions were frequent; they were also making pretence to sup. Neither remembered the flight of time.

"Of course, I have known the bare facts for a long time," said Margaret, "but only in a very vague way and in a very puzzling one. There was so much left to my imagination, and it bothered me so much to fill up the blanks. And so you are working to pay off her debts. I know it feels awfully nice to earn money for one's self. Do you know that I'm quite rich. Guess how much I made last year by my modelling?"

"How much?" he asked.

"Eighty-seven pounds, after paying all my expenses," she exclaimed. "I wanted to pay for my own frocks, but papa wouldn't let me. And so I've got it all and I don't know what to do with it; at least I know what I should like to do with it."

"But surely papa wouldn't disapprove of your doing what you liked with it?"

"Oh, papa wouldn't disapprove," she said, colouring a little, "but I'm afraid you would."

"I? You're not intending to buy me a silver chair with jewels set in it, are you?"

"I thought you might pay some of those debts with the money and let me be your creditor instead," she said hesitatingly. "Of course, you would pay me back as you saved enough, just as you are doing now with the others. And it would be a sort of symbol of the new footing on which we start from to-day."

"Dear Margaret," he said, "please don't try and press that on me. It won't help me in the least, as you see yourself. Besides, what need have we of a symbol? I want you to believe in the new footing just as much without it. And then," he added, in a gayer note, "there is another reason why I can't allow you to have such ideas. Heroines always do that sort of thing, and it's quite too conventional for you."

She laughed and did not persist, though she had coloured still more. And just then she bethought herself of the hour and drew forth her tiny watch.

"This is being wicked with a vengeance!" she exclaimed. "I really must be going back."

"You must let me come with you, else I shall be nervous all night and my hair may be grey by the morning."

"Part of the excitement of the adventure was to come alone and to go alone. But as I can't have your hair turning grey——"

"Do they know at home where you were going?" he asked, as he helped her on with her jacket.

"I didn't tell them, but I dare say they'll guess, and I mean to let them know anyway. I'm going to leave you these," and she unfastened the bunch of forget-me-nots and put them on the table.

He saw her to her own door; it was long since he had set foot in Wimpole street. She gave him a long comrade's hand-clasp, saying: "We had a charming Bohemian supper. You have made me happier to-night than I have been for years."

He turned away as she rang the bell and he walked all the way back to Southwark. Now that he had taken her into his life at last, he seemed to have unburdened himself of some overwhelming weight. Margaret knew everything at last, understood everything, and loved him through all. His self- distrust had made him keep himself hidden from the Medhursts, but she had helped him to find and know his own strength. She was right. He was strong enough to accept her friendship.

Though he would have to be at his desk at the usual hour in the morning, he could not go to bed at once. The flowers she had left seemed to fill the room with sweetness. And something of lightness and fragrance seemed to remain with him, to be flitting here and there with the silence of a phantom, to be hovering in the air, to be bending over him, to be nestling close to him. Then, as he closed his eyes dreamily, Margaret seemed to float before him. He was aware of her eyes, her hair, her voice; he saw her just as she had sat there with her face and hands showing exquisite against the silver-blue of her dress, and the forget-me-nots at her throat and waist.

CHAPTER VIII.

In the autumn of the third year of Morgan's engagement with the Upper Thames street firm of printers he found himself with enough money to pay off the balance due to his one remaining creditor. There had been a good deal of method displayed in the order in which he had enjoined Helen to settle the debts, and this particular firm had been left to the last because it had received a goodly sum in the first days when Cleo was using up their ready money.

It was Saturday, and he had just got away from the works. He had been intending to take this last instalment to Helen that very afternoon; but the idea came to him that he would rather enjoy the sensation of making this last payment in person, and he proceeded immediately to act on it.

Arrived at the business place of the firm, he explained to a clerk that he wished to clear off an old matter, and recalled the occasion to him. The man looked surprised, and went to consult his principal. An old ledger had to be looked up, and then Morgan was informed the account had been settled very shortly after the closing of the theatre. The principal now remembered the circumstances perfectly. A cheque had come from a certain firm of solicitors in the West End, much to his surprise. After some further searching the clerk was able to tell Morgan who these solicitors were.

This last piece of information simply corroborated what he had at once suspected. Helen had carried out, without consulting him, the very same suggestion that Margaret had once made to him, and was keeping the sums he had been sending her from time to time. He understood, though, that she must have done it mainly for the sake of the actors and workpeople.

He said nothing to her of his discovery when he called at Belgrave Square a couple of hours later, but just handed her the money, which she quietly placed in a drawer of her escritoire.

"And now I have to congratulate you, Morgan," she said. "You have shown the stuff you are made of. Tell me, how does it feel?"

"I feel extraordinarily light-hearted," he admitted.

"I'm sorry," she said, and looked it.

He stared at her.

"There is a story of a hungry peasant gorging himself on bread and cheese, and, when he couldn't eat any more, they brought in the stuffed geese and other delicacies."

"Well?"

"Stupid! the stuffed geese and other delicacies have yet to come in. If the coarser part of the feast has made you so joyful, the rest will be wasted on you to-day."

"I feel more stupid than ever. Still, my capacities for storing away joy are unlimited, and, what is more, I shall appreciate every crumb."

"Very well." She took up a journal from the table near her. "Let me read you this paragraph: 'In the course of the coming session an extraordinary case will be reached in the Divorce Courts. The petitioner is a lady of title belonging to one of the noblest and oldest families in the kingdom, and the respondent is a well-known novelist and dramatist. The parties were married barely three years back and the wedding was much discussed at the time. It is rumoured that facts of a strange and sensational character are likely to come to light at the trial, and the occasion will not be the first one on which the petitioner has figured in the same Court.'"

She passed him the paper—it was a gossippy society weekly—and he read the paragraph again. For a moment quick vague flashes seemed to rise in his brain as from a vain attempt to strike a flint; then light came to him.

"Ingram and Cleo," he cried. "She went back to him!"

"Precisely," smiled Helen. "You will remember my lamenting I could not be the good fairy of your life, because things were already destined to work themselves out for your happiness. You see now I was a true prophet."

But a sort of dizziness came to him on account of his stumbling efforts to think, to trace the significance of things.

"Don't faint, please. I'm only a helpless woman, and I'm sure I couldn't rise to the occasion. Perhaps I've been too precipitate. I've made you swallow the whole stuffed goose at once."

"I'm not so sure that my personal life is going to be affected by it," he began.

"Stuff and nonsense!" she cried. "Your proceedings will be reduced to the utmost simplicity. There will be no defence at all. I have been, watching affairs patiently for three years now, and what has happened was bound to come. Do you know who sent your Cleo those bank-notes she had at Dover? Do you know where she went directly after leaving you? There is a certain house in Hampstead you know quite well. It has a room in it with a fountain, and really pretty hanging lamps, and peacocks on the windows. Well, she immediately took repossession of it. And very glad her rightful lord and master was to have her back again! The distraction of his affections by the engrossing interest of ambitious matrimonial schemes had been only temporary. As for his wife—well, about the living one should be silent unless one has something nice to say. Therefore I'll say nothing about her. Before long, Morgan, you'll be a free man, and a certain chapter of your life will be erased. Fox & Kraft are an excellent firm of solicitors—almost a pity to employ such steam-hammers to crack such a very simple nut."

"You are going along much too fast, Helen. You know I am leaving Upper Thames street next week; it is an old promise made to my father. I must consult him first. Of course, I shall be glad to have this meaningless tie that binds me to Cleo cut right through, and for ever. But I do not care to let my happiness rest on such a basis. Margaret and I shall remain friends and nothing more."

"Stuff and nonsense!" she cried again. "Your father is too wise a man not to agree with me. And so I am quite content you shall abide by his counsel. Otherwise I'd have to force you into happiness even if I had to do it by threatening suicide, and you know my threats are not idle ones."

"I shall be guided by my father," he conceded. "But don't overwhelm me so much, please. My emotions at this moment are much too complex for my understanding."

"Then let me give you some tea. It will put all your notions—and your emotions—in order."

The tea certainly did soothe him. He had never known that the beverage could be so delicious.

"How did you find out about Ingram and Cleo?" he asked suddenly.

"Oh, that was very easy. The moment I heard she had bank-notes I had a very strong suspicion of the truth. As I was eager to learn whether I could be your good fairy, I had that house watched. When my suspicions were corroborated I waltzed round my room sixteen times, and, you may be sure, I was determined never to lose sight of your Cleo for a moment. But my task was not a difficult one. That delightful room seems to have been as fatal to her imagination as she was to yours. She made some desperate attempts to leave it; twice she crossed to America and made obscure appearances on the boards, and once she sojourned in Paris for several months. But all in vain—she *had* to go back and sit on her gilded couch. Do you know, I rather like her; after all, she has never tried to turn to account her connection with you, Morgan. She's no mere vulgar adventuress. There's something really taking about her. But I'd like to slap her sisters. When do you leave for the country?"

"A fortnight hence, I hope," said Morgan. "But I am rather vague about what immediately is going to follow. In a general way it is understood that I am to work in the bank, which is precisely what I refused to do thirteen years ago."

"Thirteen years! That is a good stretch out of a life," said Helen, with a half sigh, "Time flies. I scarcely realise that I am thirty-six already. And the years seem to bring nothing but perplexity and embarrassment at the increase of my fortune. It is perfectly meaningless and absurd to me, this monstrous fortune. I feel I haven't any right to it; though, as I derive no happiness from it, that feeling ought not to give me very much concern. Happiness depends on one's personal relations with others—a few others, that is—and though I shake hands with a vast crowd, I have no close personal relations; not, at least, in the sense in which I understand the phrase. A sort of subtle fusion must accompany. I should have preferred to leave my fortune to you, Morgan, but I knew you wouldn't like to benefit by my death, so I have disposed of it otherwise."

He looked hard at her.

"Why this sudden lugubriousness?" he asked.

"Well," she said enigmatically, and the enigma was repeated in the accompanying shrug of her shoulders.

He seemed, however, to pierce beyond the smiling placidity of her expression, and to be aware of something that chilled him, of something that seemed to say: "There are such things as broken hearts."

"You've never had the life you deserved to have, Helen," he cried.

"There have been those who have envied me. My biography would read like a record of every earthly happiness. I am the daughter of a rich country gentleman with whom I have always been on the best of terms, only agriculture bores me rather. I was presented to my sovereign at seventeen. I danced and rode and flirted and was supposed to be having a good time, and a Baronet thought he fell in love with me, and did really marry me. I have always had a big house, a big income, a position in society. What more can a woman want? Well, all these things do not constitute the personal life. The remembrance of the whole course of my personal life is a vivid one to me, and it seems to have run through all these things like a thin thread of silver through a mass of stuff. Looking back, this swirl of the social world, its functions, its movements, the acquaintanceships it brought me, seem to me all strangely unreal. I seem to be aware of a large, swarming vision, amid which I have lived. But nothing of it has ever in-mingled with my real sense of happiness or misery. Fortune, society—these are not the essentials. The essentials are the same for all ranks, and it is on those that personal happiness depends. Up to the age of twenty-five even a clever girl may delude herself into thinking that the hearty fun and enjoyment she may be extracting from her circumstances and her position in the world are really what make happiness, but if she have real brains, a clear vision and quick sympathies, she will inevitably stifle in her atmosphere of mere pleasure. She will not continue to set store on her material advantages, on the stage accessories by which she may be surrounded. She will long for something else—and most often not get it. If I had only been penniless and had loved and married a man who had all his fighting to do yet! I should have lived beside him, conscious of being helpful, of being valued for what my companionship meant to him, with a sense of my dignity and worth as a human being. Instead, I was born rich, I married a man who had no fighting to do, and so I was a mere mate to him. I was but a child and there was no one to warn me. Everybody about me was stupid, enslaved to ideas that are rotten at the core! We dangle baubles before our children and poison the fresh, pure fount of humanity. Thus it is I have been a waste and useless force in the world. If it had only been decreed to me to have children of my own, I feel sure I should have been a better woman than I am."

Her voice died away in a strange sweet murmur. In her face there came a look as of holy meditation; her eyes shone with a light of yearning.

"I am tired of England," she resumed in a moment. "I shall be going away before long. I want to find some secluded spot near a lovely Italian lake, where I may stay and rest indefinitely. Perhaps for years, for I am very tired. I shall wait till I see your happiness completed, Morgan, even though this may be our last meeting. Till then I dare not go; you are not to be trusted to take the happiness that is within your grasp. You know I claim to be a connoisseur of women, and I am perfectly satisfied that you shall marry your Margaret. That is the highest compliment I could pay her. There is that indefinable, unseizable something in her face which reveals the whole personality, and it won me immediately. We have met three or four times now, but, of course, I do not figure sufficiently in her consciousness that she should mention me specially to you. One thing I am grateful to you for, that you are respecting my wish that she should not know we have ever been friends. After all, I am only a sort of imaginary figure to whom you come and talk, and I haven't really counted in your life. You know I have a weakness for mysticism, and I like to think of myself as a sort of phantom that just accompanied you on your way a little and perhaps helped you a little at a critical moment and then disappeared. So promise me Margaret shall never, never know."

"She knows everything but that," he replied. "It hurts me to make the promise, but I understand why you wish me to. Besides, I must look on this one reservation from her as the penalty—the lingering symbol of the past. But there is now one thing I should like to mention, Helen, and that is, I want to recur to that money, the five hundred pounds I borrowed of you. You see I have tasted blood."

"When you feel you can spare the money, dear Morgan, I should wish you to do some good work with it. Seek out those who may need it—a struggling student, a starving poet, a brave orphaned boy or girl toiling to support the younger children. Save some human being from despair, and restore his faith and hope. That is the best repayment you could make me. And now there is one thing I should like to ask you. Do you think——"

She hesitated. His look bade her continue.

"Well," she continued, smiling a little. "I was going to ask you to kiss me—a real kiss—if you thought your Margaret could spare me one. You have never given me a real kiss, Morgan, and it would be for the last time."

She looked down almost demurely. For sole reply he took her in his arms and their lips came together. Gently she disengaged herself at length; and, as the hot tears fell from his eyes, he felt impelled to fall on his knees and cover his face with his hands.

When he looked up again he was alone in the room. His sobs broke forth afresh as he divined why she had left him.

A moment later he stole from the house.

CHAPTER IX.

The bell rang again and the passengers' gangway was hauled up on to the pier. Morgan leaned against the deck-rail and looked westwards towards a point where the Dover cliff rose highest and then swept round. It was at that spot had begun the new ordering of his life which had at last culminated in the great happiness of to-day.

On a deck-chair close by his elbow sat Margaret. As he shifted his position a little his eye caught sight of a dainty ear and a soft cheek, gleaming exquisite through her veil against the golden brown of her large velvet hat and of the stretch of velvet mantle.

"Morgan, dear," she said, pulling him playfully by the sleeve, "brides are supposed to be too excited to eat on their wedding day. So I was when I woke up, and I didn't eat any breakfast. And now the fresh air makes me as hungry as a hunter. Do get me something nice, please."

When he came back, the mails and luggage had been got on board. The water began to seethe and foam away from the paddle-wheels, and, with a pleasant hoot, the boat steamed away. And then, as Morgan leaned against the side, he fell a-musing on many things, all woven in a web of wonder at his happiness. Different parts of his life flashed at him, all out of order and irrelevantly. How near, too, had he just passed to the Ketterings! Cleo's father rose before him again with his greying hair and his good face, bent, aproned, and in corduroys, just as he was wont to stand in the Dover workshop. He remembered the kindly invitation the old man had given him when they parted, and he felt touched as he now called to mind the letter he had received from him on his ceasing to be his son-in-law. "I am glad to know you are free from her, and hope you won't think me an unnatural father; but she never tried to win my affections, whereas you won them without trying. I do hope that at no distant day you will marry a true lady, who will make up to you for the past. I know what you must have suffered."

He had been concerned about Cleo, and had so overflowed with pity for her that he had scarce had the strength to take the step that had made his happiness possible. But he knew that she was quite well and happy, living at the same house where he had first seen her, and that it had been perfectly indifferent to her whether she were tied to him or not.

And now his old fancy came to him again that he could trace a distinct unity in his life, as though it had been moulded by a guiding Power. As Helen had said, the inner spring of his life had been its own good fairy.

And as he looked at Margaret again, the dream that had sometimes come to him did not now seem so unrealisable as it had in the old days when he had been cut off from her. The burning of his old manuscripts had marked his sense that his ambition was utterly dead. But he had never regretted the burning. And now he even rejoiced at it. For, by toil and discipline and facing the fulness of the living world, he had attained to a clear sanity, to a just sense of values; the romantic blur of his early poetic vision clarifying into the strong definiteness of the Real. Assuredly he could now no longer write those nebulous, elusive word-harmonies. Nor for him the mere æsthetic toying, the dainty piece of colour-work; but poetry that should throb with vitality and humanness. From dream poetry he had passed to dream life. Now that he had won his way to true life, was he not, too, to win his way to true song?

To be a voice whose enchantment should echo down the ages, whose never-dying melody should accompany the generations on their toilsome way, ever fresh, ever sweet for human hearts!

So did he dare to aspire again, and in his fancy it was Margaret's spirit that floated on and on for ever, her fragrance immanent in the songs he should sing!

The sea was radiant with sunlight. A soft wind breathed in his face. The dwindling town nestled lazily in its valley, and the line of white cliffs stretched on either hand. And as Margaret's voice spoke to him again, something of her sweetness seemed to rise and rest on the spring world.

THE END.

www.ingramcontent.com/pod-product-compliance
Lightning Source LLC
Chambersburg PA
CBHW021426110726
47901CB00008B/2317